ROGUE WAVE

The Waterfire Saga

Deep Blue
Rogue Wave
Dark Tide

ROGUE WAVE

JENNIFER DONNELLY

Hodder
Children's
Books

a division of Hachette Children's Group

A Catalogue record for this book is available from the British Library

ISBN 978 1 444 92566 1

Printed and bound in Great Britain by Clays Ltd, St Ives plc

10 9 8 7 6 5 4 3 2 1

The paper and board used in this book are made from wood
from responsible sources.

Hodder Children's Books
an imprint of Hachette Children's Group
Carmelite House, 50 Victoria Embankment
London EC4Y 0DZ
An Hachette UK company

www.hachette.co.uk

For the awesome Steve Malk,
with gratitude

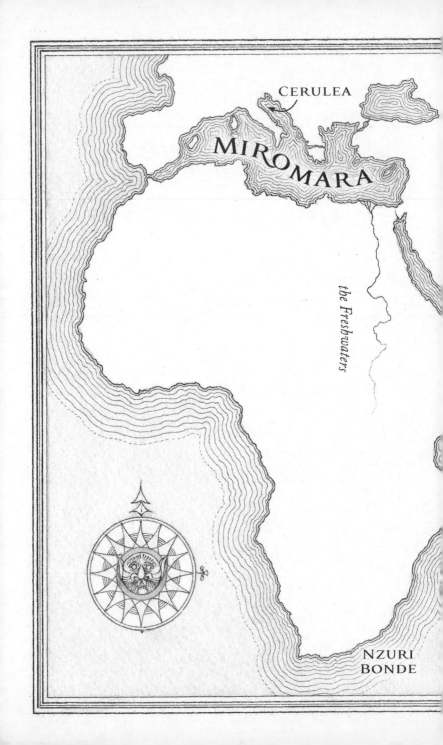

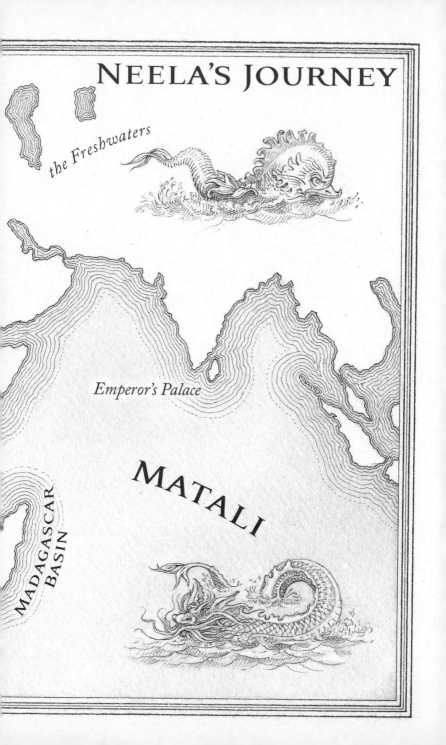

NEELA'S JOURNEY

the Freshwaters

Emperor's Palace

MADAGASCAR BASIN

MATALI

The story so far . . .

Serafina, heir to the throne of Miromara, and her best friend Neela have managed to escape the clutches of Captain Traho and his invading army. Sinister dreams have led them and four other mermaids to the hideout of the river witches, where they have been given a seemingly impossible task: find six talismans that are scattered through the oceans to prevent an ancient monster from rising. During their training the hideout is stormed by Captain Traho. The only way out for Serafina and Neela is through a mirror, and into Lord Rorrim's realm . . .

The sea is never still.
It pounds on the shore
Restless as a young heart,
Hunting.

The sea speaks
And only the stormy hearts
Know what it says . . .

—From 'Young Sea', by Carl Sandburg

PROLOGUE

BEHIND THE SILVER GLASS, the man with no eyes smiled.

She was here. She had come. As he'd known she would. Her heart was strong and true, and it had led her home.

She had come hoping that there was someone left. Her mother, the regina. Her warrior brother or fierce uncle.

The man watched the mermaid as she swam through the ruined stateroom of her mother's palace. He watched with eyes that were fathomless pits of darkness.

She looked different now. Her clothing was that of the currents, hard and edgy. She'd cut her long copper-brown hair short and dyed it black. Her green eyes were wary and guarded.

Yet, in some ways, she had not changed. Her movements were halting. There was uncertainty in her glance. The man saw that she still did not recognize the source of her power and so did not believe in it. That was good. By the time she did understand, it would be too late. For her. For the seas. For the world.

The mermaid looked at the gaping hole where the

stateroom's east wall had once stood. A current, mournful and low, swept through it. Anemones and seaweeds had begun to colonize its jagged edges. The mermaid swam to the broken throne, then bent down to touch the floor near it.

Head bowed, she stayed there for quite some time. Then she rose and backed away, moving closer to the north wall.

Closer to him.

He'd tried to kill her once, before the attack on her realm. He'd come through a mirror in her bedroom, but a servant had appeared, forcing him back into the silver.

Long, jagged cracks, running through the glass like a network of veins, held him back now. The spaces between the cracks were too small to fit his body through, but large enough for his hands.

Slowly, silently, they pushed through the mirror, hovering only inches from the mermaid. It would be so easy to wrap them around her slender neck and end what the Iele had started.

But no, the man thought, drawing back. That wouldn't be wise. Her courage and strength were greater than he'd imagined. She might yet succeed where others had failed – she might find the talismans. And if she did, he would take them from her. A merman she'd once loved and trusted would help him.

The man with no eyes had waited so long. He knew he must not lose patience now. He retreated into the glass, blending back into its liquid silver. In the hollows where his eyes once were, darkness shone, bright and alive. It was a darkness that watched and waited. A darkness that crouched. A darkness as ancient as the gods.

In her last moments, she would see it. He would turn her face to his and make her look into those bottomless black depths. She would know that she had lost.

And that the darkness had won.

ONE

'HERE, FISH! HERE, SILVERFISH!'

Serafina, breathless and trembling, called out as loudly as she dared. Liquid silver rippled around her as she moved through the Hall of Sighs in Vadus, the mirror realm. Its walls were hung with thousands of looking glasses. Light from flickering chandeliers danced inside them. Except for a few vitrina, who were gazing vacantly at their reflections, the hall was empty.

Sera had hoped her friends would be nearby, but they weren't. They must've come out in other parts of Vadus, she reasoned. At least no death riders had followed her. Baba Vrăja had seen to that by smashing the mirror Sera had swum through, allowing her to escape the soldiers, and their captain, Markus Traho.

'Come, silverfish!' she called again, her voice barely a whisper.

She had to be quiet. To make as few ripples as possible. She didn't want the mirror lord to know she was here. He was every bit as dangerous as Traho.

She remembered the beetles. Vrăja had given her a

handful of them to lure a silverfish. She pulled them out of her pocket and rattled them in her fist.

'Here, fish, fish, fish!' she called. The quicker she found one, the quicker she'd get home.

Home.

Serafina had fled Miromara two weeks before, after Cerulea – its capital city – had been invaded. The attackers had tried to assassinate her mother. They'd murdered her father. They'd been sent by Admiral Kolfinn of Ondalina, an Arctic mer realm, under the leadership of the brutal Captain Traho.

Sera had met Astrid, Kolfinn's daughter, in the Iele's caves, and Astrid had sworn that her father had not ordered an attack on Miromara, but Sera didn't trust her.

Like Serafina herself, and four other mermaids – Neela, Becca, Ling and Ava – Astrid had been summoned by the Iele, a clan of powerful river witches. From Vrăja, the Iele's leader, the mermaids had learned that they were direct descendants of the Six Who Ruled – powerful mages who had once governed the lost island empire of Atlantis.

They'd also learned that Orfeo, the most powerful of the Six, had unleashed a great evil upon the island – the monster Abbadon. The creature had destroyed Atlantis before it was finally defeated by Orfeo's five fellow mages. They had imprisoned it in the Carceron; then one of them – Sycorax – had dragged the prison to the Southern Sea, where she'd sunk it beneath the ice. But now the monster was stirring again. Someone had woken it. Serafina was convinced it was

Kolfinn. She believed he wished to use its power to take over all the mer realms.

Vrăja had told the mermaids that they needed to destroy Abbadon before whoever had woken it could free it. To do this, they would need to find ancient talismans that had belonged to the Six Who Ruled. With these objects, the mermaids could open the lock to the Carceron and go after the monster.

Sera knew her best hope of finding out where the talismans were was in Cerulea's Ostrokon, among the ancient conch recordings about Merrow's Progress. She believed that Merrow, the merfolk's first leader, had hidden the talismans during a journey she'd taken through the world's waters, and that the conchs might reveal their locations.

Though she knew it was extremely dangerous – and she was scared of seeing Cerulea in ruins – she *had* to go back home.

But not yet.

There was someplace else she had to go first.

No, Sera! a voice said forcefully.

She whirled around, looking for whoever had spoken, but no one was there.

Don't go, mina. It's too dangerous.

'Ava?' Sera whispered. 'Is that you? Where are you?'

In your head.

'Is this a convoca?' Sera asked, remembering the difficult summoning spell the Iele had taught them.

Yes . . . trying . . . can't hold it . . . ember . . . Astrid . . .

'Ava, you're breaking up! I'm losing you!' Sera said.

There was no sound for a few seconds, then Ava's voice came back. *Remember what Astrid said? 'The Opafago eat their victims alive . . . while their hearts are still beating and their blood's still pumping.'*

'I know, but I *have* to go,' Sera said.

The Ostrokon . . . safer . . . please . . . Ava was fading again.

'I can't, Ava. Not yet. Before we can find out *where* the talismans are, we have to find out *what* they are.'

Sera waited for Ava's response, but it didn't come.

'Here, silverfish!' Sera said, more urgently now. Time was passing. She had to make wake. 'Here, fish! I have a tasty treat for you!'

'How fabulous! I *love* treats!' a new voice said. From right behind her.

Serafina's blood froze. *Rorrim Drol.* He'd found her after all. She slowly turned around.

'Principessa! How lovely to see you again!' said the mirror lord. His eyes travelled over her face, taking in its pallor. He noted the deep cuts on her tail, made by the monster. His oily smile widened. 'I must say, though, you're not looking very well.'

'*You* are. Well *fed*, that is,' Serafina said, backing away from him.

His face was as round as a full moon. He wore an acid-green silk robe. Its voluminous folds couldn't conceal his girth.

'Why, thank you, my dear!' he said. 'As a matter of fact,

I've just had the most *wonderful* meal. Courtesy of a young human. A girl about your age.' He burped loudly, then covered his mouth. 'Oh, my. *Do* excuse me. I rather overdid it. There were *so* many delicious danklings to be had.'

Danklings were a person's deepest fears. Rorrim fed on them.

'So that's why you're as fat as a walrus,' Serafina said, keeping her distance.

'I couldn't resist. That silly girl made it so easy! She reads these things called *magazines*, you see. They have pictures in them of other girls, only the pictures have been enchanted to make those girls look flawless. But *she* can't see that. All she sees is that they're perfect and she's not. She spends *hours* fretting in her mirror, and I stand on the other side whispering to her that she'll *never* be thin enough, pretty enough, or good enough. And when she's utterly scared and miserable, I feast!'

Poor thing, Sera thought, remembering how bad it felt to fall short of others' expectations. How bad it *still* felt sometimes.

'Isn't it *brilliant*, Principessa? Ah, the goggs! I simply *adore* them. They do *so* much of my work for me. But enough about them. The things I hear about *you* these days!' Rorrim said, wagging a finger. 'You've got Captain Traho tearing up entire rivers looking for you. What are you doing in Vadus? Where are you going?'

'Home,' Sera lied.

Rorrim narrowed his eyes. He licked his lips. 'Surely you

don't have to leave so soon?' He was behind Serafina before she even realized he'd moved. She gasped as she felt a liquid chill run up her spine.

'Still so strong!' he said unhappily.

'Get your hands off me!' Sera cried, swimming away from him.

But he caught up with her. 'Why were you calling my silverfish? Where are you *really* going?' he asked her.

'I told you, *home*,' she said.

Sera knew she had to hide her fears from him. He would use them to keep her here forever, like a vitrina. But it was too late; she suddenly felt a sharp pain.

'Ah! *There* it is!' Rorrim whispered, his breath cold upon her neck. 'Little principessa, you think you're so clever and brave, but you're not. I know it. And so did your mother. You disappointed her time and time again. You let her down. And then you left her to die.'

'No!' Serafina cried.

Rorrim's quick fingers probed her backbone cruelly, searching for her deepest fears. 'But wait, there's more! Just *look* at what you've been up to!' He fell silent for a moment, then said, 'My *word*, what a task Vrăja's given you. And you honestly think you can do it? *You?* What will she do when you fail? I imagine she'll find someone else. Someone better. Just like Mahdi did.'

His venomous words struck at Serafina's heart like a stingray's barb. Mahdi, the crown prince of Matali, a merman she'd loved, had betrayed her for another and the wound was still raw. She looked down at the floor, paralysed by pain. She forgot why she was here. And where she was going. Her will was ebbing away. A suffocating greyness descended on her like a sea fog.

With a purr of pleasure, Rorrim plucked a small, dark thing hiding between two vertebrae. The dankling screeched and flailed as he popped it into his mouth.

'*So* delicious!' he said, swallowing. 'I shouldn't have any more, but I can't help myself.' He ate another, and then said, 'You'll *never* defeat Traho. He'll find you sooner or later.'

The brightness in Serafina's eyes dimmed. Her head dipped. Rorrim plucked more danklings, cramming them into his mouth with the heel of his hand.

'Mmm! Divine!' he said, gulping them down. A rumbling burp escaped him.

The rude noise broke through Serafina's lethargy. For a few seconds, the grey lifted and her mind was clear again. *He's taking me apart. I can't let him*, she thought desperately. *But how can I fight him? He's so strong . . .*

With great effort, she lifted her head – and gasped. Rorrim had doubled in size. His belly was hanging down to his knees. His face was grotesquely bloated. A grimace twisted his mouth.

He's eaten so much he's in pain, she thought.

She heard another voice then – Vrăja's. It sounded in her memory, loud and clear. *Instead of shunning your fear, you must let it speak*, the witch had told her.

Serafina would. She would let it *shout*.

'You're right, Rorrim,' she said. 'What Vrăja's asked of me *is* impossible.'

She was throwing her heart open to a monster. If she failed, he would devour it.

Rorrim snatched another dankling and chewed it. He burped again, wincing. His belly touched the ground now. 'Perhaps a slight pause between courses would be wise,' he said. 'A moment, please . . .'

Sera didn't give him one.

'I'm afraid I won't find my uncle. Or my brother,' she said all in a rush. 'I'm afraid of the death riders. I'm afraid for Neela, Ling, Ava and Becca. I'm afraid Astrid's telling me the truth. I'm afraid she isn't. I'm afraid of Traho. I'm afraid of the man with no eyes . . .'

Rorrim was grabbing fistfuls of danklings now. His arms were so fat, he could barely bring his hands to his mouth, yet he couldn't stop eating. His greed overwhelmed him.

'Do you know what else I'm afraid of?'

'Oh, gods, *stop*. Please!' Rorrim begged. He took a step back, lost his balance and toppled over. He tried to get up, but couldn't. His legs and arms kicked wildly, like a flipped-over turtle's. He was helpless.

Serafina bent over him. She was shouting now. 'I'm afraid I'll lose my mind if I see any more suffering! I'm afraid more Ceruleans will be killed! I'm afraid of villages being raided! I'm afraid Traho will hurt Vrăja! I'm afraid Blu is dead! I'm afraid for the merfolk trapped on Rafe Mfeme's ship!'

Rorrim closed his eyes. He whimpered and Serafina

stopped yelling. She straightened, surprised to find that the grey fog had disappeared. She had bested Rorrim. Her fear had become an ally instead of an enemy.

Smiling, she opened her hand. The beetles were still inside it. 'Silverfish! Come!' she shouted, as loudly as she could.

But no silverfish appeared. Serafina realized what she was doing wrong.

She shouted again. ' !əmoɔ ,dɛiñəvliƧ' she called.

The liquid silver stirred. Two long, quivering antennae emerged from it, followed by a head. The creature crawled all the way out of the liquid and Serafina saw that it was huge. Twice as big as a large hippokamp. Silver drops fell from its long, segmented carapace. A pair of enormous black eyes regarded her.

' ,səlɟəəd lləms I' it said.

' ,ɛɹuoʎ əɹ'ʎədɟ bns ɛiɟnslɟA oɟ əm əʞsT ' Serafina said.

The silverfish nodded and Serafina climbed onto its back. The creature folded its long antennae down so she could hold them like reins. Sera found her seat atop the silverfish just as she would if she were riding her own hippokamp, Clio. Her tail hugged its side. Her spine was straight and strong.

'To *Atlantis*? You're travelling to your own death!' Rorrim cried.

'I'm going to Atlantis to prevent death. Mine and many more,' Serafina said.

'Idiot merl!' Rorrim bellowed, flailing his arms and legs furiously. 'The Opafago will eat you alive! They'll crack your bones open and lick out the marrow! If you aren't scared, you should be!'

'I'm *not* scared, Rorrim . . .'

'*Liar*,' Rorrim hissed.

' . . . I'm terrified.'

TWO

'IT'S TOO SMALL,' Serafina told the silverfish.

The creature stared at her with his big black eyes. 'Now! Beetles!' he said.

Serafina looked at the mirror again. The silverfish had taken her a very long way down the endless Hall of Sighs and had deposited her here. The glass in front of her was broken with jagged edges, and attached to its frame on only two sides. If she sucked in her stomach and turned sideways, she might be able to swim through it, but she wasn't sure and she didn't want to take any chances.

Every mirror in the Hall of Sighs corresponded to a mirror in the terragogg or mer world. The other side of this mirror was somewhere in Atlantis, in some ruined room, but where?

It was dark inside the glass. She couldn't see what awaited her. What if she got stuck? What if she found herself half in and half out, unable to move, with Opafago on the other side? She asked the creature to take her to a different mirror.

The silverfish reared, then slammed back down. 'Beetles!' he demanded.

'¡OK! OK!' Serafina replied.

Maybe there was another way in and maybe there wasn't, but it was clear that this was as far as the silverfish would go. She slid off his back and held out the beetles she'd promised him. He ate them from her hand, then dived back under the silver. Serafina was alone.

Atlantis had been a large island. In addition to Elysia, the capital, it had boasted many towns and villages – all of which had been destroyed. Sera knew she could spend ages looking for another way in and never find it. She took a deep breath, and then – hands together over her head like a diver – she swam carefully through the mirror, mindful of its sharp edges. She pulled her tail through and found herself on a rubble-strewn floor. She'd swum out of the mirror realm, but wasn't sure what she'd swum into.

Only a thin ray of light, shining in through a crack above her, penetrated the gloom. She quietly sang an illuminata spell, pulled the ray to her and expanded it to fill the space. As her eyes adjusted to the brightness, she saw she was in what was once a large and elegant room of a terragogg house. Two walls had collapsed; the other two still stood. Above her, giant wooden beams that had supported an upper floor slanted down from the upright walls. Debris, all of it overgrown, lay heavily across the beams.

Serafina investigated the space, looking for a way out, but found none. She sang a commoveo spell – again in a quiet voice, wary of alerting anyone or anything to her presence. She used the magic to push against large chunks of stone, but it was no use; it would take a dozen songcasters to budge them. She poked and prodded at the bricks and rubble, but only succeeded in dumping silt on her head.

That's when she felt it – a vibration in the water. A strong one. Whatever was making it was big. She spun around. Three feet away from her was a large, angry moray. The eel drew herself up and hissed, baring her lethal teeth.

'Eel, please, you I trouble no give!' Serafina cried.

The terrible grammar that came out of her mouth shocked her. What shocked her even more was that her words were in Eelish – a language she didn't speak.

'What are you doing here?' the eel asked, her voice low and threatening.

I understand her! Serafina thought. *How is this possible? Ling's the only mermaid I know who speaks Eelish.*

She realized that she'd understood the silverfish too. She'd spoken Rursus with him.

Then it hit her: the bloodbind.

When the five merls had mixed their blood and made their vow to work together to defeat Abbadon, some of Ling's magic must have flowed into her. Had she got some of Ava's, Neela's and Becca's too?

'I asked you a question, mermaid,' the eel snarled, moving closer.

'Now getting out. Trying,' Serafina quickly replied.

'How did you get in?'

'Through the looking grass.'

The eel's expression changed from anger to confusion.

'Looking gas. Looking *glass*. Please, eel, show me the out.'

'There's a tunnel,' the eel said. 'But you won't fit through it. You'll have to go out the way you came in.'

'No! Can't! Bad man there. Please, you eel, the out.'

'I'll show you, but it won't do you any good,' the eel said. She swam along the floor to the remains of a collapsed wall. Among the debris was a rock, roughly a foot and a half in diameter. 'There,' she said, pointing behind the rock with her tail.

It was so murky in that part of the room that Serafina hadn't seen the rock, never mind the tunnel behind it. Tugging on the rock now, she loosened it from the surrounding silt, then cast another commoveo to push it out of the way. She took her bag off her shoulder, knelt down, put a hand inside the narrow tunnel and felt a slight current.

'How long?' she asked.

'Not very. Maybe two feet.'

'I me dig out,' Serafina said.

'Do what you need to do. Just get out of my house.'

Serafina started scooping handfuls of silt from the bottom of the tunnel. She'd enlarged it by a good six inches when she hit something hard and large. Unable to move it, she dug at the top of the tunnel instead, and then the sides, working silt, pebbles and small rocks loose. She slowly made her way through the narrow passage on her back, blinking silt from her eyes, spitting grit out of her mouth, praying she didn't loosen something major and bring an avalanche down on herself. When she finally reached the other side of the tunnel, she didn't stop to look around, but quickly wriggled back into the eel's house and grabbed her bag.

'Thank me,' she said.

'For what, exactly?' the eel asked.

'No, *you*. Thank you, eel,' Serafina said.

'Whatever. Just go,' said the eel.

Serafina pushed her bag into the tunnel. The she turned around and reversed into it herself, so that she could pull the rock she'd moved back into place. She didn't want to leave the eel with a big hole in the side of her house. Shoving her bag ahead with her tail, she squeezed through the tunnel once more. When she finally came out the other side, she saw that she was in open water. Cautiously, she checked for any signs of movement, but saw none. The waters above her were bright. From the position of the sun's rays slanting through them, she could tell that it was midday. She looked around and discovered that she was at the back of the terragogg house.

Behind it, foothills sloped gently down to the seafloor. The hills were colonized by corals and seaweeds now, but Sera knew they'd probably been terraced for grapes and olives before Atlantis had been destroyed. She swam to the front of the house, hoping to find her bearings.

There, the terrain fell away steeply into a valley. At its centre, clustered along what had once been a street, were ruins that went on for leagues. Serafina stopped dead at the sight of them, wonder-struck. She had information to gather, talismans to find and a monster to hunt down, but she was so overwhelmed, she couldn't move. Tears came to her eyes.

'Oh,' she whispered. 'Oh, great Neria, just *look* at it!'

Its houses were broken. Its temples toppled. Its palaces ruined.

It was silent. Deserted. Desolate.

But it was still so beautiful.

It was a place Serafina had long imagined, but had never hoped to see.

It was a vanished dream. A fallen empire. A paradise lost.

It was Elysia, the heart of Atlantis.

THREE

SERAFINA STARED, not moving, barely breathing.

So much had collapsed during the island's destruction, but here and there, buildings, or at least parts of them, had survived. She had studied Elysia in school, and had produced several term conchs on its art and architecture.

There in the distance, that bowl-shaped structure – that has to be the amphitheatre, she thought. *And that huge open space flanked by columns, that's the agora – the public square. And there's the ostrokon, which the Atlanteans called a* library.

Unable to contain herself a second longer, she cast a canta prax camouflage spell that allowed her to blend into her surroundings, just like an octopus. Prax, or plainsong, was the most basic mer magic and took little energy or ability. As soon as the songspell was cast, she swam for the ruins.

In minutes, she was at the outskirts of the city. She swooped down low, determined to enter it as her ancestors had, by its streets. As she swam through them – stopping to touch a column or lintel – forty centuries instantly fell away.

She swam into homes both humble and grand. Time and silt had covered much, but in one house she saw a mosaic portrait of a man, woman and three children – the family that had lived there. In another, a statue of the sea goddess Neria, miraculously intact. In a third, she saw a human skeleton – a woman's, she guessed, judging from the bracelets around her wrists and the rings on her fingers. Her delicate bones were furry with algae. Tiny fish swam in and out of her skull. *Atlantis is under an enchantment. Who was she?* Serafina wondered sadly. Had she known the six mages who had ruled Atlantis? Had she seen their talismans? How Sera wished the dead could speak.

As she was looking at the bones, a sudden movement to her left startled her. Her dagger was in her hand immediately, but it was only a crab scuttling up a wall. She sighed with relief, but the scare reminded her where she was – in the realm of the Opafago. The information she needed was here, she was sure of it, carved into a pediment or chiselled on a frieze. The faster she found it, the better.

Serafina moved on, deeper into the city, alert to sound and motion. As she swam, the camouflage spell she'd cast allowed her body to take on the colours around her – the sandy hues of rubble, the pink and white of coral, the greens and browns of seaweeds. In the centre of Elysia, she knew, was the Hall of the Six Who Ruled and temples dedicated to important gods and goddesses. The ostrokon was there, and the agora too. These public places would be more likely than private homes to have the information she was seeking.

She passed what looked like a wheelwright's shop, with barnacled hoops still leaning against its front, then a wagonmaker's and a blacksmith's. She realized she was in what must've been an artisans' quarter – like Cerulea's fabra. The street hooked to the left and narrowed; Serafina followed it. The purpose of the shops that lined it became more sombre. One had sold funeral biers. Another, shrouds.

At the bottom of the street was what looked like a temple. As Serafina neared it, she saw that its roof and walls were intact, unlike many of the neighbouring buildings'. The temple's massive doors, made of bronze, still hung on their hinges. Strangely, there was no corrosion on them. The stone columns flanking the doors were also intact. Above them were words carved in ancient Greek. Sera struggled with the letters, but eventually she deciphered them, whispering aloud the words they made: 'Temple of Morsa.'

Abbadon had uttered similar words: *Daímonas tis Morsa* – demon of Morsa. Sera's blood ran cold at the memory. Could this place contain information about the monster? Or the talismans?

No temple had ever been built for Morsa in Miromara, or in any of the mer realms. Merrow had decreed the goddess an abomination who deserved no place in a civilized society.

As she worked up the nerve to go inside, Serafina wondered if Merrow had other reasons for forbidding Morsa's worship. Just as she wondered if Merrow had other reasons for herding the bloodthirsty Opafago into the Barrens of Thira, the waters surrounding Atlantis.

According to historians, Merrow said that she'd driven the cannibals to the Barrens because the ruins were useless to merfolk. Sera, however, believed Merrow had done so to make sure the true story of Atlantis's demise was never discovered. According to Merrow's ancient bloodsong, handed down to Vrăja, the Temple of Morsa was where Orfeo had locked himself during the island's destruction. Was there something inside it that Merrow also wanted kept secret?

'There's only one way to find out,' Serafina said to herself.

It was dark inside the temple. The building's narrow windows let in little light from the waters above. Serafina cast an illuminata to see where she was going, swirling sun rays together. As the ball of light flared in her hands, her eyes widened.

The temple looked exactly as it must have four thousand years ago. Nothing was disturbed. No silt was covering the floor. No algae, anemones or seaweed had colonized the walls. It was as if even the blind, tiny creatures of the sea knew to shun the goddess.

Sera was amazed that the temple had survived, and was dazzled by its dark beauty. There were towering statues of Morsa's priests and priestesses carved out of obsidian, with polished rubies for eyes. There were painted panels on the walls depicting her shadowy realm, incense burners made of gold, and silver candelabra. But underneath Sera's amazement was a growing uneasiness. *How has the temple survived all these centuries?* she wondered.

Sera released her illuminata, leaving it to float in the dusky water. She swam to the altar, slowing as she saw what was above it – a mosaic, at least twenty feet high, of the fearsome Morsa.

It was only an image, yet it scared her. Morsa, the scavenger goddess of the dead, had once taken the form of a jackal. When she started to practise necromancy, the forbidden art of conjuring the dead, Neria transformed her into a creature so loathsome, no one could bear to look at her.

The creature staring back at Sera from the wall of the temple, with its glittering eyes, was a woman from the waist up, and a coiled serpent from the waist down. Her face was that of a corpse, mottled by decay. A crown of scorpions, their tails poised to strike, sat atop her head. On the palm of one hand rested a flawless black pearl.

What was on the floor of Morsa's altar, though, frightened Sera even more – a large, deep stain, as deeply red as garnets. She knew what it was. What she didn't know was why the seawater hadn't washed it away centuries ago. She was filled with dread as she bent down to touch it, yet strangely compelled.

Driven by the urgency of her mission, Serafina had done a foolish thing – she'd entered a place that had only one way in and one way out.

When the hand came down on her shoulder, she had absolutely nowhere to go.

FOUR

SERAFINA SCREAMED.

She whipped around and thrust her dagger up through the water, catching her attacker under the chin.

'Maybe I should have knocked.'

'*Ling?*' Serafina cried in disbelief. Her voice was shaking almost as much as her hand.

Ling tried to nod, but couldn't. The tip of Sera's dagger was poking into her skin.

'I could have *killed* you!' Serafina said, putting her dagger away. 'I almost did! What are you doing here?'

'Keeping an eye on you.'

'How did you get into the ruins?' asked Sera.

'I came out of Vrăja's mirror in Vadus. A vitrina told me I was in the Hall of Sighs. I found a mirror that led to an eel's house – a very angry eel. When she told me I was the second mermaid who'd invaded her space today, I knew I was on your tail. The tunnel was a bit tight with this thing on my arm,' she said, patting the splint she wore to protect her broken wrist, 'but I got through.'

'How did you find out I was going to Atlantis?'

'Ava. You know how she can sometimes see the future? She saw that you were coming here, then used a convoca to contact me. She was really worried, so I told her I'd go after you.'

'I'm sorry, Ling.'

'For what?'

'Almost cutting your head off.'

'No worries,' Ling said, smiling. 'If you *had* killed me,' she nodded at the mosaic, 'good old Morsa could bring me back.' Ling swam up high and peered at the ancient inscription over the goddess's head. 'It means *Soul Eater*,' she said.

Ling was much quicker at translating than Sera. She was an omnivoxa, a mermaid who could speak all languages.

'Soul eater. Wow. That's comforting,' Serafina said.

Ling swam back down and looked at the altar stone. *'Whoa.* Is that—'

'Blood? I think so.'

'Why is it still here? *How* is it still here?'

'I was wondering the same thing,' said Serafina. She reached for the dark stain again.

'What are you doing?' Ling asked.

'Pulling a bloodsong.'

Even after four thousand years, the blood came to life under Sera's hand. It brightened as if newly spilled, then spun up from the floor in a violent crimson vortex.

The mermaids heard a voice. And then another. And more. Until there were dozens of them. Screaming. Sobbing. Pleading. Shrieking. They sounded so terrified that Serafina couldn't bear to listen any longer. She ripped her hand away with such force that she toppled backwards. The blood spiralled back down into the altar.

Ling had backed herself against a wall. 'Something bad happened here,' she said, pale and shaking.

'There's got to be a way to find out what it was,' Serafina said. 'We could comb through more temples. Go to the Ostrokon and the Hall of the Six. Read every inscription we can find.'

'Yeah, we could. If we had a year or two,' said Ling. She thought for a moment, then her eyes lit up. 'We're in the wrong place, Sera. Forget ostrokons and temples. What we need is a hairdresser's. Or a toga shop. Someplace with lots of mirrors.'

'Why?' Serafina said. Then she understood. '*Vitrina!* Ling, you're a genius!'

FIVE

'So, TELL ME, does my hair look better up? Or down?'

'Four thousand years go by, and *this* is what she asks us?' Ling grumbled.

'Shh!' Serafina hissed, elbowing her. 'Up, Lady Thalia. Definitely,' she said to the figure in the mirror. 'It frames your beautiful face that way. And shows off your lovely eyes.'

The vitrina twisted her hair up and pinned it. 'Oh, you're *so* right! Now, which earrings? The ruby drops or the gold hoops?'

'You *do* remember that we're right smack in the middle of a tribe of cannibals, right?' Ling whispered.

Serafina and Ling were in the women's baths. The building, made of thick blocks of stone, had survived with little damage. One room – maybe a dressing room – contained walls that had been covered with mirror glass. Much of it had darkened, cracked or fallen away, but there was still one good-size panel that wasn't too clouded, and in it they'd found Lady Thalia, a noblewoman. She was its first and only occupant, the mermaids had learned. She'd lived in it by herself for the last four millennia.

'Poor Lady Thalia,' Sera had said. 'You must've been so lonely all this time with no one else to talk to.'

'Hardly! I have *myself* to talk to, my dear, and there's no one more charming, or lovelier, more graceful, or wittier, or more captivating in every possible way than me.'

Like all vitrina, Thalia was a ghost. She had been in love with her own reflection while alive and now her soul was trapped inside the glass forever. She'd been haughty and silent when the mermaids first found her, but Serafina had flattered her so much that she'd finally deigned to speak with them. As long as the topic of conversation was her.

Serafina smiled at the mirror. 'So, Lady Thalia . . .' she said.

'Mmm?' Talia said, fastening an earring.

'We need your help.'

'I thought you'd never ask!'

'Really? You'll help us?' Serafina said excitedly.

'Yes. First, my dear, do something about that hair,' Thalia said. 'Get a wig. Cast a spell. *Anything*. But fix it. Second, the black eye shadow has to go. And that outfit – simply unspeakable!'

'Um, that's not the kind of help we had in mind,' said Ling.

'And you,' – she pointed at Ling – 'get rid of the sword. It's unfeminine. Pluck those eyebrows. Put on some lipstick. And smile. Smiling makes you pretty.'

Ling glowered.

'Lady Thalia, thank you for all the wonderful advice.

We're very grateful for it. But we need a different kind of help,' Serafina said.

'We need to know about Orfeo,' Ling added.

'I don't wish to talk any more. Goodbye,' Thalia said, abruptly turning away.

'Lady Thalia, don't go. *Please*,' Serafina pleaded. 'If you don't help us, many will die.'

Thalia slowly turned back to the mermaids. Her vapid expression had been replaced by one of fear. 'I can't! What if he hears me?' she whispered.

'He's dead. Merrow killed him a long time ago,' said Ling.

'Are you sure?' Thalia asked, looking as if she didn't believe them.

'Yes. But his monster – Abbadon – is alive. And it's going to attack again. It's going to do to others what it did to the people of Atlantis,' Sera explained.

Thalia shuddered. 'It doesn't *feel* like Orfeo's dead. It feels like he's still here, moving through the streets of Elysia like an ill wind. We locked our doors, shuttered our windows, but it did no good.'

'Tell us what happened,' Serafina said. She squeezed Ling's hand, certain that they were on the verge of getting the answers they needed.

Thalia shook her head sadly. 'He was so beautiful. You don't call men beautiful, I know. But Orfeo was. He was tall and strong. Bronzed from the sun. Blond and blue-eyed. He had a smile that melted hearts. Every woman in Elysia was in love with him, but he loved only one: Alma, my friend. She was good and kind, as Orfeo himself was then, and he loved her more than anything in this world, or the next. They married and were very happy, but then Alma grew gravely ill and everything changed. Orfeo couldn't accept that she would die. He was a healer and he used all his powers to save her, but it was no use. She suffered so terribly that she begged for death, saying it would be a relief . . .'

Thalia stopped to dab at her eyes, and Serafina saw that the memory of her friend's death was still very painful, even after four thousand years.

'When Alma was near the end, a priest placed a white pearl under her tongue, as was the custom, to catch her soul as it left her body,' Thalia continued. 'After she passed, her body was placed on a bamboo bier and floated out to sea where Horok – the ancient coelacanth, the Keeper of Souls – would take the pearl from her mouth and carry it to the underworld. But as the bier floated away, Orfeo, insane with grief, cried out to Horok, begging him not to take Alma. Horok told Orfeo such things cannot be. That's when Orfeo went mad. He vowed to get Alma back if it took him a thousand lifetimes. He returned to his home and destroyed all his medicines. His frightened children ran to an aunt's house. He hardly spoke to anyone in the months that followed, and barely ate or slept. All his energies went to building a temple for Morsa. When it was finished, he locked himself inside it.'

'Why?' Ling asked.

'To summon the goddess. To beseech her to teach him her secrets. He gave her everything he had – his wealth, his possessions, Alma's stunning jewels, even his precious talisman, a flawless emerald given to him by Eveksion, the god of healing. I saw that emerald. It was beyond compare, a gift from a *god*, yet Orfeo destroyed it. It was said he ground it up and stirred it into the wine he gave to those he sacrificed. To tempt Morsa. Its powers made them healthy and strong, you see, and that's how she liked her victims.'

'Lady Thalia, did you say *sacrificed?*' Serafina asked, feeling sick at the very thought. She remembered the bloodstain on Morsa's altar. And the bloodsong. The voices she and Ling had heard – they were voices of human beings whose lives had been offered to the dark goddess.

'Yes, I did. He started with sailors and travellers,' Thalia said. 'Those without families in Atlantis, those who wouldn't be missed. Then he came for us. He came at night. No one knew he was doing it until it was too late. Until he was so powerful, no one could stop him.'

'But how could he have had such powers without his emerald?' Ling asked.

Thalia laughed. 'Morsa gave him another talisman ten times more powerful – a flawless black pearl. It was her symbol, a mockery of the white pearls Horok used to hold souls. Morsa's pearl held souls too – the souls of those sacrificed to her. Orfeo gave her death, and in return she gave him her forbidden knowledge. It made him so powerful that he created Abbadon and declared he would use the monster to march on the underworld and take Alma back.'

Sera's pulse was racing. She and Ling had just learned

why Orfeo had created Abbadon. Even the Iele had not known that. The vitrina had also told them what one of the talismans was.

'Lady Thalia,' she asked excitedly, 'did you ever see any of the other mages' talismans?'

'Oh, yes,' said Thalia. 'I saw all of them.'

'Can you tell us what they were?' Sera asked.

But Thalia didn't reply. She was holding up a necklace and frowning at it.

Sera panicked. She knew how vitrina were – quite a few of them had lived in her own looking glass – and she knew they had short attention spans for any topic that wasn't them. If Thalia grew bored with the conversation, she might simply drift deeper into the mirror. Sera didn't want to have to dive in after her and risk coming across Rorrim Drol again.

'That necklace is gorgeous. It'll bring out the golden flecks in your lovely eyes,' Sera quickly said, hoping to ply Thalia with more compliments.

Thalia gave her a preening smile. 'Yes, it will. You're so right, you know. About the necklace and my eyes.'

'I imagine the talismans were beautiful too. You would recognize beauty, of course, being so beautiful yourself,' said Sera, desperate to keep her talking.

'Oh, they were!' Thalia said. 'Merrow's was called the *Pétra tou Néria* – Neria's Stone. Merrow once saved the life of Neria's youngest son, Kyr, you see. He'd taken the form of a seal pup and was attacked by a shark. She was wading in the waves at the time and saw the attack. She snatched him from the water and carried him to safety. Neria was so grateful, she bestowed a magnificent blue diamond on her. It was shaped like a teardrop. I saw it. It was dazzling. As was Navi's talisman, a moonstone.'

'What did that look like?' Ling asked.

'It was silvery blue and about the size of an albatross's egg. It glowed from within like the moon.'

'Just like your complexion, Lady Thalia,' Sera said.

She couldn't believe their luck. Thalia knew what the talismans were – every one of them. Now all Sera had to do was listen to conchs on Merrow's Progress, and she'd find out *where* they were. With so much information, they'd be way ahead of Traho.

'What was Sycorax's talisman?' Ling asked.

But Thalia didn't answer. She was no longer looking at the mermaids. She was looking past them, her eyes filled with terror.

'Go! Get out of here! Hurry!' she hissed.

The mermaids turned around. In the doorway stood six creatures. They were tall and humanlike, with strong limbs, humped backs and thick necks. Their bodies were covered with scales like those of a Komodo dragon. Red eyes stared out from under thick, bony brows. Tusks curved down from either side of their noses, the better to spear their prey. Black lips parted to reveal rows of sharp, spiky teeth.

'Dinnertime,' Ling said grimly. 'And we're on the menu.'

SIX

'THE MIRROR, LING,' Serafina said quietly. 'We've got to swim into Thalia's mirror.'

Ling nodded but didn't answer. She couldn't. She was singing a spell the Iele had taught them, an apă piatră. An Opafago rushed forwards, hit the water wall Ling had created and roared. The others started to batter against it with their large clawed hands.

'Come on!' Serafina shouted.

Ling swam backwards to the mirror, keeping an eye on her water wall.

'I'll go in first,' Serafina said. 'Then I'll pull you in after me.' She started to swim through the glass. As she did, a head popped up on the other side, round and bald.

'*Darling* merl!'

'Rorrim, please, you've got to let us in,' Serafina said.

'Actually, I *don't*, but that's beside the point. I have someone here who's dying to see you.' He touched a finger to his chin. 'Or was it that he wants to see you die?'

He stepped aside and Serafina saw another figure in the silver. Her blood turned to ice. It was the man with no eyes.

He started towards her, a murderous expression on his face.

Sera was so frightened she could barely form words. 'Ling . . . trouble,' she rasped.

Ling glanced over her shoulder. 'Break the mirror!'

Sera knew that if she did that, the man would not be able to crawl out of the glass, because the pieces would be too small for him to fit through. But she also knew that they would never see Thalia again.

Vadus had few rules. The countess who lived inside Sera's mirror had told her that some vitrina stayed within the bounds of their own mirrors; others wandered through the realm. Some spoke to the living; others refused to. There was, however, one law all were bound by: when a vitrina's own mirror was broken, her soul was released from the glass.

'I *can't* break it, Ling!' Sera cried. 'We need Thalia! We need to find out what the other talismans are!'

'None of it matters if we're *dead*! Do it, Sera! *Now!*'

The man with no eyes was closer. In a few seconds, he'd be through the glass. Sera had no choice. She slapped her tail against the mirror violently, smashing it. The pieces rained down on the floor. A hundred empty eye sockets stared at her from a hundred shards, then disappeared.

'Look for another way out of here!' Ling yelled.

The water wall buckled under the force of the Opafago. Ling sang the spell again to strengthen it. As she did, Serafina looked around the room, hoping to find a hole in the ceiling, or a crack in a wall. But there was nothing.

Then she spotted a narrow doorway half hidden behind a pile of rubble. 'This way!' she shouted.

Ling followed, never taking her eyes off the cannibals.

There was a room on the other side, much bigger than the one they'd swum out of. It, too, was built of heavy stones and was intact.

Too late, they discovered that it was also a dead end.

Ling cast yet another apă piatră, concentrating her magic on the doorway. It was easier to block a smaller space, but the Opafago – slamming themselves against the water wall over and over again – were draining her strength.

'I can't keep this up much longer,' she said.

Serafina sang a commoveo and used it to push against the walls, but the room was so solidly built, nothing happened.

'I'll let the water wall down. They'll all rush in. When they do, catch them in a vortex,' Ling said.

'I can't! Any vortex big enough to catch them will catch us too.'

'Getting *tired* here. We've got to *do* something!'

Serafina swam frantically around the room. She saw that she and Ling were in the baths proper now. There were no windows and the only door was the one they'd swum through. A large sunken square, once a pool, filled most of the room and butted up against its back wall. Sera spotted stone carvings on that wall – six ornate dolphin heads. Water had flowed through pipes to their mouths and into the pool.

'Oh, wow!' she said. 'Ling, did you know that the Atlanteans were the first to figure out how to build aqueducts and bury pipes inside walls? I almost forgot that!'

'Are you *kidding* me? This is no time for a history lesson!' Ling shouted.

But it was.

The pipes would have water in them, given that they were currently under a great deal of it. And *that* water could be used for a vortex spell. It would cause an explosion. Which might blow a hole in the back wall, allowing them to escape – if everything went right. If everything went wrong, it would bring the entire bathhouse down on their heads.

Sera started to sing.

> *Water, cut off*
> *From the sea,*
> *Held here captive,*
> *Same as me,*
> *Whirl and spin*
> *And heed my call,*
> *Cause these ancient*
> *Stones to fall!*

At first, nothing happened, but then Sera heard water and sediment whirling inside the pipes. She sang the spell again, her voice growing louder. The pipes groaned. The old stones of the bathhouse rumbled. The water was spinning faster and faster, trying to spiral outward like winds in a tornado, but it couldn't and the ancient pipes screamed with the strain of containing it.

'Come *on*, Sera!' Ling yelled.

Sera sang the spell once more, with every bit of strength she had. As the last note rose, there was a deafening roar. The pipes exploded, taking most of the back wall with them. The force of the blast knocked Serafina to the floor and sent debris flying through the water, covering her in gravel and silt. She shook it off, got up and looked for Ling.

Ling was weaving back and forth, dazed. A piece of debris had sliced her cheek. She'd dropped her apă piatră, and the Opafago, dazed themselves, staggered through the doorway. Serafina grabbed her friend and pulled her through the gaping hole in the wall.

'Ling, can you swim on your own?' Sera asked. 'We've got to make wake.'

Ling blinked. She shook her head to clear it. After a few deep breaths, she said, 'Head for the surface. I hear a shoal. It's an easy meal for the Opafago. If we can get above it, we might lose them.'

Serafina and Ling streaked up into the warmer, light-filled waters. Thousands of sardines, their scales flashing, were moving through the current. The two mermaids shot through the shoal, hearts pumping, lungs straining. Sera looked back to see all six of the horrible Opafago snatching fish with their clawed hands and pushing them into their mouths.

'Could've been us,' Ling said.

A minute later, both mermaids broke the surface. Ling, panting, shaded her eyes and looked around. 'I see a cove over there,' she said, pointing west. 'It'll be evening soon. Maybe we can find a sea cave and hole up for the night.'

They swam silently for nearly half an hour. As they neared the cove, Sera noticed that Ling was cradling her bad arm.

'Are you OK? How are you feeling?' she asked her.

'I'm tired. Really, really tired,' said Ling.

'That was flat-out,' said Sera.

'Yeah, but it's more than that. I'm tired of swimming for my life. Tired of Traho and cannibals and freaks in mirrors.'

'You forgot rotters, death riders and rusalka,' Serafina added with a weary laugh.

'I just want a bubble tea, you know? Coralberry. That's my favourite flavour. I just want to hang with my friends. Go to a dance. Listen to the latest Dead Reckoners conch. Sleep in a comfy bed.' Ling paused, gazing at the horizon. 'It's not going to happen though, is it?'

Sera looked at her friend. Blood from the cut on Ling's cheek was dripping down her jaw. She was still holding her arm. This was their life now – violent encounters and narrow escapes. For a few seconds Sera was gripped by a feeling of unreality so strong, it made her dizzy.

The name of the band Ling had mentioned – the Dead Reckoners – echoed in her head. She remembered when she and Neela had found Mahdi and Yazeed, Neela's brother, passed out in the ruins of Merrow's palace after a night of partying. Yazeed, fibbing like mad, said they'd been to the Lagoon to see the Dead Reckoners. Sera couldn't believe that had happened only a few weeks ago; it felt like a lifetime. Before the attack on her realm, she'd been a pampered princess. Now she was an outlaw with a price on her head, always on the swim, always in danger. The people she'd left behind: Yaz, Mahdi, her mother, her uncle and brother . . . she had no idea if they'd even survived.

She had no idea if she would.

'No, Ling,' she finally said. 'It's not going to happen.'

Ling sighed. 'Guess we'll have to make do with the cove then. We should be safe there. I doubt anyone comes to these waters. Not with our hungry little friends in them. Whatever shelter we find probably won't be much—'

'But it'll be enough,' Sera said, her voice suddenly passionate. She turned to face her friend. 'I don't need bubble tea or a cushy bed, Ling. I lost everything I had, but I'm finding what I need. Like strength, courage . . . and most of all, merls who have my back. That's enough. It's more than enough. It's everything.'

Ling smiled at her. 'Yeah,' she said softly. 'I guess it is.'

The two mermaids dived. They swam just below the waves. Away from the Opafago. Away from Atlantis. Away from Rorrim and the man with no eyes.

Away, just for a night, from all danger.

SEVEN

'Up and at 'em, sleepyhead.'

Serafina opened her eyes. 'Morning already?' she asked.

'Yep. I scrounged some breakfast,' Ling said. 'Limpets and mussels. Reef olives too.'

She put down her scarf, which was bulging with her finds.

'Thanks. I'm famished,' Serafina said, yawning.

The sea cave where she and Ling had spent the night was thickly carpeted with seaweed and anemones. Serafina had slept well. She sat up now and stretched.

'How are your battle wounds?' she asked Ling.

'The cut on my face stopped bleeding. And my arm isn't throbbing any more. That was some tour we took of Atlantis.'

'We came *so* close to finding out what all the talismans are,' Sera said, her voice heavy with disappointment.

'We also came close to becoming a meal,' Ling added. 'At least we found out what three of the talismans are – a black pearl, a blue diamond and a moonstone. That's three more than we had. It's major.'

'I guess you're right. We should tell the others. I'll cast a convoca. See if I can get us all on the same wavelength.'

Serafina tried to cast the songspell, but nothing happened. She tried again. 'Ling, aren't you getting anything from me?' she asked, frustrated.

'Nope. Nothing. Nada. Nihilo. Nichts—'

'OK, *OK*, I get it!' Serafina huffed. She slapped her tail fin against the cave wall. 'Why can't I cast this spell?'

'Because you're tired.'

Serafina arched an eyebrow. 'You mean I'm no good at it.'

'No, I *don't* mean that. You know, I just tried to talk to an octopus. While I was out looking for our breakfast. I wanted to ask him where I could find some clams. I learned Molluska when I was, like, two years old, but I couldn't even remember how to say hello.'

'You know what's weird, though?' Serafina recalled. 'Back in Atlantis, I could talk to an eel. And I don't know Eelish. I think it happened because of the bloodbind. Because I've got some of your blood in me now.'

'Huh. I guess that explains why the illuminata I just cast when I was looking for breakfast was the best one I've ever done,' Ling said, chewing an olive. 'I've got some of Neela's skills now. I'm going to try to summon waterfire later. See if I've got some of Becca's too. But you know the deal, Sera – magic's not exact. It depends on a lot of things. Ability. Strength. The moon. The tides . . .'

'The utter lameness of the songcaster.'

'Try again in a day or two. When you're stronger. When you haven't just outswum five hundred death riders, Rorrim

Drol, a whole pack of Opafago and an eyeless gogg.'

A chill ran through Sera at the mention of the terrifying man with the black, empty eyes. He'd first appeared to her in her own mirror. He'd tried to crawl out of it, to come after her, but her nursemaid, Tavia, had scared him off. At the time, Sera had told herself he was only a hallucination. Now she knew he was real. And that he meant her – and her friends – harm.

'Who *is* he? Why is he after us?' she asked.

'I wish I knew,' Ling said, pulling a limpet from its shell. 'Promise me something though.'

'What?'

'When we go our separate ways, stay out of mirrors and Atlantis. They're too dangerous.'

'Yeah, sure,' scoffed Serafina. 'I'll just take it easy from now on. Head home to Cerulea, kick back in a war zone for a bit.'

Ling laughed.

'Actually, I might make one slight detour first.'

'Another one? It sounds like you're trying to *avoid* Cerulea, not get back to it.'

Sera bristled. Her reluctance to return home had been a bone of contention between them. They'd argued about it on their way to the Iele's cave – right before Ling was caught in one of Rafe Mfeme's fishing nets. Sera still blamed herself for the broken wrist Ling had suffered while struggling to escape.

'There's a reason for the detour. A good one,' she said, a bit defensively. 'Remember when I told you and the other merls how Neela and I had been captured by Traho? And that we escaped with the help of the Praedatori? They took us to their headquarters, to a palazzo in Venice owned by a human, Armando Contorini, duca di Venezia. Traho found out and attacked the palazzo. Because of us. I've got to go back. I've got to make sure the duca is OK.'

The duchi de Venezia, of which Duca Armando was the most recent, had been created by Merrow herself to defend the seas and their creatures from the terragoggs. They had fighters for their cause in the water – the Praedatori – and on land – the Wave Warriors.

At first Serafina had not understood why the duca had involved himself and his fighters in the attack on Cerulea. *After all*, she'd thought, *no terragoggs had been involved in the invasion, only mer*. But the duca had taught her otherwise. Traho had been aided by a human named Rafe Iaoro Mfeme. Mfeme, a cruel and brutal man who owned a fleet of trawlers and dredgers, had transported troops for Traho. In return, Traho had revealed the hiding places of tuna, swordfish and other valuable sea creatures.

Sera remembered the night Mfeme had broken into the duca's palazzo and hurled him into a wall. And how Traho's mermen, invading from the waters below the palazzo, had fired their spearguns at the Praedatori. One of them had hit Blu. The last image Sera had of him was his body twisting violently as he tried to cut the line from the gun to the spear. Grigio, another of the Praedatori, had rushed Sera and Neela into Sera's bedroom during the attack and had locked the door.

When Traho's soldiers had started battering on that door, both mermaids escaped through a mirror. Sera had been worried about the duca and his brave fighters ever since. She desperately hoped they were all right. Though she hadn't told anyone, and could barely admit it to herself, she had fallen for the mysterious Blu. He was everything Mahdi – the merman who'd broken her heart – was not.

'Just be careful,' Ling said now. 'I followed you to Atlantis, but I can't follow you to Cerulea.'

'Where are you headed?' asked Sera.

'Back to my village. I want to talk with my great-grandmother about all this. She's very wise. If there are any legends about Merrow visiting our waters, she'll know them. There might be a clue in a Qin fable or folksong. But I'm going to make a detour too. To the Great Abyss.'

Sera gave her a long look. 'And you think Atlantis is dangerous?'

'I know, I know,' Ling said. 'But it's the last place my father went before he disappeared. I feel close to him there, as if he never died.'

Ling had told Sera and Neela about her father's death. It had happened a year ago, while he was exploring the Abyss. His body was never recovered.

'I miss my father too. We used to ride together all the time,' Sera said. 'If I could, I'd go back to the palace stables. I know I'd feel his spirit there. But I don't even know if our hippokamps are still around, or if the stables are still standing.' She laughed bitterly. 'I don't even know if the palace is.'

Sera could still see the Blackclaw dragon as it tore through the palace's walls. And her father's lifeless body falling through the water. She could see the arrow as it sank into her mother's chest. And the soldiers descending from above. She knew that these images would never leave her, nor would the sorrow they made her feel. But she also knew now that she had to face her losses – as hard as that would be. Vrăja had been right when she'd told her that she needed to go home.

Someone else had been right too, and Sera hadn't acknowledged it. If she didn't do it now, she might never get the chance again.

'Hey, Ling?'

'Mmm?' Ling said, chewing a limpet.

'Before we head out, there's something I need to say . . . I'm sorry for not listening to you. Back near the Dunărea. When you said I had to face the fact that my mother might not be alive.'

'Forget it, Sera. You already apologized for that.'

'No, I didn't. I apologized for going shoaling, not for refusing to listen to you. You tried to make me see what I needed to do. You said that omnivoxas had a responsibility to speak not only words, but the truth. You never backed down from that responsibility, even when I was being angry and stupid. I just want you to know that I think that's really brave.'

Ling shrugged. 'I used to get picked on a lot. Back home. I had to develop guts early on. You need them to take on your enemies.'

'And your friends,' Sera said ruefully.

Ling laughed. The two mermaids finished eating, and then it was time to leave.

'Gotta go save the world,' Ling said, picking up her bag.

'Take care of yourself,' Serafina said, hugging her tightly.

'You too,' said Ling, hugging her back.

As Sera swam away, she glanced back at Ling. Her friend looked so small in the distance, so alone.

'Yes, we have to save the world, Ling . . . but who's going to save *us*?' she wondered aloud.

And then she turned and began the long journey home.

EIGHT

'**Y**OU ARE *NOT* the Princess Neela,' sniffed Matali's sub-assistant to the third minister of the interior under the oversecretary of the Emperor's Chamber. 'The Princess Neela wouldn't be caught *dead* dressed like that. You are an imposter. Obviously disturbed. Possibly dangerous. You must leave the palace right now or I shall call the guards.'

Neela groaned. She'd been arguing with the sub-assistant, the gatekeeper to the Emperor's Chamber, for a solid ten minutes. And that was *after* she'd argued with the executive assistant to the keeper of the portcullis, the senior assistant to the chamberlain of the Emperor's Courtyard, and the assistant chief steward, twice removed, of the exterior grand foyer.

She'd arrived at the palace an hour ago. After diving into the mirror inside the river witches' Incantarium, she'd got lost in Vadus, and it had taken her a long time to find her way out again. Finally another mirror got her to a Matali dress shop. Luckily, the place was so busy, no one noticed when she'd suddenly appeared in the dressing room. Never had she been so happy to be home. As she'd swum out of the shop, she'd spotted the palace and as always, the very sight of it – with its gleaming golden domes, its soaring rock crystal colonnades and vaulted archways – had taken her breath away.

The heart of the palace was an enormous white marble octagon, flanked by towers. Matali's flag – a red banner featuring a Razormouth dragon with a silver-blue egg in its claws – fluttered from each one. The palace had been built by Emperor Ranajit ten centuries ago, on a deepwater rock shelf off the south western coast of India. When subsequent emperors ran out of room on the original shelf, they built on nearby outcroppings and connected the old to the new with covered marble bridges. Slender and graceful, the passageways allowed the courtiers and ministers who lived on the outcroppings to travel to and from the palace without having their robes of state rumpled by the currents.

As Neela had drawn near, she'd seen that the palace looked different. Its windows had been shuttered, and its gateways locked. Members of the Pānī Yōd'dhā'ōṁ, Matali's water warriors, patrolled the perimeter.

'Excuse me, can you tell me what's going on? Why is the palace surrounded by guards?' she'd asked a passing merman.

'Have you been living under a rock? We're preparing for war! The emperor and empress have been assassinated. The crown prince is missing. All of Matali is under martial law,' the merman had said. 'Ondalina's behind it all – mark my words.'

Neela was so stunned she'd had to sit down. The man's

words felt like a knife to her heart. During the chaos of the attack on Cerulea, she had become separated from her family. In the days that followed, she'd assumed they'd been taken prisoner, but she never thought the invaders would kill them. Her Uncle Bilaal and Aunt Ahadi . . . *dead*. Grief had hit her full on. She'd lowered her head into her hands. *Why?* Her uncle had been a just ruler, and her aunt kind and good-hearted. And Mahdi . . . he was missing. That meant her parents were now emperor and empress. Was Yazeed with them? Had he escaped the carnage?

After a few minutes, Neela had picked her head up. Sitting on a bench, she realized, was helping no one. 'Get up and *do* something,' she'd told herself.

She'd fought her way through guards and bureaucrats to get to the Emperor's Chamber and now she wanted to go inside it. She needed to see her parents and tell them all that had happened. What she *didn't* need was to spend one more minute arguing with the sub-assistant.

'I *am* the princess! I was in Cerulea when it was invaded. I've been on the swim ever since. *That's* why I look like this!' she shouted, slapping her tail fin in frustration.

'Ah! You see? More evidence that you are an imposter,' the sub-assistant said smugly. 'The Princess Neela *never* shouts.'

Neela leaned in close to him. 'When my father finds out that I was here and you turned me away, you'll be guarding the door to the broom closet!'

The sub-assistant nervously tapped his chin. 'I suppose

you *could* fill out a form,' he said. He searched the shelves behind him. 'I'm sure I have one somewhere. Ah! Here we are. *Official Application for Grant of Consideration of Request for Petition of Possibility of Permission to Enter the Royal Presence.*'

Neela, seething, said, 'If I fill this out, will you let me in?'

'In six months. Give or take a week.'

At that moment, the doors to the Emperor's Chamber opened and three officials exited. Seizing her chance, Neela skirted around them and into the room, sending the sub-assistant into a tizzy.

'Wait!' he cried. 'You *must* fill out a form! That is the way things are done! That is the way things have *always* been done!'

The Emperor's Chamber was incredibly sumptuous, designed to awe both friends and enemies of the realm. Delicate coral screens covered the arched windows. The white marble walls were inlaid with piecework images of Matalin royalty in lapis, malachite, jade and pearl. Hundreds of lava torches – their glass globes tinted pink – cast a flattering glow. Murti, statues of divine sea spirits, stood in wall niches. The room's immense domed ceiling was made of faceted pieces of rock crystal that caught the light and cast it down upon the two golden thrones standing on a high dais. On those thrones sat Aran, the new emperor, and Sananda, his empress. Below them was a crowd of courtiers.

Neela caught her breath, taken aback for a second at the sight of her parents in their opulent robes of state. They looked almost engulfed by them, and so remote upon their high thrones. She knew there were rules for approaching the emperor and empress and that even she had to follow them, but joy at seeing her mother and father so overwhelmed her that she forgot about royal protocol and rushed to them.

She also forgot about the palace guards – who were stationed in a tight circle around them. As she approached, they drew their swords, stopping her.

'Who allowed this swashbuckler to come into the royal presence?' Khelefu, the grand vizier, thundered.

Neela was nearly unrecognizable. Her bleached blonde hair was coiled up on her head, and she was wearing a jacket held together with fishhooks.

'Khelefu, don't you know me?' she asked, upset.

The grand vizier, imposing in a blue jacket and gold turban, didn't even acknowledge her.

'We do not know how she got in, sir,' a guard replied.

'Forms will have to be filled out,' Khelefu said darkly. '*Many* forms. Remove her at once.'

'No, *wait*! Khelefu, it's *me*, Neela!'

Stunned by the unseemly noise, the court fell silent.

Hearing her daughter's name, Sananda turned towards the raised voices, a look of hope on her face. When she saw the young mermaid – a scruffy mess – an expression of bitter disappointment took its place.

'Take her away, Khelefu,' she said, waving a heavily jewelled hand.

'*Mata-ji!* It's *me*, your daughter!' Neela cried.

Sananda snorted, a contemptuous look on her face. 'My

daughter would never—' She stopped speaking. 'Neria be praised,' she whispered. She swam to Neela and threw her arms around her. Aran followed, and swept both his wife and daughter into a tight embrace.

After a moment, the three released one another and Sananda took Neela's face in her hands. 'I thought we would never see you again. I – I thought . . . you were . . .'

'Hush, Mata-ji. Let us not speak of it,' Aran said, his voice husky. 'She is here now.'

Sananda nodded. She kissed Neela again, then let her go.

'Is Yazeed here?' Neela asked hopefully.

'No,' Aran said sadly. 'We've heard nothing from him. Nothing from Mahdi.'

Neela nodded, swallowing her disappointment. 'I was hoping that somehow they'd escaped.'

'We must not give up hope,' Aran said firmly. 'Do you know what's become of Serafina? And Desiderio?'

'Sera's alive. I don't know about Des.'

'Where have you been all this time? We've all been worried sick!' Sananda said.

Suddenly aware of all the eyes and ears around her, Neela lowered her voice. 'The situation is very . . . *difficult*. And very urgent. I'll tell you about it over tea.'

Tea was a light afternoon meal that the royal family took in a private dining room, away from the court. Neela knew she would be able to speak without being overheard there. Her experiences had taught her to be wary. Spies could be anywhere.

'Khelefu, we will have tea now,' said Aran.

'Now, Your Grace? That would be most unusual. It is only three twenty-one, and tea is always served promptly at four fifteen,' Khelefu said.

'*Now*, Khelefu.'

Khelefu, looking unhappy, bowed his head. 'As you wish.'

Before he could act on Aran's order, however, a minister – anxious and pale – approached him and whispered in his ear. Khelefu listened, nodded gravely then said, 'An emergency meeting of the war cabinet has been called, Your Grace. Your presence has been requested.'

'I will come,' Aran said. He turned back to Neela. 'Tea will have to wait, I'm afraid.'

'*Pita-ji*, are we . . . ?' Neela couldn't bear to finish her question.

'At war?' Aran said. 'The majority of the cabinet is in favour of attacking Ondalina. Our advisers are convinced that Kolfinn is behind the assassinations of Bilaal and Ahadi. They believe he may be holding Mahdi and Yazeed as prisoners. I fear it is no longer a case of *if* we go to war, but *when*. I've sent word to the rulers of all realms asking for a Council of the Six Waters.' He shook his head. 'But with Isabella presumed dead and Kolfinn on the attack, it will be a Council of Four, if it happens at all. I must go to my own councillors now.' He kissed Neela. 'We will talk shortly, my child.'

Neela watched him swim away. His bearing was dignified and composed, but there was a stoop to his shoulders. He was a second son and had not been groomed to be emperor. Neela could see that the loss of his brother, coupled with his newfound responsibilities, weighed heavily on him.

Soon, I'll add to those worries, she thought.

'Khelefu, fetch Suma. Tell her to assist the princess. Have food and drink brought to her room, scrubbing sand readied, and clean clothing laid out,' Sananda ordered.

'Yes, Your Grace,' Khelefu said.

'But, Mata-ji, there are things I need to tell you. *Now*. They cannot wait. Can't we go to your private chambers?'

Sananda stared at Neela's face, then frowned worriedly.

'What? What is it?' asked Neela.

'There are dark shadows under your eyes! Your face is so drawn,' Sananda said. 'And – forgive me, but I'm your mother and I must say it – there is a frown line on your forehead that wasn't there before.'

Distraught, Sananda snapped her fingers and a plate of chillas was brought. She reached for one immediately. Her eyes widened when Neela did not.

'My darling, what's wrong? Are you ill?'

'I'm fine. I'm just not hungry,' Neela replied.

Neela had lost her taste for sweets during her time with the Iele. Learning convocas and other difficult spells had absorbed her so completely that she'd forgotten all about bingas, zee zees and the like.

Suma, Neela's amah, swam into the room. The old nursemaid took one look at her and paled. 'Great Neria, child, your *hair*!'

Neela sighed impatiently. She'd survived the violent attack on Cerulea, and had escaped both Traho and Mfeme. She'd crossed treacherous seas to get to the Iele, and had been given the task of destroying Abbadon – and now she had to listen to her mother lose it over a frown line and her amah freak out about her hair.

Suma, hands shaking, pulled a handful of zee zees from her pocket. She offered one to Neela.

'No, thank you, Suma,' Neela said, a note of irritation in her voice.

She didn't see her mother clutch the rope of pearls she was wearing, but Suma did. 'Child, we *must* get you out of these awful rags,' the amah said soothingly. 'You've obviously been through a great ordeal. I shall have refreshments brought, and then you can rest.'

'I don't *want* to change my clothes and I don't want to rest! I need to speak with my mother!' Neela insisted.

'The empress!' a voice shrilled.

Neela turned and saw two ladies-in-waiting rush to her mother. They caught Sananda just as she started to swoon. A third lady hurried to her with a sea fan and waved it over her face.

'Mata-ji!' Neela cried, swimming to her.

Sananda waved her away. 'It's nothing, my darling. I'm fine,' she said, smiling weakly. 'I just need to sit down.'

'Come, Princess. Let the empress breathe,' Suma said, putting an arm around Neela. 'She is quite overcome. You know how sensitive she is. Bad hair upsets her greatly.'

'But, Suma—'

'Shh, now. Let us go and see to your appearance. The sight of you in a clean sari and some pretty jewels will do her a world of good.'

Neela took a deep breath, willing herself to be patient with her mother and her amah. She was not the same mermaid who'd left Matali several weeks ago. It wasn't their fault that they didn't know that yet.

'All right, Suma,' she said. 'I'll scrub and I'll change my clothes. But I'm *not* resting. In fact, the moment my father is finished with his council, I want to see him.'

Neela started for her chamber. She was looking straight ahead, so she didn't see her amah look over her shoulder, catch the empress's eye and exchange dire glances.

NINE

'A KOOTAGULLA, *PRIYĀ*?' Aran asked, offering a platter of many-layered pastries to Neela.

'No, thank you, Pita-ji,' Neela said.

Aran cast a worried glance at his wife. He put down the platter and picked up another one.

'A pompasooma, then?'

'No, I'm not hungry. As I was saying . . .'

Neela and her parents were having tea. Neela had changed her clothes and restored her hair to its natural shade. Her mother had recovered from her fainting fit. Her father had finished his meeting. Neela had been sent for, and then they'd all met in the dining room of their residential quarters.

Finally, Neela had been able to tell her parents all that had happened to her. As she finished her story, she took a sip of her syrup-like tea and put the cup back on its delicate porcelain saucer. Her pet blowfish, Ooda – happy to see her again – swam in circles around her chair. Neela scratched the little fish's head, so relieved to be home. After days on the currents, eluding capture, she felt safe and secure in the palace. No harm could come to her here. Her parents would know how to keep her safe. They would know how to keep her friends safe too. Neela waited now for her father to tell her the best way to find the talismans and do away with Abbadon.

But Aran didn't tell her how. Instead, he sat back in his chair, his dark eyes huge in his careworn face. Then he looked at his wife, who burst into tears.

'Mata-ji, don't cry! It's all right!' Neela said. 'I'm here now. I'm fine. Everything's all right.'

'No, it is *not*,' Sananda said. 'I *knew* something was wrong the moment I saw you in that dreadful outfit. I told your father so as soon as he returned from his meeting. You're not yourself. Suma told me you actually *kept* those awful clothes, that you wouldn't let her throw them away. And you just passed up a platter of pompasoomas. You *never* say no to a pompasooma!'

Neela gritted her teeth. She took a sweet and put it on her plate. 'Forgive me,' she said, humouring her mother. 'But I'm a bit distracted, what with everything that's happened. Actually, *no*. I'm not distracted. I'm terrified. Here I am, drinking tea, while Abbadon grows stronger. I need to contact Serafina and find out if she made it back to Cerulea.'

'You'll do no such thing!' Sananda said sharply. She motioned a guard over and sent him to fetch Suma.

'But—' Neela started to say.

'You are not well, my poor daughter. You must rest,' Aran said, a pained expression on his face. 'These terrible experiences have undone your mind.'

Neela stared at her father, taken aback. 'What are you saying, Pita-ji? My mind is totally fine.'

Aran covered Neela's hand with his own. 'Think of what you just told us. That dreams are real. That make-believe witches exist. That there's an evil monster in the Southern Sea and a kind terragogg in a palazzo. You need help and you will have it. None but the best. You are not to worry. We will keep it all between ourselves, a secret. No one else will know.'

'Wait a minute,' Neela said, not believing what she was hearing. 'You think . . . You think I'm *crazy?*'

Hearing distress in her mistress's voice, Ooda started to inflate.

'No, priyā, not crazy. Your mother and I . . . we think you've had a terrible shock, that's all,' said Aran, soothingly. 'Gods only know what you've seen. The attack on Cerulea, losing your uncle and aunt, the violence you suffered at the invaders' hands – these things would have undone anyone. It's amazing you were able to escape from this terrible Traho and swim back to us from his camp.'

'But I *didn't* swim back to you from his camp. I swam back from the Iele's cave!' Neela said. Loudly.

Aran looked at Sananda. 'Rest and quiet,' he said.

'Everything I said was true! Someone is trying to set the monster free. Don't you see what danger we're in?' Neela asked, upset.

'Bland food. Soft colours,' Sananda said.

'I have to contact Serafina! *Now!*' Neela protested, desperation in her voice.

Suma appeared in the doorway. 'You sent for me, Your Grace?'

'The princess is unwell. Take her back to her room and see that she is not disturbed.'

'Yes, Your Grace,' Suma said. She swam to Neela and took her arm. 'Come, Princess.'

'It will be all right. You'll see,' Sananda told her daughter. 'Kiraat, the medica magus, will examine you. Under his care, you'll return to your senses.'

'No, I *won't!*' Neela said. 'Because I haven't left them!'

'Come now, Princess,' Suma soothed. 'There's no need for a fuss.'

'Neela, child, go peacefully. *Please*,' Sananda said, fresh tears in her eyes. 'Don't make me ask the guards to escort you. No one wants that.'

Neela opened her mouth to argue, then closed it again, seeing that it was futile. The more she disagreed with her parents, the more she confirmed their belief that she'd lost her mind.

'You're making a terrible mistake,' she said.

Her mother kissed her. Then her father did. Neela did not kiss them back.

Suma led her out of the dining room, clucking over her just as she had when Neela was a child, but Neela barely heard her. Ooda, as round as a full moon now, followed them. As she swam down the long, mirrored hallway to her room, Suma firmly gripping her arm, Neela heard something else.

Something dark. Something low and gurgling.

It sounded like Abbadon laughing.

TEN

'D ID YOU HEAR THAT?' Neela asked.

'Hear what?' Suma asked.

'Laughter.'

'I'm sure it's the grooms. The stables are underneath us.'

Neela broke free of Suma's iron grip and swam to a nearby window. A groom was swimming across the stable yard, leading an unruly hippokamp. He wasn't laughing.

It was Abbadon, I'm sure of it. But how did I hear him? she wondered uneasily. *I didn't cast an ochi to spy on him and, unlike Ava, I don't have the gift of vision. Maybe they're right. Maybe I am going insane.*

Suma took Neela's arm again and pulled her along.

'Let *go* of me! You're treating me like a baby!'

'Because you're acting like one. Come along now. This uncooperative behaviour is yet another symptom of your derangement,' Suma said sagely.

'*Derangement?!*' Neela sputtered. 'I'm not deranged!'

'Ha. There is the proof. Crazy people never think they're crazy,' Suma said.

'I'm worried and scared, Suma. Because there are things

going on in the seas. Bad things. And my parents aren't dealing with them.'

Suma tsk-tsked. 'It is all this worry that has ruined your face and your mind. But of course your face is more important. You *must* stop fretting, child. Emperor Aran will not let harm come to us. He will speak with his councillors and they will sort everything out. That is the way things are done. That is the way things have always been done.'

Neela, realizing she would get nowhere with her amah, fell silent. A few minutes later, they reached her rooms. 'Here we are,' Suma said. 'I sent for a cup of walrus milk before I fetched you. Everything will look better after a nice hot drink, you'll see. Ooda, *stop* that!'

Ooda was so distressed by Neela's unhappiness that she'd inflated herself to painful proportions. As Suma and Neela watched, she started spinning around in circles and floated up to the ceiling.

'Leave her. She'll come down when she's ready,' Neela said. She was used to Ooda's antics.

Suma bustled about the chamber, drawing the curtains. Then she brushed Neela's long hair until it gleamed. As she finished, a servant arrived with the walrus milk and a platter of sweets.

'Rest now, Princess,' she said. 'Soon the learned Kiraat will come and put you to rights.'

Neela forced a smile. She stretched out on a soft tufted chaise. Suma smoothed a sea-silk throw over her, then left, quietly closing the door.

As soon as it clicked shut, Neela threw off her cover. She swam to her closet and got her messenger bag down from a shelf. The transparensea pebbles Vrăja had given her were still in it. She put some currensea into the bag, along with her black swashbuckler's outfit and a few more pieces of clothing.

Her anger hadn't abated any; it had only grown. Drink walrus milk? Eat sweets? Rest? Hardly! She was going to sneak out and head for Cerulea.

She took a transparensea pebble from her bag. She would cast it, then make her way out of the palace. But were there guards outside in the hallway? If so, they would see her door open and close. She would have to check.

Neela grasped the doorknob and turned it, but nothing happened. The door wouldn't open.

Suma had locked her in.

ELEVEN

THE UNDERWATER ENTRANCE to the duca's palazzo was shrouded in darkness. The lava globes flanking the tall double doors had gone out. The carved stone faces were silent.

Serafina knocked on one of the doors. It swung open at her touch. *That's odd*, she thought. *Why isn't it locked?*

She looked up and down the current, feeling uneasy. Here and there, a shadowy figure came or went, but most of the palazzos were locked up tight, their windows shuttered. The Lagoon looked very different from the last time she'd been here.

Serafina looked different too. Swimming for weeks on end had made her body lean and taut. Her cheekbones were sharper under her skin. Her clothing was frayed and silt-stained. She was getting the hard, rangy look of a merl who'd been on the currents too long.

She'd left Ling a week before and swum west to the Mediterranean, then north to the Adriatic, sticking to lonely back currents the whole way. She knew that returning to Cerulea would be extremely dangerous. Before she attempted it, she wanted to get as much information as she could from the duca on the number of troops still in the city and the locations of any safe houses. She hoped he might have news of her family, too. Of the Matalis. And of Blu.

'Hello?' she called out, swimming through the doorway. 'Is anyone here? Blu? Grigio?'

No one answered. She moved down the hallway warily. Her fins started to prickle. As soon as she broke the surface of the duca's pool, she knew something was seriously wrong. It was dark inside the library. There were no lamps lit, no fire blazing. She hoisted herself up on the edge of the pool, and cut her palm on a shard of broken glass.

'Ouch!' she yelped, shaking her hand. 'Duca Armando?' she called out. 'Are you here?'

There was no answer. A dozen or so bioluminescent jellyfish were floating in the pool. She cast an illuminata over them and they lit up brightly. In their blue glow, she could see the library properly. She gasped as her eyes travelled over the broken statues and slashed paintings. Bookshelves had been pulled over and their contents trampled. Furniture had been smashed.

Suddenly, she heard footsteps. They were coming fast. Something swished through the air over her head. She flipped backwards into the pool. When she surfaced, she saw a pan floating on the water and a terrified woman standing at its edge.

'Filomena? It's me, Serafina!'

'*Oh, mio Dio! Che cosa ho fatto? Mi dispiace tanto!*' Filomena said tearfully.

'You're talking too fast. I can't understand you. Do you speak Mermish?'

Filomena nodded. 'Forgive me, Principessa,' she said, her voice halting and uncertain. 'I no see it was you. I think Traho and his soldiers come again.' She began to cry. 'The duca, he is dead. Oh, Principessa, he is *dead*.' She sat down heavily.

'No!' Serafina cried. With shaking arms she pushed herself out of the water and sat on the pool's edge, next to Filomena.

'It happen the night you and the Princess Neela are here,' Filomena said. 'The men who came . . . the humans . . . they torture him. Then they kill him.'

Sera was stricken by guilt. 'It was because of us, wasn't it?' she said. 'Neela and me. The duca died because of us.'

Filomena shook her head. 'No, child. They know you escape and still they kill him. They want information. They think the duca have it.'

The talismans, Serafina thought.

'Please, Filomena, it's very important,' Serafina said as gently as she could. 'The men who came here, did you hear what they said?'

Filomena pressed the heels of her hands against her brow, as if she'd like to pound the memories out of her brain. 'The one man . . . he have sunglasses,' she said.

'Rafe Mfeme,' Serafina said.

'Yes. He shout at the duca. Same thing, over and over. He beat him . . . an old man, a gentle man . . .' She dissolved into tears again.

Serafina took her hand. 'What did he say?'

'He say, "Where is it? Where is Neria's Stone?" And the duca, he tell him he do not know. But Mfeme, he no believe it.'

Serafina swore silently. Now she was certain that Traho knew what the talismans were. He'd told Mfeme and sent him after them. But *how* did he know? Not even the Iele knew. Had he gone to Atlantis and found Lady Thalia? No, he couldn't have. Thalia had said she'd been alone ever since the island was destroyed.

'Did Mfeme say anything else?' Serafina asked.

'No, but he take something – a painting. Of Maria Theresa.'

Serafina remembered the portrait of the beautiful, sad-eyed infanta of Spain in her sumptuous clothing and magnificent jewels. She'd drowned centuries ago when her ship was attacked by pirates.

'Do you have any idea why?' Sera asked.

Filomena shook her head.

Serafina had one more question. It took all her courage to ask it. 'Do you know what happened to the Praedatori? One of them, Blu, was badly wounded.'

'No. There was big fight. Some Praedatori are hurt. Some are killed. There are bodies in the water. I cannot look at them. I am sorry.'

Her voice broke off and Serafina knew she couldn't press her any further.

'Thank you for telling me all this, Filomena,' she said.

'What will you do now? Will you stay here?'

'*Si, si*. The duca's son, he come from Roma soon. He is duca now. He ask me to stay.' She squeezed Serafina's hand. 'But you, you go now, Principessa. It is not safe for you here.'

Serafina hugged her and was about to say goodbye when Filomena said, 'Oh, Principessa, I forget! The duca, he leave something for you.'

She hurried out of the room, then returned with a small wooden box. 'He give this to me. The night you and the Princess Neela come. After you go to bed. "In case something happen to me, you give this to the principessa," he say. I hide it in my kitchen under tomatoes.'

Serafina opened the box. It contained twenty gold trocus coins and a small conch. She held it to her ear. The sound of the duca's voice made her heart clench.

> *My dearest Principessa,*
>
> *I've received news tonight. Your uncle is alive and was seen at the Straits of Gibraltar. My source says he is indeed heading to the North Sea to seek an alliance with the Kobold. We must wait with hope to see what the days ahead bring. If something happens, if I am taken or killed, do not go home. Go to Matali. The Praedatori will escort you and the Princess Neela to the palace. The Matalis are stalwart friends of Miromara and will offer you sanctuary. If you will not heed my advice – and I fear you will not – know that Cerulea is a very dangerous place. Do not allow yourself to be seen. There*

*is a safe house in the fabra. 16 Basalt Street. The password is
starfish.*

Be brave, Principessa. Be wary. Trust no one.

Ever yours,

Armando

Serafina lowered the conch. Her Uncle Vallerio – her
mother's brother and Miromara's high commander – was
alive. Happiness and hope flooded through her. If he
succeeded in his efforts with the Kobold, he'd be able to
assemble an army and take Cerulea back. The sea goblins
were fearsome fighters. If anyone could force the invaders
out, they could.

Serafina's happiness abruptly dimmed, however, as the
memory of Ava's vision – the one they had shared when
Ava had cast a convoca in the caves of the Iele – returned
to her. In it, the goblins had been her foes, not her allies.
She'd seen herself on a battlefield, moving soldiers into
position. On the other end of the field was a goblin army.
One of its soldiers had crept up behind Serafina and swung
an axe at her.

Sera told herself that there was a simple explanation.
There were four goblin tribes – the Feuerkumpel, the
Höllebläser, the Meerteufel and the Ekelshmutz. Perhaps
one of them had sided with Traho, and it was that tribe she'd
been preparing to fight in the vision.

'You go some place safe now?' Filomena asked.

'I'm going to Cerulea,' Serafina replied. Despite what the

duca had advised, she knew it was what she had to do.

'How do you get there? The Lagoon is full of soldiers. You never make it like that,' Filomena said, pointing at Serafina's swashbuckler outfit. 'If you swim through Lagoon, you must look like Lagoona.'

Serafina cast an illusio songspell. Her hair turned pink.

'No,' Filomena said. 'Now you look like anemone.'

Serafina cast another spell. It turned green.

'Now you look like frog. Make hair black again. But long.'

Serafina tried it and Filomena smiled. She took the red silk scarf she was wearing around her neck and tied it around Serafina's head, knotting it at the nape of her neck and letting the ends trail. Next, she went to the kitchen for her handbag, and returned with a selection of make-up.

'Gogg make-up? It'll wash off,' Serafina said.

'This make-up is waterproof. What else would Venetian lady use?' Filomena asked.

She outlined Serafina's eyes heavily with a black kohl stick, then gave her a beauty spot. Next she painted her lips a deep crimson. Lastly, she put her own gold hoop earrings in Serafina's ears.

She stood back, appraised her work and frowned. 'The clothes, no good. Can you not make song on them too?'

Serafina looked at her black tunic. She transformed it to a long black dress. A flowery tunic. A red gown.

Filomena shook her head at each transformation. 'No, make it like *this*,' she said. She undid the top buttons of her blouse. Underneath it, she was wearing a pretty bustier.

'All right,' Serafina said sceptically. She sang a new songspell and the next minute, the top of her tunic had become a bustier and the bottom a short, floaty skirt.

'*Si!* Much better!' Filomena said. 'Only the top, make bigger.'

Serafina sang again. The bustier expanded and nearly slipped off her.

Filomena shook her head impatiently. '*No, cara, no. La tua sfaldamento!*' She placed her hands at the sides of her enormous bosom and hiked it up. '*Capito?*' she said.

'Make them *bigger?* They're already up under my chin in this thing as it is!'

'*Si! Maggiore!* Bigger!' Filomena said.

Serafina tightened the bustier, then looked down at her cleavage. 'It looks like I have two sea mounts stuck on the front of me. With an abyss between them,' she said. She peered at her reflection in the pool water. 'All I can see is my chest!'

'*Buono!* This is what *soldati* will see too,' Filomena said. 'Not the face.' She stood. 'Now, you *no* swim like this, all elbows,' she said, mimicking Serafina's brisk stroke. 'Lagoona swim like *this*.' She held her head high, smiled invitingly and led with her chest. 'When in Rome, do as Romans. When in Lagoon, do as Lagoona. Swing the hips! Flutter the fins!'

'I'll try,' Serafina said uncertainly, wondering how she'd ever get her hips to sway like Filomena's. 'Thank you,' she added, putting the currensea the duca had left for her into her pocket. 'For everything.'

Filomena waved her words away. 'Take this,' she said, handing Serafina her make-up. 'No thank me now. You thank when you get to other side.'

'*If* I get to the other side,' Serafina said.

Then she dived into the pool, and disappeared under the water.

TWELVE

'HEY, MERLIE, OVER HERE!' the death rider called to Serafina. He and some fellow soldiers were floating outside a bar on the Corrente Largo, the Lagoon's main thoroughfare, goggling at her.

Sera's heart was slamming, but her face showed no fear. She flipped her tail at them and swam on, chest out, head high, black tresses swirling behind her like ribbonworms in a riptide.

My gods, what if they'd recognized me? she thought.

Traho's soldiers were everywhere. Serafina knew she had to get out of the Lagoon, and fast. She thanked Neria that it was night-time. The darkness, her make-up, and her clothing made her look totally different from the naive young princess staring out from the wanted posters all over the place. The soldiers had been drinking; that helped too. Sera saw bottles of posidonia, a sweet wine made from fermented seaweed; and brack, a frothy ale brewed from sour sea apples.

There were more whistles and catfishcalls as she swam down the current. She ignored them haughtily. Shops were open. Through their windows, she saw shopmerls briskly wrapping purchases. Cafés and restaurants were busy too. Their signs – made of tiny bioluminescents – flashed brightly. Trouncers – large jellyfish with long, dangling tentacles – floated above entrances to nightclubs, zapping anyone who tried to sneak in without paying.

None of the Lagoon's residents had been taken away, it seemed, and Serafina soon realized why – the Lagoon had become one big barracks for many of Traho's troops, and the Lagoonas were needed to cater to them. The sight of the invaders carrying on in Miromaran waters as if they owned them put her into a seething rage.

Stay cool. You don't have much further to go, she told herself.

She passed another café. Two more bars. She saw a fancy wine shop up ahead in the bottom of a large yellow coral. Ten yards past it was a fork in the current. She wanted the stream on the left, which led south. Once she was off the busy Corrente Largo, she'd be able to swim away fast.

Slow and steady, Serafina, she cautioned herself. *One fin in front of the other. Don't give the game away. You're almost there.*

Just as she passed the last nightclub on the current, a soldier – milling around with his friends outside it – reached out and grabbed her wrist. Startled, Serafina tried to pull free but couldn't.

'Not so fast, *bella*,' he said. 'I feel like hearing a siren's song tonight.'

A siren? Serafina thought, horrified. She'd obviously overdone it with the make-up and the cleavage. Sirens sang for currensea – and this walrus-faced lump thought she was one. *What am I going to do?* She decided to go along with him. She had no choice. She couldn't afford to make a scene and draw attention.

'What have you caught there, Sergeant?' one of his friends shouted.

Serafina panicked. If he pulled her into the midst of his group, she was dead. She might deceive one drunken fool, but the rest of the sergeant's companions might not be so far gone. Instead of bringing her over to the others, though, the sergeant led her into the glow of a streetlamp. There was a poster of her attached to it.

Oh, no, Serafina thought. *This is even worse.*

'What's your name, *cara?*' he asked. His breath stank. His jacket was unbuttoned and his large gut spilled out of it.

'Lisabetta,' Serafina said, trying to lead him away from the lamppost.

'Ah, a shy one, are you? Let me see you,' he said, pulling her back towards the light. His eyes crawled over her. 'Oh, yes. You'll do. If your voice is half as pretty as your face, you'll do very nicely,' he said.

Serafina prayed he wouldn't see the wanted sign, but the gods weren't listening. His eyes suddenly flickered from her face to the sign and back again.

'You look a little bit like the outlaw princess,' he said, lifting her chin with his finger.

'Must be because I always give my audience the royal treatment,' Serafina purred.

'How much?'

Serafina had no idea. 'Ten trocii,' she said.

'That's an outrageous amount!'

Oh, thank goodness, she thought. *He doesn't have the money.*

'Maybe another time,' she said, trying to move off.

'Here,' the sergeant said, handing her ten gold coins. 'And it had better be worth every cowrie.' Still holding her wrist, he pulled her towards the nightclub. 'Come on. Me and my mermen want a song.'

Sera had to think fast, but she was so scared, she couldn't think at all. She had to get away. She couldn't go through with this. The soldiers would know she wasn't a siren as soon as she opened her mouth.

Sera's voice was strong and pretty and it carried magic well, but a siren's voice had a very particular magic. Their voices, and the songs they sang, were so achingly beautiful that listeners forgot everything: their disappointments and heartaches, their lost loves and broken dreams. Some became so deeply enchanted they forgot their own names.

What would they do when they found out who she really was? They'd put her in irons and deliver her to Traho.

The sergeant pulled her down a dimly-lit hallway. There were a few sputtering lava torches on the wall. *I could grab one and hit him over the head with it*, she thought. *But what if I miss? Or what if I manage to hit him, but don't knock him out? He'll shout and more death riders will come.* Her fear was yammering so loudly now, it threatened to overwhelm her.

Then she heard a different voice in her head.

Think, Serafina, think. Ruling is like playing chess. Danger comes from many directions, from a pawn as well as a queen. You must play the board, not the piece.

Those were her mother's words. Isabella had said them to her on the morning of her Dokimí.

Play the board, Sera, she repeated silently to herself. *Think.*

She and the sergeant were approaching a set of double doors at the end of the hallway. Loud voices and laughter were coming from behind them. She tried to slow down, to stall for more time, but the sergeant yanked her hard. As he did, her bag banged against her side. Something inside it rattled.

Vrăja's gifts! The witch had given her and the other four mermaids magical items right before they fled the caves: transparensea pebbles, ink bombs and vials of potion.

Sera knew a transparensea pebble wouldn't help her. The death riders would see her cast it. They could simply block her exit until the spell of invisibility wore off. She doubted the ink bomb would help, either. Soldiers who dealt with dragons and lava bombs wouldn't even blink at an ink bomb.

That left the vial of potion. *It's Moses potion, from the Moses sole in the Red Sea. Sharks hate it. Maybe death riders do too*, Vrăja had said.

Why did sharks hate it? What did it do? Sera wondered. There hadn't been time to ask. She would have to release it inside the nightclub and hope it spread quickly through the water to each and every death rider. But she would be in the water too. How could she protect herself from the potion's effects?

The sergeant pushed the doors open. Sera was out of time. She reached into her bag, pulled out the vial and secreted it in her hand.

A loud, raucous cheer went up as the sergeant entered the room, dragging her behind him. The soldiers applauded loudly. Sera forced herself to smile. The sergeant cleared a space for her by the bar, shooing all the mermen to the other side of the room. As they settled themselves, Sera folded her hands behind her back and worked the top of the vial off. She knew she had to act fast, before the noise died down.

'Help me,' she said quietly in Pesca to a stargazer swimming by. 'Take this vial and pour it out in the waters above the soldiers' heads.'

The fish fearfully darted away.

'Help me, *please*,' she said in Tortoisha to a loggerhead turtle carrying a bottle of wine on his back. 'I'm not a siren. I need to escape before they find out.'

Far too slowly the turtle said, 'If . . . I . . . help . . . you . . . they'll . . . kill . . . me . . . I'm . . . a . . . prisoner . . . here.'

Serafina felt a soft touch on her hand. She risked a glance behind her. It was an octopus.

'I'll help you,' the creature said in Molluska, 'if you get us out too. They took us from our homes and use us as slaves. I want to see my children again.'

'I will, I promise,' Serafina said.

The octopus took the vial and swam off.

The sergeant stopped speaking. He swept a hand towards Serafina. The soldiers started pounding on tables. 'Sing!

Sing! Sing! Sing!' they shouted.

Sera, a smile pasted on her face, held up a hand for silence. Out of the corner of her eye, she saw the octopus move along the floor, pass under some tables, then creep up a wall behind the soldiers, her colour blending with her surroundings. The creature tipped the vial, then swam over the death riders' heads, trailing a milky ribbon of potion behind her.

Sera desperately hoped that no one looked up. *How long does it take for the Moses potion to work?* she wondered.

'Whatcha waiting for, merlie? Sing!' someone shouted.

Sera tried not to show any of the panic rising up inside her. She bowed her head and slowly lifted it again – stalling for time.

'It will be my pleasure,' she said. 'But first, I'd like to tell you a story about the very special song I'm going to sing for you . . .'

'Stuff the story, sister!' someone else yelled. 'Sing!'

And then Sera saw one of the soldiers frown. He nudged his companion and pointed at a wanted poster on the wall. Sera didn't have to look closely to know whose face was on it. The soldier shot out of his chair and pointed at her. Sera's stomach tightened with terror. It was over. He would shout out her name now. She would be seized and taken to Traho.

But that didn't happen.

Instead of shouting, the soldier yawned. His eyes fluttered shut. He swayed back and forth, then toppled back into his chair.

Another soldier fell over, and another, until almost every merman in the room was out cold. Only the sergeant was still upright.

'You . . . Youdidthis,' he said, slurring his words. He took a few strokes towards her, then crashed to the floor.

As Sera looked around, in a state of disbelief, she felt a heavy sleepiness steal over her.

That's how the potion works! she thought.

She knew if she breathed much more of it, she would pass out too – right here next to a hundred of her enemies. She ripped Filomena's scarf out of her hair and tied it over her nose and mouth.

At that moment, the bartender, who'd gone to the basement to fetch more wine, came back into the room. He promptly dropped the bottles. 'You crazy-wrasse merl! What have you *done?*' he shouted, looking at the motionless bodies. 'I'm not going down for this. No way,' he said. He grabbed a rag off the bar, tied it over his nose and mouth as Sera had, and then started for the door.

In the blink of an eye, Serafina had the sleeping sergeant's speargun out of its holster. 'Not another stroke or I'll shoot,' she said, training it on the barman.

He stopped short, only a foot or so from the door, and slowly turned around. As his eyes met hers, they widened in recognition.

'You're her. The principessa.'

'Back away from the door,' Sera said. 'Now.'

The merman didn't move.

Serafina raised the speargun so it was level with his head. 'You can't spend the bounty money if you're dead,' she said, moving closer to him.

It was a total bluff. She had no idea how to shoot the thing. But it worked. The merman backed away.

'Sit down,' Sera said, motioning to a nearby chair. 'Put your arms at your sides.'

The merman did so.

There was a string of tiny, twinkling lava lights behind the bar. Sera sang a vortex spell and wound the string around him, binding him to the chair.

'I can't let you sell me to Traho,' she said.

'I would never do that, Principessa. I swear,' he protested. 'I only want to help you.'

Serafina laughed, remembering how, only a few weeks ago, she had trusted a merman named Zeno Piscor and his offer of help. She glanced at the sergeant who'd brought her into the club. He was still out cold.

'The royal treatment,' she said under her breath. '*As if.* What you got, lumpsucker, was the royal flush.'

She put the speargun down on the bar. It was too dangerous to carry. If she was stopped by another death rider, she wouldn't be able to explain how she got it.

Moving quickly, she threw open the double doors. 'Go, all of you! Get out of here before the soldiers wake up!'

The stargazer and half a dozen turtles swam by her, struggling against the effects of the potion. They were followed by three octopuses.

'Thank you, Principessa!' the one who'd helped her called out. 'We won't forget this!'

Sera was just about to leave when she saw a flag hanging on the wall behind the bar. It was not Miromara's.

'Whose banner is that?' she demanded of the barman.

'The invaders',' he replied.

'That can't be right,' she murmured. The flag was not Ondalina's – a black and white orca against a red background; it was merely a black circle on a red background. What if Astrid had been telling her the truth back when they were with the Iele? What if the Arctic realm wasn't behind the invasion of Cerulea?

It's probably a regimental flag, Sera thought.

She tore it off the wall and threw it on the floor. Then she took a bottle of wine from the bar and doused the flag, ruining it. She pulled the lipstick Filomena had given her out of her bag and scrawled *Merrovingia regere hic* on the wall. She used Latin, the language of history. Because she was determined to make some.

'When the sea scum come to, translate for them,' she said to the barman. 'Tell them what this says: the Merrovingia rule here.'

And then she was gone, out of the club and down the dark current, swimming fast for the open waters of the Adriatic. For Cerulea.

For home.

THIRTEEN

I T WAS NEARLY MIDNIGHT when Serafina reached the walls of her city – or what was left of them. The route had been difficult to navigate because familiar landmarks had been destroyed or obscured and lava globes had been broken. She'd taken a back current and swum low to avoid detection. She hadn't seen another soul on the way.

Only a few globes sputtered weakly above the East Gate now. Sera swam through the archway and stopped dead. She took a few more stumbling strokes then slowly sank through the water until she was sitting in the silt.

'No,' she said, unable to believe her eyes. '*No.*'

Her beloved city was in ruins.

Serafina had fled when Cerulea first fell under attack. She hadn't witnessed the full force of the invaders' destruction. All that remained of the thicket of Devil's Tail that once floated protectively above the city were stumps where the vines had been hacked away. Huge sections of the wall that surrounded Cerulea had caved in. The ancient stone houses that once lined the Corrente Regina were now piles of rubble. Temples to the sea gods and goddesses had been pulled down.

Worst of all, a terrible silence had descended. Serafina knew that the heart of a city was its people, and Cerulea's were gone.

Tears threatened, but she held them back. Grief was a luxury she could no longer afford. The sun would be up in only a few hours and the waters would lighten. She remembered the duca's warning not to be seen, to find a safe house. She had come here to find the locations of the talismans. That's what would defeat her enemies. That's what would help her people. Not sitting in the silt, crying.

She started up the Corrente Regina. There were only a few lava globes left to light her way. In their flickering half-light she could see the broken windows of looted shops and the remains of hippokamps killed in the fighting. Wild dogfish roamed in packs, feasting on carrion, or growling from the shadows.

Sera swam across a deserted intersection, turned a bend and saw the royal palace, high on its hill. It was the only building that was still illuminated. Some of the damage inflicted by the Blackclaws had been repaired, but not all of it. A large chunk of the east outer wall was still missing. Sera remembered how the dragons had battered their way through it and into her mother's stateroom.

Scores of soldiers rode in and out of the west wing of the palace on hippokamps. *They must be using it as their base*, she thought. Her eyes followed the riders. She wondered if her own hippokamp, Clio, now belonged to them. And her pet octopus, Sylvestre – had he survived the attack?

Staying in the shadows, she continued up the current until she reached the Ostrokon. Its large, ornate pediment had fallen to the seafloor, and its entrance was filled with debris. She thought about Fossegrim, the elderly liber magus, the keeper of knowledge. He would never have willingly allowed the invaders to enter this place of learning and peace. The death riders had surely killed him.

Sera peered up and down the current, then shot across it. She skimmed over the rubble, darted inside the Ostrokon and hid behind a pillar, hoping no one had seen her. Much of the first level was still intact. The front desk was undamaged. A pair of glasses still rested upon it, as if their owner had just swum away for a minute. Here and there, broken conchs littered the floor.

Like all ostrokons, Cerulea's was modelled on the nautilus shell. It had twelve levels, in honour of the twelve full moons of the year and their importance to the seas. While the nautilus's chambers were sealed off from one another, those of the Ostrokon opened off a tall central hallway, and it was this hallway Serafina swam down now. She knew where she needed to go – to Level Six, where the collection of conchs on early Merrovingian history were kept.

The water became inky as she descended, so she grabbed a lava torch off a wall. The spiralling hallway, usually so familiar to her, felt eerie now. Doorways loomed at the left and right like giant, gaping mouths. Schools of thick-lipped blennies and bright-orange wrasses – usually shooed out by the ostroki – swam silently through them.

As she rounded the bend to the fifth level, a movement startled her. She whipped her dagger out.

'Who's there?' she called out.

There was no answer.

'I'm not afraid to use this!' she shouted.

A low growl rose. Serafina slowly raised her torch, holding it – and her knife – out in front of her. She saw sleek grey bodies flash by, black eyes, sharp teeth. It was a pack of dogfish. She didn't know what they were doing in here. Or why they were so aggressive. And then the stench told her. She lowered her torch to illuminate the floor and saw the dead merman they'd been eating.

'Easy, pups,' she said with a shiver, moving on. 'I'm not here to steal your dinner.'

Finally she arrived at Level Six. She hurried inside and swam to the shelves where the conchs on Merrow's Progress were stored. When she reached them, she held up her torch, ready to grab a conch and start listening.

But she couldn't, because there weren't any. The shelves were bare.

Where were they? Could Traho have taken them? But how had he come up with the idea to search for clues to the whereabouts of the talismans in the conchs on Merrow's Progress? He didn't know the truth about Atlantis. Vrăja hadn't shown him Merrow's bloodsong. How could it be that he was *always* one stroke ahead of her?

Serafina was crushed. Everything depended on those conchs. She had come all this way only to find herself back at square one.

A group of sea bass swam by, heading for an unlit corner of the room. Sera knew that they were nocturnal feeders. If they were seeking darker waters, it meant that dawn was coming. It was time for her to find the safe house, while she still could. With a heavy heart, she swam back to the first level and returned the lava torch to its bracket on the wall. She was just about to swim out of the Ostrokon when light played over the rubble in front of the building. Voices shouted orders.

Oh, no! she thought. *Death riders. It's a patrol!*

Her hands went to her bag, where she'd put the transparensea pebbles from Vrăja, but it was too late. There was no way to cast them without being heard. She quickly crouched down behind a broken stone pillar. Her hiding place wasn't great. If the soldiers searched the entry thoroughly, she was done for. A group of six passed by and swept into the first level. Sera heard their voices and saw their lava lanterns bobbing around inside. After a few minutes, they came back out.

'All clear?' a voice shouted. It belonged to an officer. He was inside the entry. Serafina hadn't seen him. She prayed that he hadn't seen her either.

'First level's clear, sir!' one of the searchers shouted back. 'Should we sweep the sub-levels?'

The officer, closer now, told him not to bother. 'I doubt the rebels are down there studying. Move out,' he ordered. His voice sounded familiar to Serafina. It was muffled by the column, but still, she was certain she'd heard it before.

Slowly, carefully, Sera moved her head to the left, trying to identify the speaker.

'We'll head to the fabra next,' he announced as he followed his mermen outside. She could see his back now. He was wearing the same black uniform as the others.

'Sir!' one of his soldiers said. 'Sergeant Attamino is outside. He just arrived. His patrol just found two rebels hiding near the South Gate.'

'Take them to Traho,' the officer said. 'He'll want to question them.'

He turned around and cast one more glance over the Ostrokon's entrance. At last, Serafina could see his face. Her hands clenched into fists as she recognised it. She bit back a wounded cry.

The officer was Mahdi.

FOURTEEN

SERAFINA DUCKED DOWN, terrified she'd been seen. She waited for the sound of fins coming through the water, for the light of a lava lantern to fall across her.

'All clear! Let's go!' Mahdi shouted.

And then he and his soldiers were gone.

Sera couldn't move. She had suffered so many shocks and so many losses already. But *this* . . . this defied all understanding. She remembered the duca's warning – *trust no one*. But *Mahdi*? He'd betrayed her with Lucia, yes, but how could he betray her people? And his own? The invaders had probably killed his parents, and now he was on their side?

She tried to tell herself that she was wrong. That it was all just a trick of the light. But she'd seen him clearly. He was wearing the enemy's uniform. She had to accept it – Mahdi was a *traitor*.

Aching inside, she swam out of the Ostrokon into the current, expecting to run into a patrol at every turn. Basalt Street, where the safe house was, was at the northern edge of the fabra. When she finally reached it, still dazed by Mahdi's betrayal, she wondered if, in her shock, she'd made a mistake. The house itself – number 16 – looked like a wreck. Its top floors were gone. What was left of the facade was cracked and sagging. She peered in through a broken window and saw an empty interior. Hesitantly, she knocked on the door. Nothing happened. She knocked again.

'Starfish,' she whispered.

The door was wrenched open. A hand grabbed her and yanked her inside.

'Who sent you?' growled a burly merman.

'The duca di Venezia,' Serafina said. 'The *late* duca di Venezia.'

The merman nodded. He released her. 'Find a spot wherever you can. We're full tonight,' he said.

'How many others are here?' Serafina asked, following him down a narrow hallway.

'Forty-three.'

'Where are they? The house looks empty.'

'We slapped a big-time illusio on it to fool the patrols,' the merman said. 'It's working. So far.'

The hall led into what had once been a living room. Now it appeared more like a hospital ward. Sick and wounded merpeople lay on the floor. The able-bodied were doing all they could to take care of them. No one recognized Serafina. No one even glanced at her.

A tiny mermaid cried out in her sleep. Sera forgot all about her own heartache and instinctively bent down to her. She stroked the child's head, murmuring soothing words, and the little merl settled back into sleep. Another child moaned that he was cold. Sera adjusted his blankets. Then she swam to the next room – once a dining room. It, too, was full of broken merpeople. So were the upper rooms. Only the kitchen had no beds in it, because it was being used as both mess hall and makeshift surgery.

I'm their principessa and I don't have the first clue how to help them, she thought. 'What do I *do*?' she said out loud.

'Do what you can. Like the rest of us,' came a gruff reply. Sera turned around. An older mermaid, harried and distracted, handed her a cup of tea. 'My name's Gia. I'm in charge here. Take this to Matteo. He's in the living room near the front wall. Black hair. Blue eyes. Fever.'

Serafina took the cup. She found Matteo, sat him up and helped him drink the tea. She held him when a fit of coughing overtook him, then eased him back down on his mattress. After that she went back into the kitchen, looking for more work.

'Take this to Aldo. He's the guy on the door. He hasn't eaten all night,' said a man dishing up stew.

Serafina dutifully carried the bowl through the house to the front door.

'Thank you,' Aldo said as she held it out to him. He was just about to take it when there was a knock.

'Starfish,' a voice on the other side of the door said.

'Hang on to that a minute, will you?' Aldo said. Sera nodded.

He looked through a small peephole, then opened the

door. A merman in black, hunched over, swam inside. Aldo locked the door behind him. The merman straightened.

Serafina's eyes widened at the sight of him. She dropped the bowl. 'Sea scum!' she shouted. 'Traitor!'

In a flash, her dagger was in her hand. A split second later, it was hurtling through the water.

Heading straight towards Mahdi.

FIFTEEN

'WOW, MAN. You really have a way with the ladies,' Aldo said.

'Not funny, Al,' Mahdi replied, holding Serafina off with one arm. His other arm was immobilized, because her dagger had pinned his sleeve to the door. 'How about some help here?'

'He has death riders with him!' Serafina cried. 'He's a traitor! Aldo, *help* me!'

'Pipe down, merl, before every soldier in Cerulea hears you. That's no traitor, that's Mahdi,' Aldo said. He hooked a meaty arm around Serafina's waist and pulled her off him.

'Don't touch me!' Sera shouted. She broke free of Aldo and backed away.

Mahdi pulled the dagger out of his sleeve. 'Hi,' he said to Serafina. 'Nice to see you too.'

'Are you going to turn me in?' Sera hissed. 'Hand me over to your master? You may have Aldo fooled, but I *saw* you. In the Ostrokon with your soldiers.'

Anger darkened Mahdi's features. 'You're kidding, right? If I'd wanted to turn you in, I would have done it then.

I saw *you* too, you know.'

'You saw *me*?' Serafina said uncertainly.

'You were hiding behind a pillar. Thank gods the idiots I was with didn't see you. I didn't recognize you at first. That's quite an outfit you're wearing,' he said, nodding at her Lagoona get-up.

Sera bristled. 'How about *your* outfit, Mahdi? Decided to join the invaders, I see. The same ones who destroyed Cerulea and murdered its citizens. Ladies love a merman in uniform. Lucia must be beside herself.'

Aldo, who was picking up Sera's bowl, looked at Mahdi and blinked.

'Lucia? Lucia Volnero? *Really?*'

'Aldo . . .' Mahdi said through gritted teeth.

Aldo looked from Mahdi to Serafina, sensing the anger between them. He quickly invented a reason to get back to the kitchen.

'Serafina,' Mahdi said as soon as he left, 'haven't you figured it out yet?' He was about to say more, but a child's wail, coming from within the house, cut him off. He ran a hand through his hair. 'This place is overflowing tonight. And there's probably not enough food. There's *never* enough food. Are you here by yourself? Where's Neela?'

'None of your business,' Serafina snapped.

'You still don't trust me.'

Serafina snorted. 'Haven't you figured *that* out yet?'

Mahdi swam close to her. 'Do you have so little faith in me? What kind of merman do you think I am?' he asked, furious now. He grabbed the front of his jacket and ripped it open. His chest was bare underneath it.

'That move might work on Lucia, but it doesn't do a lot for me,' Serafina said.

He held her dagger out. 'Take it,' he said. 'Go ahead, Serafina – take it!'

When she didn't, he took her hand, put the knife in it and pressed the tip to his heart. It pierced his skin. A thin rivulet of blood floated from his chest.

'What are you doing? Stop it, Mahdi!' she said. She tried to pull her hand away, but he held it fast.

'Go ahead. Use it,' he said. 'Take me out. You can kill the enemy. If that's who you really think I am.'

'Let go of me. Let *go*!' Serafina said.

Mahdi released her. She threw the dagger down.

'I don't *know* who you are!' she cried angrily. 'Not any more! All I know is that I saw you with death riders. Rounding up merpeople. *My* merpeople. So tell me, Mahdi, who *are* you?'

'Serafina, you didn't—' he started to say.

'Are you actually going to deny it? I *saw* you!'

'No, Serafina, you didn't. You didn't see *me*. What you saw was a lie. Like this uniform. Like my earring. Like the Lagoon and Lucia.'

He took Serafina's hand again, gently this time. He reached into his pocket, pulled something out of it and slipped it onto her finger. It was the little shell ring. The one he'd made for her two years ago.

'You're still my choice. Always,' he said. 'Even if I'm not yours any more.'

Serafina stared at the ring, incredulous. 'How did you get this?' she asked.

'I picked it up after you threw it away.'

'But you couldn't have. You weren't there. I threw it away when I was with the Praedatori. I don't . . . I don't understand.'

Then suddenly she did.

She grabbed the lapels of his jacket and pushed it off his shoulders. Under his right shoulder, just below the outer edge of his collarbone, was a bandage. It covered the place where the death rider's spear had gone through him. When he was in the duca's palazzo. When he was fighting for her life.

When he was Blu.

SIXTEEN

MAHDI CUPPED Sera's face.

'Don't touch me, Mahdi. I'm mad. No, I'm *furious*! After what happened at the duca's, I thought you were *dead*!' Sera said, slapping his hand away. 'You let me believe you were.'

'Maybe it was wishful thinking,' Mahdi said.

Sera ignored that. 'How long have you been with the Praedatori? What's the death rider uniform all about?'

Mahdi was silent.

'You need to tell me. My life's in danger, Mahdi. I *have* to know what's going on.'

'I've been a member of the Praedatori for a year. I've been pretending to be a death rider for the last few weeks.'

'Why didn't you say something at the duca's?' Serafina asked. 'Why didn't you tell me it was you?'

Her head was spinning. Until a minute ago, she'd thought that her betrothed had abandoned her. And that an outlaw had sacrificed himself for her. Now they were both the same merman, and right here before her.

'I couldn't say anything, Sera. We take a vow—'

'I don't *care*!' she said, slapping her tail. 'You took another vow. To me. Or you were about to.'

'I only wanted to protect you. It's dangerous to know things. Knowing things can get you killed these days.'

'It's more dangerous not to know. I just lunged at you with a knife, Mahdi. I . . . I could have . . .' Serafina's voice caught.

'It's all right. I'm fine.'

'Is Yazeed in the Praedatori too? Is he alive?'

Mahdi said nothing.

'I'll take that as a yes. Tell him he's got to get word to Matali. Neela's worried sick.'

'I can't. Yaz is missing in action. He was directing guerilla operations outside Cerulea. His base was raided a week ago. No one's seen him since.'

Serafina fell silent now, and Mahdi kept trying to explain.

'I wanted to say something. The whole time I was with you, I was wishing I could. But I couldn't, even if I hadn't taken a vow. If you'd known it was me, you might've made decisions based on my safety, not your own. I didn't want that. I wanted you to be able to swim away. To leave me behind if you had to. I was also worried about my cover. What if you'd been captured? You might've been forced to tell Traho the truth.'

'*Never*. I never would have told that sea scum anything.'

'Traho can be very persuasive.'

'I don't care if he tortured me. I *never* would have betrayed you.'

'What if it wasn't you he tortured? What if it was Neela?

What if he cut off *her* fingers and made you watch? Could you stay silent then? Four days ago, he cut a finger off a child – a *child*, Sera – to make her mother tell him where her father was hiding. I saw him do it. And I couldn't do anything. I couldn't stop him. It would have blown my cover. I would have saved one, maybe – and sacrificed thousands more. I still see her. That little merl. I see her at night when I try to sleep. I still *hear* her.'

Mahdi leaned his head against the wall and closed his eyes.

'Oh, Mahdi,' she said, her heart hurting for him.

He looked at her, then touched a tendril of her hair, following its curve across her temple and down her cheek. 'It suits you,' he said, smiling. 'So does the outfit.'

Serafina looked down at her clothing. The illusios she'd cast at the duca's had finally worn off. She was back to short hair and swash clothes. 'Thanks,' she said. 'It's all Neela's doing. We needed disguises and she came up with some.'

'I was so worried about you, Sera. After we fought off the attackers at the palazzo, we hunted for you. All the Praedatori did. The ones who survived, at least. We couldn't find you anywhere. How did you get out?'

'Through a mirror.'

'Seriously?'

'Yes.'

'But only the very best mages can do that. How did you—'

'Look, Mahdi, I'm asking the questions right now, OK?'

Sera was wary. The lessons of the last few weeks had taught her not to give her trust until it had been earned. Who was the real Mahdi? Was it the shy, serious boy she'd fallen in love with two years before? The party boy she'd found passed out in the ruins of the reggia? Or the solemn, selfless warrior she now found herself talking to?

'Why did you join the Praedatori?' she asked. She wanted to hear the whole story, from the beginning.

'Serafina, I can't break—'

'Your vow? Sorry, that catfish is out of the bag. And besides, you didn't break it. Not technically. You didn't tell me. I guessed.'

Mahdi took a deep breath. 'It all started soon after I returned home from Miromara. After it was decided we were to be betrothed. I sent you conchs at first, do you remember?'

'*Remember?* I lived for them,' Serafina said.

'I didn't choose to stop sending them. My messenger – Kamau – was taken. With two of my closest friends – Ravi and Jai.'

'What do you mean *taken?*'

'They were travelling back together from Miromara and stopped for the night at a village about twenty leagues from Matali City. The village was raided. Khelefu, the grand vizier, came to tell me. He brought me Kamau's bag. It was found at the inn where they'd stayed. There was a conch in it for me from you, a necklace he'd bought for his merlfriend, and a study conch. Kamau was cramming for the entrance exam to our military college. Ravi and Jai had been on a year abroad at the university in Tsarno . . .'

Mahdi shook his head, overcome by emotion. 'Yaz and I, we grew up with those guys. They were more than friends; they were our brothers. We asked Khelefu what was being done. He said the proper forms had been filled out and a battalion of soldiers had been sent to the village, but they'd found nothing. Other villages had been raided too. No one knew who was behind it. I asked him to send more soldiers. To widen the search area. He told me that would be highly unusual and that additional forms would have to be submitted.'

Serafina knew that Mahdi chafed under the burden of Matali's archaic bureaucracy.

'I couldn't just sit there while my people were being stolen,' Mahdi continued. 'I asked our high commander if Yaz and I could go out with the soldiers, but he said it was too dangerous. So we went to the chief of the Secret Service. He asked us how we were going to help – by going undercover? He laughed at the idea. Everyone in the entire kingdom knew who we were. I got angry then. Really angry. I'd lost three friends and couldn't do a thing about it. Yaz felt the same way. In fact, the thing we did? It was his idea.'

Serafina raised an eyebrow. 'What thing that you did?' she asked.

'We sneaked to the stables with four more friends, got hippokamps and took off. We went to search for Kamau, Ravi and Jai. We were gone for two days. No one could find us. It kind of caused an uproar.'

'I bet it did,' said Serafina. 'You're the heir to the throne! What were you thinking?'

'I wasn't thinking. Not then, and not for a long time after,' he said.

'What do you mean?'

Mahdi looked up at the ceiling. 'I knew about the raids. They'd been happening in Matali for over a year. I'd heard the reports. But I'd never actually seen one of the raided villages. It was horrible, Sera. The worst thing I'd ever seen. Some of the villagers must've tried to fight. There were bloodstains on the walls and floors of houses. They scribbled notes and left them behind. *Please tell my wife . . . Please help us . . . They've got my children . . .*'

Serafina leaned her head against Mahdi's shoulder. She was silent. She had learned that when pain was very deep, you shouldn't talk. You should listen.

'I lost it,' Mahdi said. 'Totally. I was grieving for my friends and for the stolen villagers. I wished I could talk to you and missed you like crazy and I couldn't even get a conch to you, not without Kamau. He was the only one I trusted with something so private. I was first in line to the throne, the second most powerful merman in the realm, but I couldn't do anything to help anyone. I kind of went off the deep end.' His jacket was still open. He touched his fingers to his chest, to the place over his heart, and drew out a bloodsong, wincing slightly.

Serafina watched the crimson swirl through the water and the images coalesce. A few seconds later, she sat up straight. Her jaw dropped open. She could not *believe* what she was seeing.

Mahdi and Yaz were at a club playing a spirited game of drupes, in which players took turns trying to bounce a shiny silver coin into a cup of brack. Whoever got the coin in handed the cup to another player to drink. The two of them had obviously been handed most of the cups, because a minute later, they were on the club's stage, kicking up their tails in the middle of a showmerl chorus line. A few hours later, they were at a piercing parlour getting gold hoops in their ears.

Serafina saw other memories. Of breakneck hippokamp races and games of Dump the Dude, in which they knocked gogg surfers off their boards. Of raucous shoals, and huge bets made on caballabong matches. There were memories of out-of-control waves that went on all night and ended up with Yaz passed out on top of a turret and Mahdi hanging off a spire one-handed, yelling, 'Serafina! SERAFINA!' before he was stopped by the Imperial Guards.

'*Wow*,' Serafina said now, as the bloodsong faded into the water.

'Yep,' Mahdi said. ''Fraid so. That went on for about a year and then one night – or morning, rather – when the two of us woke up on the floor of a nightclub, a man was standing there. The duca. In trousers, leather shoes and a tweed jacket.'

'Underwater? How did he—'

'I don't know. I can't explain most of the things he did.'

'Does he – *did* he – have magic?' Serafina asked.

Mahdi thought for a minute, then said. 'He had love, Sera. So much love. For the sea and all of its creatures. I think that was his magic.'

Serafina nodded.

'He stood there, leaning on his walking stick, looking down at us,' Mahdi continued. 'And then he told us that we were disgraceful. "Is this how you honour the memory of your friends? Of those villagers?" he said. We asked him who he was and how he knew about the villagers. He told us about the duchi di Venezia, the Praedatori and the Wave Warriors. We explained to him that we'd approached the high commander, and the Secret Service. We said we'd even tried to find the villagers.' Mahdi shook his head again, embarrassed. 'It sounds as lame now as it did then. The duca told us we needed to do more than try, we needed to succeed. And we would if we joined his Praedatori. So we did. We took the vow. We promised we'd shape up, but he didn't want us to. He wanted us to keep doing exactly what we were doing. To hang out in clubs. Rub elbows with caballabong players, sirens, club kids, and the lowtiders who hang around them.'

'Why?'

'So we could watch and listen and pick up info. If some lowtider was suddenly throwing currensea around, it was a pretty sure thing he'd sold out a swordfish shoal, or given up a shark to the finners. We'd tell the duca, and he'd have other Praeds follow the guy, nab him in the act and hand him over to the authorities. That's what we were doing in the Lagoon the night before Cerulea was attacked. We were hanging out in a club in the hopes of connecting with some sea scum who help seal hunters. I wanted to explain, Sera. So badly. I couldn't tell you the truth, but I wanted to at least tell you that what you were seeing wasn't me. Not the real me. But then, well . . . the whole world fell apart and I never got the chance.'

Sera looked at him now, and knew in her heart that she was seeing the real Mahdi. She wondered if she would ever have a chance again to know that Mahdi, to be as close as they once were, to make up for all the time they'd lost.

'I'd heard so many stories,' she said. 'That morning, in my chambers, Lucia was talking about what a great time you'd all had in the Lagoon. And then when I saw you, with her scarf tied around your head—'

'—you thought we had a thing,' Mahdi said.

Serafina nodded.

'I don't want Lucia.'

'She wants you.'

'Yeah, I know she does. She told me so.'

Serafina's fins flared. '*What?* When?'

'In prison. Right before I was going to be executed. Lucia Volnero's the only reason I'm alive.'

SEVENTEEN

'SERA, LISTEN. Just listen this time, OK?'

'OK, Mahdi,' Serafina said, trying not to be angry. 'I'm listening.'

'When the invasion of Cerulea started, Yaz and I cast transparensea pearls so we could fight without being seen. It was pretty pointless. I mean, two merboys were no match for Traho's forces. Then we heard you and Neela had been captured, so we went after you and got you to the duca's. After he was killed, and you disappeared, Verde ordered Yaz to remain underground to direct guerilla operations. He ordered me to get myself captured.'

'Seriously?'

'Yes. He thought I'd make a valuable political prisoner. He figured I'd be treated well and could pick up information about the invaders. So I did it. But the plan failed. Traho didn't think I was valuable at all. He thought I was an idiot. Can't blame him – I've worked really hard to give the world that impression. He threw me in prison and was going to have me shot. Like he . . . like he had my parents shot.'

Mahdi's jaw clenched. He couldn't continue.

Serafina ached for him. She touched her forehead to his

and put her arms around him. She knew what he was feeling, knew his pain all too well.

When he could, he spoke again.

'Lucia found out what was happening and got me out. I have no idea how. I do know that the Volneros and their friends have Traho's favour though. He spared their houses in the Golden Fathom and they get to come and go when they want. Lucia had me brought to Traho. I saw my chance to win his favour, to get close to him, so I bargained away Matali. I told him I'd give it to him bloodlessly, if he'd let me be a figurehead emperor. I said I didn't care about the realm as long as I had plenty of currensea so I could keep partying. He agreed to try my plan. He said it would save him the time and expense of an attack.'

Serafina paled. 'My gods, Mahdi . . . a takeover of Matali? *When?*'

'I don't know. He's not ready just yet. He's still testing me, seeing whether he can fully trust me. He gave me command of two patrols to start with. I must've done something right, because he upped it to twenty right before he left Miromara to hunt you and Neela down. Now I'm in charge of sweeping the city. I go out three, sometimes four, times a day. He's nervous, I think.'

'About what?'

'Talk of a Cerulean resistance.'

Hope leapt in Serafina's heart. 'Really, Mahdi? Who's leading it?' she asked, hopefully.

'We don't know.'

'I – I thought maybe it was my mother or brother,' she said, her hope fading.

Mahdi looked at her, but didn't say anything.

Serafina understood. She lowered her head. All these weeks, she'd refused to believe it. All these weeks, she'd held on to the possibility that her mother was still alive.

'Both of them?' she asked softly. 'For sure?'

'We know Isabella is dead. We think Des is. No one's seen any sign of him. You know what he's like. He's fierce. If he was alive, no one could have kept him from Cerulea. He would have taken on Traho single-handedly. I'm sorry, Sera.'

Serafina nodded. Tears stung her eyes, but she blinked them away. 'I never got to say goodbye,' she said. 'To my father, to Des or to my mother. She died fighting, Mahdi. Did you know that? She died protecting me. I wish I could say thank you. I wish I could tell her how much I loved her . . .'

A low moan of grief escaped her. Mahdi pulled her to him and held her tightly. She balled her hands into fists and pounded them against him. He took her blows and continued to hold her, rocking her, saying nothing, for there was nothing to say. Her pain was too deep for words.

After some time, he released her. 'There is some good news,' he said. 'About your uncle. There have been sightings, and talk that he's—'

'Heading north. To the Kobold.'

'You've heard. Word must be spreading. I'm not

surprised. It's talked about a lot here. In the Golden Fathom. At dinner parties at the di Remoras' and the Volneros'. The nobles believe he'll return.'

'You go to the Volneros'?' Serafina asked.

Mahdi nodded. Serafina looked away.

'Look at me, Sera,' Mahdi said, turning her face back to his. 'Here's the truth: I kissed Lucia that night in the Lagoon, OK? It meant nothing to me. I'm still kissing her . . .'

Sera winced.

'. . . and it still means nothing. It's part of my job. Verde wants me to play up to Lucia because she and her mother are close to Traho. I'm going to keep playing up to her until I find out if Kolfinn's the one who's backing him.'

'Do you think he isn't?'

'We haven't been able to create a clear trail from Traho to Kolfinn. The death riders – they're not Ondalinian. They're all mercenaries, bought and paid for.'

'So it's *not* Kolfinn.'

'I didn't say that. It may just be that Kolfinn's good at covering his wake. That way, he can take over realms and all the while tell the Council of Six that he's not.'

Serafina nodded.

'That's why I hang with Lucia. I'm hoping to see something, or hear something, that will help us stop Kolfinn. Can you understand that? Can you forgive me?'

Serafina wanted to tell him no, until she thought of the drunken sergeant in the Lagoon and the dangerous game she'd played with him. She'd done what she had to do to escape. To survive another day. To fight for her people. And she knew she would do it again if she had to.

'Yes, I can,' she said.

Mahdi touched her cheek with the back of his hand. 'I don't want Lucia. I want *you*. I told you that two years ago and I'm telling you now. I've lost my parents. I may lose Matali. I can't lose you too. You have to believe me, Sera. Say you do.'

Serafina looked at him then, searching his beautiful dark eyes for the truth. What she saw in them made her believe. 'I do, Mahdi.'

And then she was in his arms and his lips were on hers, silently telling her who he was. *Hers*. Always. And for a moment, there was no safe house, no danger, no grief. All she knew was the heat of his kiss and the feel of his heart beating under her hand.

Mahdi broke the kiss. 'I have to go,' he said. 'I took a big risk in coming here. But I had to see if you were here.'

Serafina, who'd been clutching his jacket, reluctantly let go of it. 'I hate seeing this thing on you,' she said.

'Me too. Sometimes, when I first wake up in the morning, I don't know where I am. Or who I am,' he said. 'This uniform, everything I say, everything I do . . . It's all a lie. Only one thing is real and true – my feelings for you.' He kissed her again. 'Stay here where it's safe, Sera. Please. No more trips to the Ostrokon. Promise me.'

'I can't, Mahdi,' Serafina said. 'I have to go back to the Ostrokon. I have to find some conchs there.'

'It's too dangerous. Traho's patrols—'

'—aren't going to stop me. Traho was on my tail all the way to the Freshwaters, but I stayed one stroke ahead of him. I won't let him catch me,' Sera said, bristling. 'I have work to do here, Mahdi. Just like you do.'

'The *Freshwaters?*' Mahdi said, disbelief in his voice. 'Sera, where have you been all this time? What have you been doing?'

Sera was about to reply when a thunderous crash cut her off. It was followed by the sound of splintering wood. The front door shuddered. Shouts and commands came from outside the house.

Mahdi swore. A second later, Aldo came barrelling down the hallway. He picked up a heavy board that was propped against the wall and slid it into two brackets on either side of the door, bracing it. 'That'll give us a minute,' he said.

'What's that noise? What's happening?' Serafina asked, frightened.

'Death riders,' Aldo said grimly. 'Get the hell out of here.'

EIGHTEEN

I sing to you this spell of strength,
To shore you up both breadth and length.

My song your cracks and breaks will heal,
And change your boards from wood to steel.

Keep evil out, keep death away.
Keep all enemies well at bay.

Away to safety, we must speed.
Give us, door, the time we need . . .

Aldo was casting a robus songspell. Eyes closed, sweat streaming down his face, he was pushing his voice against the safe-house door with all his might.

But the death riders were pushing back.

There was terror and confusion as everyone hurried to the basement. Sera had learned that a door there opened onto a network of tunnels that led to another safe house.

'Get out of here, Mahdi!' a voice hissed. It was Gia. 'You're our only link to Traho. If you're taken, we won't get any more info on the patrols!'

'What about you and Aldo?' Mahdi shouted, trying to make himself heard above frightened screams and the pounding on the door. 'What happens to you when they break through?'

'Don't worry about us. We'll make it to the tunnels,' Gia said.

But Sera saw the fear in her eyes. *She's trying to sound convincing for Mahdi's sake. To get him to leave*, she thought. *She knows it's hopeless.*

Despite Aldo's robus, the door – made of shipwreck wood – was splintering under the death riders' attack.

'Traho's not getting these people. He's *not*,' Sera said aloud. But how could she stop him? She tried to think, but her ears were ringing with the mer people's cries and the shrieks of her own fear.

I have to help them, she thought. *There* must *be a way.*

And then it happened again – just as it had in the Iele's caves when Abbadon tried to break through the waterfire: a cold, crystalline clarity descended upon her. It quieted the chaos in her head, focused her mind and enabled her to play the board, not the piece.

'Forget the tunnels. Here,' she said to Gia, pulling two of the three small, precious chunks of quartz Vrăja had given her out of her bag. 'Transparensea pebbles for you and Aldo. Cast them. Now. Hold the death riders back for as long as you can. When they break the door down, swim upstairs and get out through a window.'

Gia nodded, her eyes alight with renewed courage. 'Will do. Thanks, merl. Now, *go*!'

As Sera and Mahdi raced through the house to the basement, they heard a small, frightened sob. They stopped, turned back and swam to its source. In what had once been the living room, two little merls, no more than a year old, were sitting in a crib, crying.

In the frenzied rush to escape, orphaned children had been left behind. Two merboys were sitting up in their beds, wide-eyed. Another was still lying down, his eyes closed. It was Matteo, the one with the fever.

'Matteo? Can you hear me?' Sera asked, gently shaking him awake.

The merboy opened his eyes. They were glassy and unseeing.

'We can't leave them here,' Mahdi said, casting an anxious glance back at the hallway.

'Come on, Matteo, don't be afraid,' Sera coaxed. 'We've got to go. Put your arms around my neck.'

The merboy did so and Sera lifted him out of his bed. Mahdi hoisted the two merls out of their crib and tucked them under his arms. He roused the other two merboys – Franco and Giancarlo – and told them to follow him because they were going on an adventure. Then he swam for the basement.

Sera was right behind them. Aldo and Gia were still songcasting, but their voices were ragged now, and the sound of battering was deafening.

'What about the upstairs rooms? What if someone's still up there?' Sera said as they reached the basement door.

'We don't have time to check. We have to get these kids to safety,' Mahdi said.

The last few inhabitants of the safe house were hurrying into the tunnels. Mahdi shepherded Sera and the children ahead of him, then closed the basement door. It was flimsy, made of worm-ridden wood, and not worth enchanting. The door to the tunnel was made of iron, so spells to strengthen or camouflage it would be useless, as iron repelled magic, but it did have a strong lock. As soon as everyone was inside the passage, Mahdi closed the heavy door and shot the bolt.

'That'll slow them down,' he said to Sera. Then he turned to the children. 'Come on, kids. We're going to race. First one to the fork in the tunnel wins. On your marks, get set, go!'

Franco and Giancarlo tore off. Sera was next with Matteo. Mahdi brought up the rear with the two tiny merls in his arms. Their group didn't have any lava torches, but they were able to follow the glow of those being carried by people up ahead.

They swam for about a quarter of an hour, through a tunnel that was dark, narrow and full of brittle stars and spider crabs. After bearing right at two separate forks, they followed a bend to the left and found themselves in a heavily graffitied section. Within a giant picture of Captain Kidd, a door opened for them.

'You knock on Kidd's chest four times,' Mahdi explained.

'The password is urchin. Just case you ever come here on your own.'

A merman named Marco hurried them inside. 'You the last ones?' he asked.

Mahdi nodded and Marco locked the door behind them. Sera found herself in another basement.

'I have a sick child here,' she said, breathing heavily. Carrying Matteo through the tunnels had exhausted her.

Another merman took the child from her and carried him off to the infirmary. Marco told Mahdi and Sera where they could find beds for the other children. As they settled them in, the boy named Franco asked, 'Where's Cira?'

Sera's stomach knotted. She prayed that Cira was a toy.

'Who's Cira?' Mahdi asked.

'She's my friend. Her mama's not well. She's going to have a baby. They sleep upstairs.'

'I'm going back,' Sera said.

'No way. It's suicide. The death riders will be in the house by now,' Mahdi said.

'We should have checked the upstairs.'

'What if we had, and the death riders had broken in while we were up there? How would these kids have got out?'

'Anyone left in that house will be interrogated by Traho.'

'So will you if his soldiers capture you.'

'A *child*, Mahdi. A pregnant mermaid and a little child!' Sera's voice was rising. With fear. And fury.

'If you go back and you're taken, Traho will make you tell him where *this* house is and *these* people.'

'They're *mine*, Mahdi. *My* people,' she shouted. 'He can't have them!'

'Sera . . .'

But she was already speeding back to the basement.

'Let me out. I'm going back to Basalt Street. We left two behind,' she said to Marco.

'That's a really bad idea,' said Marco.

'Let me out *now*!' Sera demanded.

Marco gave her a long look, then said, 'This door has a peephole. If I see, hear or smell any soldiers behind you, I'm not opening it. You're out in the cold, merl.'

Sera nodded. She picked up a lantern lit by glowing moon jellies. Marco opened the door and she swam out of it.

Mahdi was right behind her.

NINETEEN

SERA TENSED, ready to throw a frag or whirl a vortex.

'You good to go?' Mahdi whispered.

She nodded. They were back at Basalt Street, in the tunnel, with no idea of what awaited them on the other side of the iron door.

Mahdi pressed his ear to it. He listened for a few seconds, then slowly drew the bolt back. Taking a deep breath, he swung the door open.

The basement was empty.

Sera put her lantern down and cautiously swam inside. She crossed the basement and started for the ground floor, but a noise stopped her short. It was the sound of furniture being toppled and smashed.

Mahdi caught up with her. 'Death riders. Upstairs,' he said, mouthing the words.

Sera glanced at the rickety wooden door that led out of the basement. It was ajar. Mahdi had closed it when they'd fled. She was sure of it. She touched his hand then pointed at the door. He nodded. He understood what she was trying to say: *someone else is down here.*

Sera turned in a slow circle, expecting to see Traho

lurking in the shadows, a smile on his face, a speargun in his hand, but he wasn't there.

Another crash from above froze her in place.

Mahdi, eyes on the door, motioned to her to follow him back inside the tunnel, but she shook her head. 'They're *here*. Cira and her mother. I know they are,' she whispered. 'They're the ones who left the door open.'

Mahdi held up a finger, indicating that she had one minute.

She moved through the basement like a whirlwind, looking in every corner, behind the lava furnace, around piles of old furniture. Mahdi did the same, keeping a wary eye on the doorway. After a minute had elapsed, he motioned that it was time to go.

Sera nodded, heartsick. Traho must've found Cira and her mother. Their risky trip back here had been for nothing. She headed back towards the tunnel.

As she did, a movement caught her eye. An old coral-frame sofa, its sea-silk cushions rotted long ago, had been pushed close – but not all the way – to a wall. The tip of a small green tail fin was sticking out from underneath it. Sera grabbed Mahdi's arm and pointed.

They swam closer. Cowering in the gap between the sofa and the wall was a mermaid, her belly large and round, holding a trembling little merl. The mother's eyes widened in fear when she saw Mahdi in his death rider's uniform. She tightened her grip on her daughter and shrank against the wall.

'It's OK,' Sera whispered. 'He's not one of them. It's just a disguise. Come with us. We'll get you out of here.'

The mother looked from Sera to Mahdi uncertainly. As she did, another crash was heard above their heads.

'Please,' Sera said. 'We don't have much time.'

But the mother, paralysed by fear, wouldn't budge.

'Search the basement!' a voice commanded.

Sera recognized that voice. She heard it in her nightmares. 'Traho,' she said. 'We've *got* to go.'

'Cira,' Mahdi said to the little merl, 'your friends are waiting for you. Franco and Giancarlo. They told me you were here. They're safe and they want you to be safe too.'

The young mermaid gave Mahdi a brave smile. She took his hand. 'Come on, Mama,' she said. 'It's OK.'

Mahdi hurried mother and child into the tunnel. Sera followed. She was about to pull the tunnel door closed when four death riders swam into the basement.

'You, there! Stop!' one of them shouted.

'Call Captain Traho!' another yelled.

One reached for his speargun, holstered at his hip. Two more rushed at Sera. They were both holding lava torches.

Sera realized that they had only seconds in which to live or die. She needed more than canta mirus now; she needed canta malus. She didn't hesitate. Her voice swooped into a low, dark key as she focused on the glass globes of lava set atop the torches.

Lava hot and lava bright,

Hide us from our enemy's sight.

Bubble, leap, hiss and burn.
Make these soldiers quickly turn.

Deadly lava, do your worst.
Through the goblin glass now burst!

Mahdi lunged for Sera just as the last note of the songspell left her lips. He pulled her into the tunnel and yanked the door closed. His quick thinking saved her life.

The explosion was instantaneous. The concussive force was so great, it shook the ground. Sera saw a blinding flash of white light in the crack under the door; she heard the impact of debris as it was flung against the iron, and the bubbling and hissing of lava.

Then she heard nothing at all.

'They're . . .' she started to say.

'Yeah, they are,' Mahdi said. 'No one could survive a blast like that. I doubt the safe house survived it. My gods, Sera, what *was* that?'

'Darksong,' Sera replied. 'It's legal if used against an enemy during wartime. I had no choice, Mahdi. It was us or them.'

'I know *that*. I meant *you*. When did you learn how to cast such a powerful frag? I know seasoned commanders who couldn't do what you just did.'

The bloodbind, Sera thought. *It gave me Neela's skills with light and Becca's with fire.* She was about to explain her newfound powers, or try to, when shouts carried through the door.

'More death riders,' Mahdi said tensely. 'Traho must've had extra troops outside the safe house. Time to go, everyone.'

'Thank you,' Cira's mother said as they started off. 'Thank you for coming back for us.' In the light of Sera's lantern, her face looked pale and pinched. She was breathing heavily.

'I'm Kallista, by the way.'

'Are you OK?' Sera asked.

'I'm in labour.'

'Oh, wow. Oh, boy,' Mahdi said, running his hands through his hair.

'There's an infirmary in the new safe house. It's not far from here. Half a league,' Sera said. 'Can you make it?'

Kallista laughed weakly. 'Do I have a choice?'

'Sera, you take one of her arms. I'll take the other. Cira, you stay right on our tails,' said Mahdi.

Sera hoped they could move faster than before since they knew where they were going this time, but that wasn't the case. The tunnels were too narrow to allow them to swim three abreast. She and Mahdi often had to turn sideways, which slowed them down. She was glad when the first fork appeared ahead of them.

Before they reached it, however, Mahdi stopped abruptly. 'Hold up a minute,' he said.

'What is it?' asked Sera.

Then she heard it: the sound of voices. Closing in fast.

'They got through,' said Mahdi. 'We're going to split up at the fork. You three go right and swim as fast as you can to the safe house. I'll go left and draw them off.'

'Mahdi, no!' Serafina said.

'*Go!*' he hissed. He fished a moon jelly out of Sera's lantern to light his way, picked up a rock off the floor then shot into the opposite tunnel. A second later, Sera heard a scraping sound. He was dragging the rock against the tunnel wall.

'Come on,' Sera said to Cira and Kallista, remembering Marco's dire warning about not letting her back in if soldiers were on her tail. 'We've got to swim. Fast.'

They took off up the right-hand tunnel, moving as quickly as they could. A few minutes later, Sera spotted the second turn-off. As they reached it, she heard voices again.

Mahdi's plan hadn't worked. The death riders weren't following him; they were following *them*.

Sera took Cira by the shoulders. The child couldn't have been more than eight. 'Cira, listen to me. You've got to get your mum the rest of the way there, OK? You can do it. I know you can.' She explained how to get inside the safe house, then she scooped another glowing moon jelly out of her lantern and put it in Cira's hands. 'Go!' she hissed.

As Cira and her mother hurried off, Sera swam into the other tunnel. 'Help!' she shouted. 'We can't find the safe house! *Please!* Is anyone there?'

This time, the plan *did* work. The death riders chased her, not Cira and Kallista.

'I've got her!' she heard one of them yell. A silver spear hit the tunnel wall, missing her tail by a hair's breadth. The death riders were fast, but Sera – strong and lean from weeks on the currents – was faster. A few minutes later, she saw the end of the tunnel. Rays of sun slanted through the water outside. She put on a final burst of speed, shot out into the open daylit waters and found herself across the current from the Ostrokon. She darted into its ruined entry and down to its dim depths. Heart pounding, lungs heaving, she swam into a listening room and hid under a table.

A few minutes passed. And then a few more. When half an hour had elapsed, Sera finally allowed herself to believe that she'd escaped her pursuers. Her muscles were trembling. Painful cramps knotted her tail. She stretched out and closed her eyes.

'Please,' she whispered. 'Please let Cira and Kallista have made it to the safe house. Please let Mahdi be OK.'

She remembered the trust in the little merl's eyes. And the desperate relief in her mother's. What if the death riders had split up and searched both forks? What if Cira and Kallista had led them right to the Market Street safe house? Had she endangered scores of people for the sake of two?

A good ruler will never sacrifice the many for the few, her uncle once told her.

She'd tried to argue with him. *But, Uncle, the few are no less . . .*

Important, she was going to say. *Valuable. Beloved.*

But Vallerio had cut her off. *The few are fewer, Serafina. And in war, numbers are all that matter.*

She couldn't understand that. Not then. Not now. Kallista mattered. And the tiny baby she was carrying. Little Cira mattered. The many *and* the few.

She'd made the right choice. She'd done the right thing.

As sleep stole over her, Serafina held on to that.

And tried her best to believe it.

TWENTY

'THERE YOU GO, PRIYĀ,' Suma said, helping Neela into a soft sea-silk robe. 'A nice scrub makes everything better.'

Neela did not reply. She simply sat down by a window, in the same place she'd been sitting for the better part of three days, and stared out of it.

She had just scrubbed her body with soft white sand. Then she'd rubbed driftnut oil into her hair and brushed it until it gleamed. Suma had brought a tray of her favourite foods for dinner, and a plate of sweets for dessert. Soon she would lie down in her soft bed and sleep. She was safe. She was warm and well fed.

She was furious.

'Is there anything else you require?' asked Suma.

Neela shook her head.

'May I take the nasty black clothing away?'

'You may not.'

'You know what the medica magus said, Princess,' Suma reminded. 'The sooner you admit you need help, the sooner he can help you. Promise to behave yourself and get rid of those awful things, and Kiraat will allow you to leave your room. Give them to me. I'll put them in the incinerator. The lava will make short work of them.'

'Leave them, Suma. And me.'

'And the mirrors? What about the mirrors?' Suma asked.

Neela had draped every single mirror in her room with saris. 'Leave those too,' she said.

Suma shook her head mournfully. She dabbed at her eyes. 'Covering your mirrors! Oh, Princess, it's worse than any of us thought. You *have* lost your mind! I thought that when you started eating bingas again you were making progress, but I was wrong.'

She bade Neela a tearful good night and left her.

Neela mindlessly unwrapped a sweet and ate it. Boredom and anxiety had driven her back to them. She glanced at the offending garments – her black lace top and skirt, her jacket, her messenger bag. They were draped over a chair. Kiraat had demanded she get rid of them, and she'd refused. He'd declared her dangerously deranged and advised she be confined to her room so she couldn't do damage to herself or to anyone else. Kiraat and her parents thought they were protecting her. They thought they were helping her come back to her senses, but all they were doing was killing her spirit, bit by bit.

How could she explain to them what her swashbuckler clothes meant to her? When she looked at them, she didn't see frays and tears, she saw Sera and Ling eating stew in Lena's kitchen after Ling had almost been captured by Rafe

Mfeme. She saw Becca and Ava in the River Olt, fighting off the rusalka. She saw fierce Astrid battling Abbadon in the Incantarium with only her sword.

And she saw herself – being braver and stronger than she'd ever thought she could be.

And now they wanted her to go back. Back to pink. Back to smiling until her face hurt. Back to chatting about the tides. Back to never doing anything important, or saying anything honest. Back to the eternal beauty contest.

Neela had tried to get out. She'd tried to pick the lock on her door, just as she'd picked the locks on the iron collars that she, Sera and Thalassa had been forced to wear when they were Traho's prisoners. But this lock had been enchanted. It could only be opened by the key Suma carried. Neela's entire bedchamber had been spellproofed. She couldn't get the windows open. Or blow them out. She couldn't cast the tiniest vortex, or throw a weak frag. Even the convoca she'd tried to cast, to inform the others of her predicament, failed. She'd thought about escaping through one of her mirrors, but fear of meeting up with Rorrim had stopped her. In fact, she'd covered all her mirrors to keep him from spying on her.

So Neela sat, staring listlessly out of the window, watching the Matali flags flap in the current. She unwrapped another sweet, wondering who was going to break first. Kiraat? Her parents?

Or her.

TWENTY-ONE

SERAFINA WOKE WITH A GASP. For a moment, she panicked. She didn't know where she was. Then she remembered – the Ostrokon. She'd swum under a table to hide, and passed out from exhaustion. Now she rolled over onto her back and opened her eyes. How long had she been here? She felt as if she'd slept for three days. Her body was numb from the hard floor. Her mind was numb too – from all the questions still plaguing her, the ones that had no answers.

She thought of Mahdi, Cira and Kallista. Had they escaped? Maybe she could make her way back to the Market Street safe house and find out.

She recalled the lethal darksong spell she'd cast against the death riders. She'd had no choice; she knew she'd do it again if she had to.

When the Praedatori had killed a prison guard in order to free her from Traho's camp, Sera had been traumatized by his death. She'd felt sorrow for him. More death riders had died at the Basalt Street safe house. Because of her this time. But she felt no sorrow for them. She felt nothing.

I'm changing, she thought, *and not entirely for the better*.

There were barnacles on the underside of the table, glowing whitely in the darkness. She pressed her palm against their sharp edges. She wanted the pain. Wanted to know she could still feel *something*.

Voices drifted through her mind, hers and her mother's.

Mum, can you just be a mum *for once? And forget you're the regina?* Sera had shouted on the morning of her Dokimí.

Isabella had smiled sadly. *No, Sera*, she'd said. *I can't*.

Serafina had been so angry at her for that. But now she understood that Isabella had loved her people so fiercely she'd given up many things for them – including time with her family. She now understood that Mahdi loved the seas so much, he was risking his life to defend them.

Sera was beginning to see that love wasn't pretty words and easy promises. Love was hard. It challenged you and changed you. It filled your heart and sometimes hardened it too. Love demanded sacrifices. She'd made many over the last few weeks, and knew she would be called upon to make many more.

As she lay on her back, her palm still pressed against the barnacles, her stomach growled. It sounded insanely loud in the large, empty room. Sera was hungry and had no idea what to do about it. She hadn't eaten anything more than a handful of reef olives and eel berries in days.

I'll starve to death under this table, she said to herself. *Years from now, someone will find my bones here. They'll feel so sorry for me*.

No, they won't, a voice said. *They'll think what a total loser you were.*

'Ling!' Sera said out loud.

Want a meal with your whine?

'Ha. *So* funny. Where are you?'

Close to the Abyss. Just thought I'd cast a convoca and check in, see how you're doing. Not so good, I gather.

'That would be the understatement of the century. I was chased by Traho's soldiers this morning. At least, I think it was this morning. Maybe it was yesterday. Anyway, I also found out that the conchs we need are gone, Cerulea's been destroyed, and my people – the ones who are left – are suffering badly. And what am I doing? Lying under a table.'

Any good news?

'As a matter of fact, yes. It turns out that I still love the merboy I used to love even though I'm in love with somebody else.'

What?

Sera explained. She told Ling everything that had happened since they had last seen each other.

Wow, Sera. Never a dull moment in Miromara. Seriously, though, the Traho thing sounds scary. You OK?

'I'm fine. It *was* scary. What about the others? Have you heard from them?'

Becca's already crossed the Mid-Atlantic Ridge. Ava's in the Ceara Abyssal Plain. They're fine. Baby is too, you'll be happy to know.

'How could he not be? That monster-on-a-leash bites

anyone who looks at him. What about Neela?'

Ling's voice took on a worried tone. *I can't get through to her, Sera. No matter how many times I cast a convoca, she doesn't answer. Have you heard from her?*

'No, but then again, I haven't tried to contact her. I haven't cast a convoca since I failed back in the sea cave. I'll try when I leave the Ostrokon. You can't cast in here. The acoustics make songspells fall flat. Fossegrim, our liber magus, wanted it that way. He always said knowledge is its own magic.'

Serafina's stomach growled again.

You sound like a sick walrus! Look, maybe you can't overthrow Traho at this particular point in time, but you can get up and find something to eat, so we don't have to listen to any more disgusting noises.

'How? I'm in an ostrokon!'

Doesn't it have a TideSide? The ones in Qin do.

'Yes, it does! A little one on Level Four. I totally forgot! Ling, you're a genius!'

Of course . . . am . . . careful, Sera . . .

'I'm losing you, Ling.'

. . . hear you . . . later . . .

'Yeah, merl. Later,' Sera said as the convoca faded.

Now that Ling was gone, the room seemed twice as large and twice as dark and Sera felt more alone than ever. Sighing, she swam out from under the table.

TideSides were small freestanding snack bars that sold drinks and finger foods. Serafina had visited the one in the Ostrokon whenever she'd stayed late to study, her royal guards trailing discreetly behind her. She swam to one of the listening room's walls and took a lava torch down. The lava needed to be replaced. It was cooling, giving off only a dull orange light, but it still allowed her to see where she was going. She poked her head out of the doorway and cautiously looked up the spiralling hallway. It was empty and sad. There were no students in it now, no black-robed professors, no ostroki carrying baskets with conchs in them, shushing everyone.

Moving slowly, Serafina made her way up the hall. She paused now and again to listen for voices. She was almost at the fourth level when she felt vibrations in the water. She stuffed the lava globe under her skirt, dousing its light, and ducked into an empty doorway. A few seconds later, a small school of blennies swam by. Her shoulders sagged with relief.

The TideSide was tucked between the geology and biology collections. When Sera reached it, she saw that it was dark and deserted, like the rest of the Ostrokon. She swam to the counter, hoping for a bag of mussel chips or some snail gums, but there was nothing to be had. Not even a salted sandworm.

'Great,' she said out loud. Now she would have to risk a trip outside. She tried to recall if there were any cafés nearby. If so, maybe she could break into one and find some beach plums. Clam puffs. *Anything*.

That's when the net went over her head.

Serafina screamed. She dropped her torch. Its globe smashed on the floor. Lava oozed over the stone, hissing and bubbling and sending up steam through the water.

'Let me go!' she shouted, as the net enveloped her. She struggled and tried to swim away, but only succeeded in tangling herself so badly that she could hardly move.

A face, pale and bespectacled, came close to hers. It belonged to a young merman. 'She's one of us, Magistro, not a death rider,' he said. 'I *think*. At least, she hasn't got a uniform on.'

Serafina recognized him as an ostroko who used to work in the literature section. Another face came into view – an older merman's. He wore glasses too. His long hair and beard were grey. His broad, magnificent fins were black. He was pointing a spear. At her.

'Magistro Fossegrim?' she cried. 'It's me, Serafina!'

A third face peered down at her. A child's. She looked about twelve. Serafina had seen her before. If she could only gather her wits, she might remember where.

'It *is* her, Magistro!' the young mermaid said. 'She's cut her hair off!'

'Good gods! What have we done? Release her!' Fossegrim ordered.

The net was removed. Serafina, who'd sunk to the floor, looked up at her would-be captors – Fossegrim, the young merman, two other mermen, two grown mermaids and the young one.

'Cosima!' she said, the child's name finally coming back to her. 'Lady Elettra's little sister. I remember you from the court.'

'Coco, Your Grace,' the merl said, with a quick dip of her head. 'I *hate* Cosima.'

'Coco, Fossegrim, what are you doing here?' Serafina asked.

'This is our headquarters, Your Grace. I'm sorry about the rude welcome. We were only trying to defend it,' Fossegrim replied.

'I don't understand,' Serafina said. '*Whose* headquarters?'

Fossegrim pulled himself up to his full height, swept a hand towards his companions and grandly said, 'The Black Fin resistance.'

TWENTY-TWO

'PLEASE, PRINCIPESSA, take more snails. Have more worms,' Fossegrim said.

'Thank you, Magistro, they were delicious, but I'm full.'

It was a lie. Serafina was still hungry. But Fossegrim and the others were too. She could tell. They were thin. Their clothing was baggy.

She was sitting with the liber magus in the Ostrokon's sub-basement. It was nearly ten at night now. The others had gone off on their rounds. Sera had slept for most of a day.

They'd all introduced themselves on Level Four – after Serafina had got up off the floor. She already knew Fossegrim and Coco. Then came Niccolo, the young merman with the glasses. The others were Calvino, Domenico, Alessandra, and Sophia.

A handful of ostroki and a child. That was the resistance.

'Cerulea is very lucky to have you fighting for her,' Serafina had said, smiling.

Cerulea is totally doomed, she'd thought.

But that was before they'd taken her through a trapdoor in the floor of the basement. There she'd discovered a clean, warm, fairly large chamber that contained cots, a small lava stove, medical supplies and a stockpile of food. The walls were covered with maps of the city.

'The war room,' Fossegrim had said proudly. 'From here, we've managed to cut lava lines to the palace, release a lava flow that destroyed the kitchens and let crabs loose in the food stores.'

'How did you know to do all these things? Did the acqua guerrieri help you?' Serafina had asked, amazed. She regretted underestimating them. These ostroki were as formidable as the Praedatori.

'Conchs!' Coco had piped.

'We listened to field marshals from the Hundred Years War, Qin's Yŏnggǎn Dynasty generals, guerilla fighters from Atlantica's swamps and a lot of early Merrovingian commanders. There's *nothing* Quintus Ligarius can't teach you about sabotage!' Niccolo had said cheerfully.

'We're a large and sharp sea thorn in Traho's side,' said Fossegrim now, as he put the uneaten snails and worms away. 'We shall rout him and return Cerulea to the Merrovingia!'

'Magistro, I'm afraid that the battle is much bigger than Cerulea,' Serafina said gently. 'I know a way to fight it. But I need your help.'

'Anything, Principessa,' he said. 'Say the word.'

'I came here last night to listen to conchs on Merrow's Progress, but they were gone.'

'Yes, Traho took them. I don't know why.'

'I do, but I can't tell you without putting you at even

more risk. Are there any other conchs here on the same topic?'

'On what topic?' Coco asked.

She had just returned from her rounds carrying a sack full of sea cucumbers. A grey sand shark, small and quick with sparkling copper eyes, followed her.

'Where did you get those? I told you not leave the Ostrokon, young lady! It's far too dangerous!' Fossegrim scolded.

Coco ignored him. 'What information are you looking for, Principessa?' she asked.

'Conchs on Merrow's Progress,' Serafina replied, to be polite. She doubted very much that the merl had even heard of the Progress. Sera had studied post-fall Atlantean history extensively and she knew that ten years after Atlantis was destroyed, Merrow, Miromara's first regina, had made a long journey through the waters of the world. The official story was that she was seeking safe new places for her people to live, as they were thriving and needed space. Sera was certain, however, that there was an unofficial reason for the trip – to hide the six talismans.

'Try Baltazaar, first minister of finance from the start of Merrow's reign to the year 62,' Coco said matter-of-factly. 'He's a great source, but hardly anyone knows about him. I think it's because his conchs aren't shelved on Five in Early Merrovingian History. They're on Three, with Governmental Records. In the expenditures section for 10 anno Merrow, the year Merrow made her Progress.'

Serafina's jaw dropped. '*What?*' she said.

'Bal-ta-zaar,' Coco slowly repeated, as if speaking to an idiot. 'First minister—'

'Yes, I heard you. How do you *know* that?'

'I've listened to lots of conchs since I came here. We can't go out during the daytime, and there's not much else to do. I like listening to conchs. I like the Ostrokon too. A lot better than I liked the court. Sorry.'

Serafina smiled. 'Don't be. I do too,' she said.

'So as I was saying,' Coco continued. 'Baltazaar was, like, Merrow's accountant. He went on the Progress and conched *everything*. It took me two days to get through just five of those conchs. He is *so* boring. He talked about everything they packed. Everything they used. Everything they wore. Everything they said. Everything they did. Everything they saw. Everywhere they stopped—'

'Everywhere they stopped?' Serafina cut in.

'Yes.'

'Can you show me where those conchs are?' Serafina asked, trying to hide her excitement.

'Sure,' Coco said. 'Come on.'

'One moment, please,' said Fossegrim. 'The death riders sweep the Ostrokon regularly. Coco, you must act as lookout while the principessa studies the conchs. We can take no chances. You're both to be back here by midnight.'

Coco saluted.

But Serafina protested. 'I can't do that, Magistro. I have to get through these conchs as fast as I can. I'm going to work through the night, the day and the next night too, if I have to.'

Fossegrim shook his head. 'Too dangerous,' he said. 'For you and us.'

'I have no choice. I need to find some very important information before Traho does.'

Fossegrim thought about this, then said, 'Take two baskets with you. Put as many conchs as you can carry in them and bring them back here. It won't be as quiet, but it will be safer.'

Coco grabbed a couple of baskets that were on the floor, then swam up to the trapdoor. Serafina picked up two lava torches and followed her, desperately hoping that First Minister Baltazaar could tell her what she needed to know.

TWENTY-THREE

'HE SUFFERS. A LOT,' Coco said as she and Serafina swam to Level Three. Both mermaids carried a basket in one hand and a lava torch in the other.

'Who?'

'Fossegrim. He hardly sleeps. Barely eats. He blames himself for everything that's happened. For the destruction of the Ostrokon. For the theft of the conchs. Niccolo tells him there was nothing he could have done, but Fossegrim doesn't listen.'

'Poor Fossegrim,' Serafina said. 'My grandmother once told me how protective he was of the Ostrokon and its collections, even as a young ostroko. She said it was always clear that he would become a liber magus.'

Fossegrim had described Traho's attack on the Ostrokon to Sera after he'd led her to the bunker. Several ostroki had been killed trying to fight him off.

'I bet Fossegrim didn't tell you how hard *he* fought. Or what they did to him,' Coco said. 'Traho's soldiers beat him so badly, he lost consciousness. Then they left him for dead. Luckily, Niccolo and the others were hiding in the stacks.

They waited until Traho left, then they dragged Fossegrim to the sub-basement. They saved his life. We've all been down there ever since. Teaching ourselves how to fight back. We named ourselves Black Fins in honour of Fossegrim. We enchanted our fins to match his. Outside, of course. You know how he is about casting in the Ostrokon.' She held up her tail fins. They were a deep, glossy black. 'We're doing pretty well,' she added, smiling proudly. 'Cutting off the lava supply *really* screwed things up at the palace. Finding enough food is the hardest thing for us. I'm better than anyone else at it. I find a lot of stuff in the wrecked houses.' Her smile faded. 'I find the owners sometimes too. But I'm getting used to dead people.'

'Why are you in the Ostrokon, Coco? Where's your family?' asked Serafina.

'Gone.'

Serafina heard a catch in the merl's voice. She glanced at her – in time to see her brush at her eyes.

'What happened?'

Coco shook her head. The grey sand shark who'd been following in their wake circled worriedly around her.

'Please tell me,' Serafina said, putting an arm around her.

'They came into the palace,' she said. 'The death riders. They were rounding everyone up. My parents heard them coming and tried to protect us. My mother cast a transparensea pearl for me and told me to swim up to the ceiling. She was casting one for Ellie when the death riders broke the door down. Ellie was screaming. My mum too. My dad tried to

ROGUE WAVE

146

fight them off, but they beat him up. I watched it all happen. Then they took them.'

Coco was looking ahead into the dark waters as she spoke, but Serafina knew she wasn't seeing anything nearby. She was seeing her family being brutalized.

'I was so scared,' Coco said. 'As soon as the soldiers left, I swam out of the palace. I went straight to the Ostrokon, because it was the safest place I could think of. I hid on Level Four for days. I ate the food at the TideSide. Alessandra and Domenico found me.'

'I'm so sorry, Coco,' Serafina said, her heart aching for the child.

Coco nodded. 'Come on, we should keep going,' she said, swimming off.

She doesn't want me to see her cry, Serafina thought. Rage burned constantly in her heart these days, but once in a while – like now – it flared high. What had happened to Fossegrim and Coco were two more crimes to add to Traho's tally. She would tell her uncle of them when he swam home with his goblin armies. Traho would pay for his crimes. Vallerio would make sure of it.

'We're here. Level Three,' Coco said a few minutes later, shining her globe on the writing over the doorway. 'We'll need a sentry,' she added. 'Abby, go keep an eye out up top, will you?' The little sand shark nodded. 'Abelard's the best lookout ever. He senses movement way before I do. If the death riders show up, he'll be down here in two seconds flat.'

Abelard took off. Sera watched him go. 'You haven't seen

Sylvestre, have you?' she asked wistfully.

'Not since the attack,' Coco replied. 'I sneak into the palace as often as I can to look for medicine, food, weapons – anything the resistance can use. He's not there.'

Sera nodded sadly. She missed Sylvestre and hoped he'd somehow escaped the death riders, but she realized she'd probably never find out what had happened to him.

'Come on, Coco. We've got a lot to do,' she said.

The two mermaids entered the listening room. It was as black as the abyss inside. All the lava globes had burned out.

'The government records are shelved by year, and then subject – *ouch!*' Coco yelped as she whacked her tail against an overturned chair. 'I can't see a *thing* in here.' She held up her torch, and then swam to the back of the room. 'One thirty-six . . . no, that's not what we want,' she said, peering at the shelves. She moved to the right. Serafina followed her. 'There's ninety-eight . . . sixty-seven . . . twenty-nine . . . Here we go . . . ten anno Merrow.'

Coco ran her index finger along the front of the shelves as she spoke. '*K . . . L . . .* We need the *P*s . . . Here they are . . . Parliamentary Minutes . . . Prison Budget . . . Privy Council . . . Progress, Merrow's!' She shone her light over the shelf. 'Looks like about twenty conchs in all. We'll be able to fit them into—'

Her words were cut off by the sudden arrival of Abelard. He nipped her shoulder.

'Death riders?'

Abelard nodded.

'Hurry, Principessa,' Coco said, sweeping shells into the basket. Serafina followed her lead.

The mermaids couldn't carry the heavy baskets and the lava torches, so they put the torches on top of the baskets, then swam out of the listening room as fast as they could.

When they got into the hallway, they heard voices. Sera guessed the death riders were only a level away. She could feel their heavy vibrations.

Go! she mouthed, hoping she and Coco could get far enough down the hallway so that the glow from the torches didn't give them away.

Coco lurched forwards, struggling with the weight of her basket. The jerky motion unbalanced the torch, with its round glass globe. It started rocking from side to side. Coco tried to steady it by moving the basket, but that only made things worse. The torch rolled across the conchs to the side of the basket.

Serafina gasped. If it slipped off and hit the floor, the death riders would hear it.

'Abby!' Coco hissed.

Abelard turned around just as the torch fell. He zipped over to it and managed to catch the globe on the tip of his nose just inches off the floor. He nudged it back up into the basket, did a quick about-face and shot off down the hallway. Serafina and Coco followed, swimming flat out.

'Hang on a minute . . . do you feel something?' a voice said.

A death rider's voice.

'No, do you?'

'I thought so. Maybe not.' There was a pause, then, 'Tell Fabio to bring the hound sharks down. Better safe than sorry.'

'Fabi-*o*!'

'What?'

'Unleash the hounds!'

'Do I have to? I want to get out of here. I hate this place.'

'Gotta do it. If the Ostrokon blows up tomorrow and we didn't sweep it, it's our tails.'

'Go, Coco! *Swim!*' Serafina whispered, wild with fear.

Finally, they got to the basement. Abelard had alerted Fossegrim by butting his nose against the trapdoor.

'Get inside,' Fossegrim said, holding the door open. 'Hurry!'

As Serafina passed him, he opened a reed cage full of fish. 'Go!' he ordered them in Pesca. 'Head for the surface.' The fish rushed out – forty at least.

He looked at the far side of the basement. 'Hide us. Hurry!' he said in RaySay. As he pulled the trapdoor closed, two rays rose from the floor. They nudged a basket filled with broken conchs over the door, then disappeared back into the gloom.

Only seconds later, Sera, Fossegrim and the others heard hound sharks baying overhead and death riders yelling at them.

No one moved. They barely dared to breathe.

'It was nothing, you dumbwrasse!' one of the death riders yelled. 'Just a bunch of blennies! I'll *never* get the hounds back now. They'll chase those fish all the way to Tsarno.'

The soldiers' voices trailed off. Fossegrim waited. A minute went by, then another. No more sounds were heard. He leaned his head against the door, let out a sigh of relief and turned to Serafina.

'I hope those conchs were worth it,' he said.

Trembling, Sera said, 'So do I.'

TWENTY-FOUR

SERAFINA STRETCHED. She yawned. She leaned her head from side to side and cracked the bones in her neck.

'You should get some sleep,' Niccolo said. He nodded at the conchs she'd spread out on a table. 'How's it going?'

'Not so well,' Serafina replied.

She was losing hope in Baltazaar. She only had two more conchs to go, and still had no idea where Merrow had hidden the talismans.

She'd begun listening to the conchs as soon as the death riders left the Ostrokon. She'd worked through the remainder of that night, and the following day – stopping only once to nap for a few hours. That day was now ending and her second night in the bunker was beginning.

Meanwhile, Niccolo and the others, who'd slept all day, were beginning to stir. They'd tunnelled under the palace and had placed a large pile of explosives under the Janiçari's old barracks – which now housed some of Traho's troops. They planned to detonate the explosives in a few days' time and blow the barracks to bits.

Serafina picked up another conch, cracked and yellowed

with age. Only the one listening to a conch could hear the sounds within it, and Sera was glad of that. Knowledge of the talismans was dangerous, and she didn't want to put Fossegrim and the others at any additional risk.

As she pressed the shell to her ear, Baltazaar's now all-too-familiar voice started speaking.

Last night, when she'd listened to the first conch, it had been amazing to hear the faint words of a long-dead merman coming to her across the millennia. She'd struggled a little at first to understand him since he spoke an old form of Mermish, but the more she listened, the more familiar his ancient words became. He told of how Merrow went on a progress to find new waters for the mer. The regina and her ministers had investigated everything, he explained: kelp forests, plankton-rich shallows, abyssal plains, seamounts and crevasses, and hazards too.

She was very brave, Baltazaar said, *and examined all dangers with no regard for her personal safety, noting size, location and description of each, so that she might warn her people away from them.*

Coco was right – Baltazaar *was* boring. He went on and on, exhaustively listing every tent, bowl, cup, spear, pen, spoon and saddle taken on the expedition. Every water apple, flatworm and eel berry eaten. Every boulder, reef and cave they saw. One hour in, Serafina wanted to bang the conch on the table. Two hours in, she wanted to bang her head on the table.

She had persevered, however, writing down on a piece of

kelp parchment every hazard Baltazaar mentioned. The Deathlands of Qin, where underwater vents spewed sulphur and smoke; freshwater lakes so hot they boiled anything that fell into them; the lands of the Kobold goblins; and the caves of the Näkki – murderous shapeshifters in the northern Atlantic.

Now Niccolo and his fellow resistance fighters waved goodbye to Fossegrim and Sera as they headed out on their night's duties. Fossegrim gave them stern warnings to be careful. Sera waved back, then continued adding to her list of hazards, noting down the EisGeists of the Arctic Ocean, the Grindylows of the English Channel, the Gates of Hell in the Congo River. Three hours later, she picked up the last of Baltazaar's conchs. She'd written down over a hundred dangerous places.

This is totally hopeless, she thought, looking at the list. *We couldn't search all these places if we had a thousand years. I've wasted so much time.* She wondered what Traho had learned from the conchs he'd taken. He might be holding one of the talismans in his hands right now.

Sighing, she looked at the very last shell. *On the acquisition and maintenance of hippokamps*, was written on it. *With special regard to expenditures on provender and medicaments.*

No way, Serafina thought. *I can't do it. I can't waste any more time on this.* She was about to put the conch back into the basket, but something made her stop. *I've started this; I should finish it*, she thought. Her mother had always insisted on that, whether it meant practising a songspell until it

ROGUE WAVE

154

was perfect, reworking a thesis until it was polished or brushing Clio herself after a long ride, instead of handing her off to a groom.

Sera held the conch to her ear, expecting to hear Baltazaar drone on about the high price of sea straw. Instead, his voice was brisk and aggrieved.

'I attended the meeting of the regina's privy council in her tent this morning,' he said, 'in order to raise the topic of her evening rides, the too-frequent destruction of good hippokamps on said rides, and the high cost of procuring new animals in foreign waters. Since there are no mer where we go, we must buy from Kobold or Näkki traders. They know we have no alternative and price their stock accordingly. I pointed out that the rides are dangerous not only to our animals, but to the regina herself. Several times we've had to engage the services of local healers for her as well as her mounts. She would not be dissuaded by me, however, and claimed she needs time alone at the end of the day to order her thoughts. These rides are a reckless occupation and I note it here so that upon our return, any charges of profligacy with the realm's monies will be levelled at the deserving party, not the innocent one.'

Serafina sat up, puzzled. Good riders didn't injure their animals, never mind *destroy* them. And Merrow had been many things, but reckless was not one of them. What had she been doing during these rides? How many mounts had she lost? Sera continued to listen, writing down the casualties as Baltazaar dictated them.

White stallion bought to replace animal lost to the maelstrom off the coast of Lochlanach, 500 trocii.

'Lochlanach . . . that's an old mer name for Greenland,' Serafina said. She remembered Vrăja saying that Orfeo had come from Greenland. Her fins started to prickle.

Paint gelding bought to replace animal lost to a dragon in its breeding grounds, 400 trocii. Healer's charges for the regina's injuries, 30 trocii.

Dragons lived and bred in one place only – the Indian Ocean. Navi had come from India.

Grey mare bought to replace animal swept away by the wind spirit Williwaw in the waters of Hornos, 350 trocii.

Hornos was what the early mer called Cape Horn, on the shores of Atlantica – Pyrrha's home.

Bay stallion to replace animal eaten by Okwa Naholo in swamps of the River Mechasipi, 600 trocii.

'The Mississippi. A Freshwater realm,' Serafina said. 'Nyx lived on its banks.'

Roan mare to replace animal lost on slopes of Great Abyss, 400 trocii.

That was in Qin, upon whose shores Sycorax had dwelt.

Dapple gelding bought to replace animal stranded on the shores of Iberia, 700 trocii. Healer's services to regina for wound from terra gogg fishing spear, 40 trocii.

That would be the Spanish coast of the Mediterranean sea, Merrow's realm. *Iberia* was an old word for *Spain*.

As Baltazaar began complaining about the cost of saddles, Serafina put the conch down. Merrow had ridden to places so dangerous they led to the deaths of her hippokamps six times. In each of the six water realms.

'For each of the six talismans,' Sera said aloud. Her pulse quickened. She was certain there had been a method to Merrow's madness. Merrow had been close to the other five mages – even Orfeo, before he became evil – and she'd lost them all during the destruction of Atlantis. Their bodies had not been recovered. She'd had no remains to mourn. No funeral dirges had been sung. Had she carried their talismans to hiding places in waters near their original homes as a way of putting the souls to rest? Sera wondered.

If so, then it was Orfeo's black pearl that was in the maelstrom off the coast of Greenland. Navi's moonstone was in the dragon breeding grounds of Matali. And Merrow's talisman – Neria's Stone – was somewhere on the coast of Spain. Lady Thalia hadn't had time to tell Sera and Ling what the remaining three talismans were, but Sera was willing to bet that Nyx's – whatever it was – was in the Mississippi swamps, Pyrrha's was at Cape Horn, and Sycorax's was in the Great Abyss.

Sera was excited she had learned so much, but dismayed that she still didn't have all the answers she needed. It made sense that she should search for her own ancestor's talisman, as it was hidden in her own realm's waters – but where should she begin? Baltazaar had mentioned no specific hazard in connection with Neria's Stone. He'd only stated that Merrow had been wounded by a fisherman along Spain's coast, and that her hippokamp had been stranded. But Spain's coast was hundreds of miles long. It would be impossible to search every inch of it.

Serafina groaned in frustration. What she desperately needed to know was right in front of her, in her notes. It had to be. Why couldn't she see it?

But which talisman was in which realm? Was there a connection between the objects and their hiding places? Or none at all?

Serafina pressed her hands to her temples, trying to clear her mind. It made sense that out of all the hiding places, all over the world, Sera herself should search for the one in Spanish waters, as they were part of her own realm. Merrow's hippokamp had been stranded on the Spanish coast. But where, exactly? Spain's coastline was hundreds of miles long.

Serafina was closer to unlocking the mysteries of the talismans than ever before; she felt it, she *knew* it. Words from her notes, faces and names and places from the past few weeks swirled in her head. *Lochlanach . . . Merrow . . . dragons . . . Nyx . . . a moonstone . . . Traho . . . Sycorax . . . Hornos . . . Mfeme . . . Navi . . . Morsa's black pearl . . . the duca's palazzo . . . Pyrrha . . . swamps . . . Thalia . . . the Abyss . . . Spain . . . Orfeo . . . Neria's Stone . . .*

What she needed to know was right in front of her, in the words, the names – why couldn't she see it?

Her frustration was growing. 'Calm down. Take them one at a time,' she told herself.

She picked up her pen and doodled a picture of a large diamond on her parchment. She drew it as Lady Thalia had described it – in the shape of a teardrop.

'Come on, Merrow, help me out here,' she whispered. '*Please*. Where is Neria's Stone?'

The trapdoor to the bunker suddenly opened. Niccolo and Domenico swam in, agitated. Serafina soon saw why. They had found a baby. A little merboy. Only two or three months old. He was howling. Niccolo was holding him. Domenico was babbling like a lunatic.

'We found in him in the fabra. We heard him crying. I can't believe the death riders didn't. He was hidden under some coral. We don't know how he got there. He's a *baby*, Magistro! What do we *do*?'

Before Fossegrim could answer, Alessandra swam to Niccolo and swept the baby out of his arms.

She tried to quiet him. '*Oh, povero piccolo infante!*' she cooed. She was from the Lagoon and often lapsed into Italian. '*Dolce bambino! Poveretto! Dolce infante!*'

Infante.

'Oh. My. *Gods*,' Serafina whispered. 'I know where the talisman is.'

TWENTY-FIVE

Serafina Jumped up out of her chair so fast, she knocked it over.

'Magistro!' she shouted.

'My goodness, child, what is it?' Fossegrim asked, startled.

'Where can I find conchs on shipwrecks in Miromara?'

'Level Eight,' he said. 'Why?'

Serafina grabbed her bag and slung it over her shoulder. She headed to the door.

'Principessa, wait! Where are you going? It's not safe outside,' Fossegrim protested.

'I have to go, Magistro. I'll return as soon as I can. Hopefully in a few days. Tell the others goodbye for me. Can I borrow a compass?' she asked, grabbing one from a shelf.

'Yes, of course. But why?' Fossegrim asked.

'I'll tell you when I get back!' Serafina said. She hugged the old merman, grabbed a lava globe and swam out of the bunker. A few minutes later, she was on Level Eight.

Infante.

The word had triggered a memory – an image of a

painting that had hung on the wall of the duca's library before it was stolen by Rafe Mfeme. It was a portrait of one of the duca's ancestors, Maria Theresa, an infanta of Spain. Around her neck was a magnificent blue diamond – a jewel that had been passed down through generations of Spanish queens. Was *that* why Merrow had gone to the Spanish coast? To give her very own talisman to a human?

The more Serafina thought about it, the more sense it made. Merrow chose a human because there was nothing more dangerous. That human must have been an ancestor of the infanta's, which is how the infanta had come to own the diamond. And Rafe Mfeme had stolen the infanta's portrait to show it to Traho, so he could see exactly what the talisman he was searching for looked like.

The only thing Sera couldn't figure out was how Traho had made the same connections without having seen Merrow's bloodsong in the Iele's caves, or talking to Lady Thalia. Once again, he was one stroke ahead of her.

Sera found the shipwreck section easily and soon located a conch containing information on the ship. She remembered that the duca had said that the infanta sailed to France in 1582 on board the *Demeter*, and the conch revealed where it sank – twenty-five leagues due south of the French town of Santes-Maries. She also learned that the ship was a three-masted caravel. The pirate who'd attacked it was from Cathay. His name was Amarrefe Mei Foo. Contemporary sources believed that Mei Foo did not obtain the diamond, but no one knew what actually happened to it, only that it was never seen again.

'Hopefully because it's still around the infanta's neck,' Serafina said aloud, putting the conch back.

She slung her bag over her shoulder. She had what she needed. Dawn was still hours away. She'd leave Cerulea under cover of darkness. Later, she'd contact Neela, Ava, Ling and Becca to tell them what she'd learned.

'Where are you going? Can I come with you?' a voice said.

Serafina nearly jumped out of her skin. She spun around, reaching for her knife, but it was only Coco. And Abelard.

'Don't *do* that! You scared me half to death!'

Coco eyes travelled to the bag slung over Serafina's shoulder. 'You're going somewhere, aren't you? Take me with you.'

'No, it's much too dangerous. And besides, who would take care of Fossegrim?'

The little merl threw her arms around Sera's neck. 'Promise me you'll come back. Promise me,' she said fiercely.

'I promise,' Serafina said. She hugged her hard, then said, 'I've got to go now, Coco. Get back to the bunker where it's safe.'

Serafina said goodbye, then swam away. Time was not on her side. Traho also believed that the infanta's blue diamond and Neria's Stone were one and the same. Plus he had the portrait. He knew what the diamond looked like. He probably knew about the *Demeter* too, and that the infanta had gone down with it.

Serafina could only hope that he *didn't* know the wreck lay twenty-five leagues due south of Saintes-Maries.

TWENTY-SIX

NEELA YAWNED. Another day had passed. The waters outside her windows were growing dusky. She'd lost track of how many days she'd been confined to her room now. Five? Six? Did it matter? Did anything?

There were zee zees and bingas nearby. Bags of them. Their wrappers littered her floor. There were shaptas. And pink, lots of pink. Pink saris. Pink bangle bracelets. Pink scarves. Was pink really so bad? Maybe she should do what they wanted. Maybe she should give in, a little voice inside her said. Before she truly lost her mind – from boredom.

'No way,' she said out loud, countering the voice. 'I won't.'

Giving in was impossible. Not because she'd have to surrender her swashbuckler clothes, though she'd miss them greatly, but because Kiraat wanted promises of good behaviour. That meant she wasn't supposed to talk about Abbadon or swim off to find Sera the first chance she got.

Neela rose from her chair. She was just about to pour herself yet another cup of tea when she heard a tapping at her window. Startled by the noise, Ooda puffed up in alarm. Neela swam to the window and saw that a pelican was swimming back and forth outside it. He tapped again.

'I can't open it!' she told him. 'I'm sorry!'

Kiraat had enchanted her windows so she couldn't swim out through them, but he'd left one open a crack, just wide enough to allow fresh water in. Or a conch.

As Neela watched, the pelican nudged a white shell through the space.

'Thank you!' she said, taking it. She unwrapped a few zee zees and pushed them through the crack. Pelicans, she knew, were partial to them. He caught them in his pouch, then headed back to the surface. Neela held the conch to her ear excitedly. She recognized the voice inside it.

'*Hey, Neels,*' Serafina said. '*I made it home. I hope you did too. Are you OK? Ling and I tried to convoca you, but we couldn't get through, so I sent this conch. It's a risky move, I know, but I instructed the pelican to crack it if any death riders came after him. I can't explain everything now, but I think my theory about Merrow was correct: she hid the talismans during her Progress. What's more, I think she hid all but one in waters near each mage's original home. A vitrina told Ling and me that Navi's talisman was an egg-shaped moonstone. I think it's somewhere in Matali's dragon breeding grounds. If you go searching for it, don't go alone. You'll need soldiers with weapons or you'll be eaten alive. I'm setting off after Neria's Stone. Wish me luck. It's hard here in Cerulea. We're really in trouble. And I don't know how to do this, you know? I miss you. A lot. But I've got you with me, kind of. Because of the bloodbind. I throw a mean frag now, and I can speak to eels and silverfish. I think the vow gave each of us some of everyone else's magic.'* There was a pause and then, *'Mahdi's alive. He's OK. That's all I can say for now. We're trying to find out anything we can about Yaz. Don't give up hope. We'll find him. I know we will. I love you, Neels. Smash this when you're done listening to it, OK?'*

Neela laughed out loud, so happy to know that Sera and Mahdi were both OK. She wished Sera could have told her that her brother was too, but she would keep hoping. Knowing Yazeed, he would turn up in a nightclub somewhere.

She thought about what else Sera had said – that Navi's talisman was a moonstone and that it was in dragon breeding grounds . . . but which ones? Matali had dozens of them.

Dragons were the main source of Matali's wealth. Its temperate waters provided ideal breeding conditions for many types, including the Bengalese Bluefin – gentle, calm and good for pulling wagons and carriages; the Lakshadwa Blackclaw, huge, powerful and used by the military; and the Royal Arabian – a creature so dazzling, and so costly, that only the wealthiest mer could afford them. There were many more, all bred and exported. All, that is, except the Razormouths, who were feral and murderous. In centuries past, attempts had been made to domesticate them, but they'd always ended badly. The Razormouths nonetheless served an important purpose. They bred in the Madagascar Basin, in western Matali, near Kandina. Attempts to invade Matali via the Basin always ended badly too, because no invaders could slip by them. The Razormouths' importance to the realm's defence was the reason their image was on the Matalin flag.

Neela swam back and forth now, trying to figure out which breeding ground Merrow would have picked. The Razormouths' was the obvious choice, but other breeds could be vicious too. She stopped at her windows and stared out, biting her lip. The sun was almost down now. Its last, weak rays were fading in the water and a strong westerly current was rising. It was tearing at the Matali flags, making them flap. Neela looked at the national symbol – the Razormouth queen holding her 'special' egg – the only one that wasn't an ugly brown. As she continued to stare at the flags, Neela's tail fin began to twitch and her skin started to glow bright blue. Something had just occurred to her.

'Ooda!' she said aloud. 'Navi's moonstone was egg-shaped too. That's what Sera said. Maybe it's *not* an egg that the Razormouth queen is holding . . . maybe it's the moonstone! What if Merrow gave it to the reigning dragon queen – because there's nothing more treacherous than a Razormouth, right? And the queen passed it down to the queens who came after her. Whoever made the first Matali flag must've seen the dragon queen with it. He didn't know it was a moonstone . . . why would he? He probably just thought it was an egg. *It's there*, Ooda! The moonstone's with the Razormouths. I *know* it is.'

You'll need soldiers . . . Serafina had said.

Yes, Neela thought, *thousands of them. With spears and shields and lava launchers.*

'How am I going to do this? It's impossible,' she said out loud. 'Even with soldiers, I may as well hang a sign around my neck that says Lunch.' She paused for a minute, thinking, then said, 'Maybe Kora can help. Do you remember her, Ooda?'

Ooda quickly shook her head.

'Yes, you do. You just don't want to go.'

Neela had met Kora during the many trips she'd taken with the royal family to the western waters. Kora – nineteen now – ruled a sizeable portion of Matali as a vassal of the emperor. When Kandinian teens came of age – at sixteen – they were required to prove themselves by swimming through the breeding grounds of the Razormouths. Those who made it to the other side were welcomed into the community as adults. Those who did not were mourned.

'If anyone knows about the Razormouths' breeding grounds and how to negotiate them, it's Kora,' Neela said. 'I'll leave for Kandina as soon as I can. There *has* to be a way out of here. There just *has* to be.'

Ooda, looking worried, started to inflate. Soon she'd risen so high, she bumped the ceiling. Neela was annoyed with her. She had no time for the little fish's antics right now. She had much bigger problems to worry about.

'Ooda, *stop* it!' she said. 'Come down right now! Don't make me come up there after you! Oh, Ooda! You are *so* . . .'

Neela stopped talking. She stared at the blowfish, then said, '. . . *brilliant!*'

She swam up to the ceiling, kissed the fish on her lips and brought her down.

'I think I just figured out how to get out of here, Ooda,' she said. 'And you're going to help me.'

TWENTY-SEVEN

Early THE NEXT MORNING, Neela heard the key turn in the lock of her bedchamber door. She'd barely slept all night.

'Here she comes, Ooda. Get ready!' she whispered.

Ooda darted under the bed.

Suma entered the room, carrying a tray. She put it down on a table, then swam back to the door and locked it. The key was on a silver ribbon. Suma dropped it into the side pocket of the long, flowing jacket she was wearing.

'How are you, darling Princess?' she asked. 'Did you sleep well?'

Neela stretched, blinked sleepily and said, 'I did, thank you, but I still feel tired. I think I'm coming down with something. Do I feel warm to you?'

Suma hurried to Neela. As she felt her forehead, Ooda swam out from under the bed. The end of the silver ribbon was hanging out of Suma's pocket. Ooda bit down it and started swimming backwards.

'My goodness, child!' she said. 'You're burning up!'

She sat down on the bed, yanking the ribbon out of Ooda's mouth.

Oh, no! Neela thought. 'My cheeks are warm too,' she quickly said. 'Don't you think?'

As Suma felt one, Ooda rooted for the ribbon. The key had slipped deeper into Suma's pocket and the little fish had to delve for it.

'Feel the other one too, Suma,' Neela said, stalling.

Ooda finally got hold of the ribbon again and tugged with all her might until she'd pulled it out of Suma's pocket. She was so pleased with herself that she hovered behind Suma, beaming, the key dangling from her mouth.

'We, um, have to get the fever *down*,' Neela said, shooting Ooda a look.

Ooda darted under the bed once more, dragging the key with her.

'Could you bring the bottle of nettle elixir from my grotto?' Neela asked. 'It's on one of the shelves in the cabinet.'

'Of course, Princess,' said Suma, hurrying off.

It wasn't. Neela had hidden the bottle in her closet.

She swam out of her bed, snatched the lava globe from underneath her pillow and put it back in its holder on the wall. It had heated her pillow and her head – so much so that she'd been able to fool Suma. Next, she ripped off her robe. She was wearing her swashbuckler clothes underneath it. Her messenger bag was packed and under her bed. She reached for it now, just as Ooda swam out with the key.

'Good girl!' she whispered, taking the key. 'Let's go!' She

lifted the flap of her messenger bag. The little fish zipped inside.

'I don't see the nettle elixir!' Suma shouted from the grotto.

'Keep looking. I'm sure it's there!' Neela called back.

With nervous hands, she pulled one of Vrăja's transparensea pebbles out of her pocket and cast it. Almost instantly, she was invisible. She unlocked the door, let herself out and locked it again. Luckily there were no guards in the hall to see it open and close.

Swimming just below the ceiling, as Ooda had done last night, Neela moved swiftly through the palace. It would have made things easier if she could have swum out of a window, but every one she saw was shuttered in preparation for war. She kept going, down long hallways, through staterooms and over the heads of courtiers.

'Almost there,' she whispered to Ooda, as a pair of arched doors leading out of the palace came into sight.

And then a cry, loud and urgent, ripped through the water. 'Close the doors! The emperor commands it! Princess Neela has escaped from her room!'

'Oh, silt!' Neela said.

She was still a good twenty feet from the exit. It took two guards to push each massive door closed and they were now hurrying to do so. There was a gap of about thirty inches between the doors and it was narrowing every second. Neela put on a burst of speed and aimed straight for it. She brought her hands together over her head, turned sideways in the water and shot through it. The doors closed with a boom behind her.

She didn't look back as she raced through the Emperor's Courtyard towards the open water. She felt bad about locking Suma in, bad about the worry she knew she'd cause her parents, but they didn't understand what was happening. Hopefully, when they discovered that everything she'd told them was true, they'd forgive her.

As Neela swam, she heard the sub-assistant's voice in her head. Khelefu's, too. Suma's. And her parents'. They were all saying the same thing: *That is the way things are done! That is the way things have always been done!*

Neela knew that if she wanted to find Navi's talisman and defeat the monster, she would have to bypass *the way things are done*.

She would have to find a new way of doing things.

Her way.

TWENTY-EIGHT

'AND HOW WAS your stay with us, Miss Singh?'

'Invincible. If I could get the bill? I'm, like, *way* in a rush, you know?' Neela said, snapping her chewing sponge.

'Right away,' the clerk said, totalling her charges. 'One room for one night, room service twice . . .'

As he continued, Neela glanced nervously at the shiny mica-covered wall behind him. In it she could see a group of Matalin guards. They were still in the street outside. How much longer before they came into the hotel?

'Here we are! It comes to six trocii, five drupes.'

Neela paid him. As she did, the guards came in. One was holding a piece of parchment. She knew her picture was on it. There was no time to swim to an upper floor or cast a transparensea pebble. She would have to front her way out of here. Praying the illusio spell she'd cast would hold, she turned around and sashayed towards the door. She'd changed her messenger bag into a flashy designer bag, her black hair blonde again, her blue skin pink and her nails a sparkly silver. Her black swashbuckler's outfit was now a long, neon-blue, boyfriend-size caballabong jersey with GO GOA! across the front and the number 2 on the back. A pair of enormous round glasses was perched on her nose. Shiny gold hoops dangled from her ears. The guards were looking for a princess disguised as a swashbuckler. They wouldn't look twice at a caballabong merl.

As the guards approached, she pretended to talk into a small message conch. 'This is, like, totally woeful!' she said. 'Could this thing maybe actually work for once in its shabby little life? Hello? *Hel-lo?* OK, I think it's recording now. Hey, merl! Hope you can hear this. Meet me in an hour at the Skinny Manatee for a bubble tea, yah? If you get there first, get me a water apple. Fat free. See you soon. Mwah!'

She swam out of the hotel in a leisurely fashion, as if she had all day. As soon as she turned the corner, though, she spat out her chewing sponge and tore down the current like a marlin. Twenty minutes later she was out of town and in the open water.

'Wow, that was close,' she said, stopping to open her bag and let Ooda out. 'Scary. We're only about half a day from Nzuri Bonde now. Let's swim the backcurrent all the way. It's a little bit longer, but safer, I think. We'll have to push hard. You ready?'

Ooda nodded and they set off. Neela and her pet had spent four days on the currents, staying overnight in hotels, paying her bills with currensea she'd packed. So far, she'd avoided three separate search parties of palace guards, all of whom were sent – she was certain – by her parents to fetch her home.

It was hard staying one stroke ahead of the guards, but oddly, Neela found she was able to think on her fins like never before. She could see what was coming, like Ava could, and then see how to deal with it, like Sera. She remembered what Sera had said about the bloodbind in the conch she'd sent. Sera was certain the vow had given them all bits of each other's magical abilities.

She must be right, Neela thought. *It's the only thing that explains how I've managed to not get myself captured.*

She knew she couldn't afford to get caught. She had to find Navi's talisman. A few more leagues' hard swimming and she'd be in Nzuri Bonde, Kandina's royal village, and that much closer to the moonstone.

Or so she thought.

Eight hours later, the backcurrent they'd taken had weakened to nothing, and she and Ooda were totally lost in the middle of a flat, grey wasteland with scrubby vegetation and no signposts, only warning signs about dragons.

She knew that the Razormouths' breeding grounds were near Nzuri Bonde, and she was certain she and Ooda had to be close to the village, but high above the water's surface, the sun's rays were already lengthening; it would be dark in only a few hours. Dragons hunted at night. If she and Ooda didn't find the village soon, they'd be sleeping out here – lost, alone and very visible.

Neela consulted a map she'd bought. As she did, she noticed that her hands were glowing. The soft, pale-blue light she often gave off had brightened.

'That's weird,' she said.

Neela only lit up brightly when she was emotional or when other bioluminescents were around. Bios could sense each other, and when they did, their photocytes kicked in, causing them to glow.

She turned her attention back to the map. She was sure it showed the way to Nzuri Bonde from where they were, but she didn't *know* where they were and she wasn't terribly good at reading maps anyway. She'd never had to. There had always been officials for that. She turned the map this way and that, and finally decided to head in the direction she thought was west.

She and Ooda swam for another fifteen minutes without coming across any sign whatsoever of the village. Just as she was getting really worried, Ooda nipped her arm and pointed ahead of them with her fin. As Neela rubbed the bite, she noticed that her skin had darkened to cobalt. 'What is going on with me?'

Ooda nipped her again. 'Ow! Stop it!' she scolded. 'What is *with* you?' She looked ahead, squinting at the dusky water. And then she saw it – a large silt cloud rising in the distance. 'Good girl!' she said. 'Let's go!'

Neela knew a cloud of that size was a sign of life. Many things could be stirring up the silt – caballabong players, a factory, farmers ploughing. Maybe it was a sea-cow ranch. At this time of day, the ranchers would be herding their animals into barns to be milked, then bedding them down.

She hurried along, relieved to have found merpeople and hopefully a place where she and Ooda could shelter for the night. But as they drew closer, Neela slowed to a halt.

It was no sea-cow ranch or caballabong game that was raising the silt cloud.

It was an enormous prison.

Full of merfolk.

TWENTY-NINE

'MY GODS!' Neela whispered, stunned.

She swam a little closer, crouched down behind a rock, and peered out from behind it. She'd seen prisons before – every realm had them – but she'd never seen a prison like this.

Mermen and mermaids – thousands of them – were inside. They had the darker skin of the West Matalin mer, and they were digging. Neela could see them. She could see *everything*, because the fence surrounding the prison was made of dozens of sea whips, monstrous bioluminescent jellyfish that were almost entirely translucent. There were hundreds of them, each about twenty-five feet long and eight feet wide. They were floating in a tight circle. Their lethal tentacles formed the bars of the prison.

'*That's* why I'm glowing!' she said to herself.

More sea whips, even bigger than the others, floated above, alert for any movement.

'Living guard towers,' Neela whispered.

As she watched the prisoners, one of them – an older mermaid – stopped to lean on her shovel, obviously exhausted. Immediately a death rider was on her. He yelled at her and hit her with a crop. She cried out, then quickly resumed digging. Nearby, a reed-thin merman, his clothing in rags, collapsed. More death riders dragged him away.

And then Neela saw something far worse – *children*. Hundreds of them. She couldn't tell what they were doing from where she was, but they weren't digging. Upset, she opened her bag, took out one of her two remaining transparensea pebbles and cast it. She wanted to have a closer look.

'Stay here, Ooda,' she said, as soon as she was invisible. Careful to stay out of striking range of any tentacles, she swam to the fence. Sea whips were the most deadly jellyfish in the world. The pain of their sting was so excruciating it could stop a mermaid's heart in minutes. The sea whips couldn't see her, but they could still feel her movements in the water and would lash out if she got too close.

From her new vantage point, Neela could see a group of children clearly. They were shaking large rectangular sieves full of mud. Inside the sieves, crabs and lobsters scuttled back and forth, picking through pebbles and shells. The mud was brought to the children's work area in carts pulled by thin, frightened-looking hippokamps. The children, too, were thin and fearful. Many were crying.

Neela swam the entire perimeter of the prison, seeing misery everywhere she looked. Barracks stood at the far side of the prison. They were little more than sheds. Behind them, two guards stood close to the sea whip fence, talking. She could hear what they were saying.

'We've dug up every damn inch of the mud in this godsforsaken hellhole. Traho says these are the old breeding grounds, and it might be here, but I say different.'

'We have orders to move the whole prison five leagues north if we've found nothing by Moonday,' the second guard said.

'The further we get from the dragon caves, the better. We're only three leagues east of them now,' he said, hooking his thumb to his right. 'It's sheer bloody luck they haven't discovered us yet.'

'Traho came yesterday. Did you see him?'

The first guard shook his head.

'He wasn't happy. He wants the moonstone and he wants it now,' the second guard said. 'He says the prisoners need to work harder. Smaller rations. Harsher punishments and—'

The guard stopped talking and looked up. A huge shadow passed overhead. 'It's him,' the guard said. 'Mfeme. With more prisoners.'

'We better get moving,' said the second guard. 'We'll be needed to help herd them in.'

Neela followed their gaze. For a moment, she saw nothing but the silhouetted hull of an enormous ship. As she kept watching, though, she saw things dropping down through the water. They looked like big black squares. As they got closer, Neela saw that they were cages filled with merpeople.

The jellyfish floating over the prison parted, and the cages landed roughly on the seafloor inside it. Guards opened the cage doors, shouting at the prisoners, hitting them with crops, driving them to a central assembly area. As the guards herded the prisoners, they tore any remaining personal effects off of them – beaded armbands, head wraps, belts – and tossed them through the sea whips' tentacles. An armband landed near Neela. She picked it up when the guards' backs were turned and put it in her pocket. The prisoners, gaunt and sick-looking, were frightened. Once they'd all been crowded together, they were told they were here to dig for a valuable object, a large moonstone, and that whoever found it would be set free. They were all given shovels – old and young, strong and weak. A man protested that his wife was too ill to dig. He was promptly beaten.

Neela reeled back from the fence, sickened, and saw that her tail was shimmering. The transparensea pebbles were not as strong as transparensea pearls. The spell was wearing off. She swam back behind the rock where Ooda was waiting and sat down on the ground to collect herself.

'Sera was wrong, Ooda,' she said, her voice shaking. 'Mfeme has the people from the raided villages on his ship, yes, but he's not taking them to Ondalina. He's taking them to prison camps. To dig for the talismans. I've got to send messages to the others, but we have to get out of here first, before we end up inside the prison too. Or inside a dragon.'

Neela leaned back against the rock and closed her eyes. She didn't know what to do and there was no one here to tell her. No Sera. No Ling. No sub-assistants with their forms. No grand vizier. No Suma to make everything better with a cup of tea and a plate of bingas. She would have to figure it out herself. But how?

She opened her eyes, then opened her bag and did what she always did when she was angry or scared – she hunted for a sweet.

There has to be one in here, she thought desperately. Her craving was terrible. She pushed aside make-up, her hairbrush, a little sack of currensea . . . and then she spotted a shiny green wrapper.

'A zee zee! Oh, thank gods!' she said.

It was a bit squashed from being at the bottom of her bag, but it was still a zee zee. Sweets made it all better. Sweets always made it better. She unwrapped the shiny candy with shaking hands and popped it into her mouth, waiting for it to make her feel calmer, happier . . . but it was so cloying, it made her feel sick instead.

She spat it out.

As she did, she heard a voice speaking from inside her head. *Here, just for you. A shapta*, it said. *Swallow it, darling. Just like you swallow all your fears and frustrations. They leave such a bitter taste, don't they?*

It was Rorrim's voice. He was right. That's what she'd always done – swallowed her fears, with the help of a little candy to sweeten them.

She looked at the prison again, and the people in it, and realized that there was no *better*. Not from a binga. If she wanted things to be better, she would have to make them so.

She got up, brushed the silt off her backside and slung her bag over her shoulder. 'Thanks to the sea-scum guards, we know which direction to swim in, at least,' she said to Ooda, remembering how one of them had hooked his thumb to his right. If we're lucky, we'll make Nzuri Bonde by morning.'

THIRTY

'**H**I-*YAAAAAH*!'

The cry – high and terrifying – carried piercingly through the water.

'That's Kora,' Neela said. 'I'd know her voice anywhere. Come on, Ooda. We're almost there.'

Neela and Ooda had been on the move all night, ever since they'd left the prison camp. Neela was dragging. She was desperately in need of a rest and a good meal, but hearing Kora's voice gave her new energy.

The morning sun's soft rays illuminated the waters of Nzuri Bonde. As Neela and Ooda approached it, they saw low houses made of stones mortared with a mixture of silt and crushed shell, and surrounded by lush vegetation. The doorways and windows were bordered by stark, geometric designs in red, white and yellow. Simple and spare, they were in harmony with their remote, wild surroundings. Outbuildings made from the bones of whales collected from the seafloor held dugongs placidly waiting to be taken out to graze.

Neela thought about how you could see the shining domes

and turrets of Matali City long before you were in it. Nzuri Bonde was just the opposite; you were practically in it before you saw it.

There was a large open arena on the outskirts of the village. Kora was there, drilling with the Askari, her personal guard. They lived apart from all others in the ngome ya jeshi, their own compound. They were practising haraka now, a form of martial arts that was lightning fast. Tall bamboo poles were used for whacking the enemy across his body, or taking his tail out from under him. Neela watched the fighters as she approached the arena. The Askari were lean, fast and lethal – and none more so than their leader.

Dark-skinned and regal, Kora had high cheekbones, a full mouth and hazel eyes flecked with gold. Her powerful tail was striped brown and white, like a lionfish's. Her pectoral fins fanned out at her sides when she was angry, rising in tall, barbed spikes. She wore a turban of red sea silk and a chestplate of cowrie shells and beads. Her armband, made of white coral, was notched for every sea dragon she'd killed.

'*Mgeni anakuja!*' one of the Askari cried out. They all stopped drilling and looked where she was pointing – at Neela. Ooda, frightened of them, zipped into Neela's bag.

Neela, who spoke some Kandinian but not a lot, was surprised to find that she understood the guard. He'd just warned Kora that a stranger was approaching. *It's the bloodbind*, she thought.

Kora spun around. Her eyes narrowed at first, then

widened in recognition.

'*Salamu kubwa, Malkia!*' Neela called out, bowing her head. *Greetings, Great Queen.*

'Princess Neela? Can it be?' Kora said, speaking Mermish now. She swam over to her. A smile, broad and beautiful, spread across her face. She took Neela by her shoulders and kissed her cheeks.

'You have a new look! I was not aware that you followed Goa!'

Neela was still in her caballabong outfit.

'I don't. Even though it looks that way,' Neela said. 'I've been—'

Swimming all night she was going to say, but Kora cut her off. She playfully tugged one of Neela's large hoop earrings.

'You are the only mermaid I know who would make such a dangerous trip so well accessorized!' she said. 'Had I known you were coming, I would have had my nails done.'

Kora, who had little interest in fashion, liked to tease Neela about her passion for clothing and jewellery. Neela always played along good-naturedly, but not this time.

'Kora, this isn't a social call. I'm here because I need your help.'

'What kind of help?'

A wave of exhaustion washed over Neela. She had no idea where to start. 'Um, well, we need to save the world, basically,' she said.

'And the right accessories will aid you in that?' Kora asked, raising an eyebrow. The Askari laughed uproariously.

Neela glared. 'The right accessories,' she said testily, 'help with everything.' She needed Kora to help her, not mock her.

Kora wrapped an arm around her neck and put her into a headlock – a Kandinian sign of affection. 'Do you remember the last time you came to Kandina? With the entire Matalin royal family? The entourage continued behind you for two leagues! Where are your trunks? Where are your retainers?'

'Oh, Kora, there are no retainers. That's what I'm trying to tell you. This visit isn't like the last time. Not at all. There's trouble, big trouble . . .' Neela said. Her voice broke on the last word. She was so upset by what she'd seen at the prison camp, so worn out from hours of swimming, that she was about to collapse.

Kora snapped into action. She led Neela to a shaded part of the arena, made her sit down in a cushioned chair and called for food and drink. The Askari followed, and sat in a circle around their queen and her guest.

'Now, tell me,' Kora said.

Neela glanced at the guards.

'I trust them with my life,' Kora said, reading her thoughts. 'We cannot help you if you cannot trust us. All of us.'

Neela nodded. And then she told them everything – about the dream, the attack on Cerulea, the duca, the death riders, the Iele, the Six Who Ruled, the monster, the talismans and her escape from her own palace.

'I need you to help me find the moonstone. Sera and I believe it's with the dragon queen. And there's something else too,' she said. She took a deep breath, readying herself to tell them about the prison camp, when she realized the Askari had gone dead quiet. They looked at one another, then at her. She recognized their expressions. She'd seen them very recently – on the faces of her mother and father.

'Wait, don't tell me,' she said. 'You think I'm crazy, don't you?' She looked from the guards to Kora.

'Neela,' Kora began, 'you come in very strange clothes, telling us a wild story . . .'

'It's a true story. Every word of it,' Neela said.

'Where is your proof?' Kora asked.

Neela remembered the beaded armband. It was in her pocket.

'You want proof? OK. Have any of your villages been raided? Have any of your people been taken?'

Kora looked at her for a few seconds before answering. 'Yes,' she finally said. 'Jua Maji was raided. My *kiongozi* – my general – is out along the southern borders of the realm as we speak, searching for the villagers. Why do you ask? How do you know this?'

'Your general won't find them. They're west of here, not south. I've seen them. A gogg took them. They're being used as slaves.'

'Neela, you are not making any sense. Food has arrived. Perhaps you should eat something,' Kora said, motioning for her servants to put their platters near her.

They set out pitchers of spiced dugong milk, bowls of seasnake eggs in a blue anemone sauce, plates of moon jellies stewed with shoal peppers, and a spongecake studded with candied honeycomb worms. Neela ignored it all.

'Your people, Kora, are in a prison camp,' she said. 'They're being forced to search for a moonstone, the talisman I just told you about. I've *seen* them. They're being worked to death.' She pulled the armband from her pocket and handed it to Kora. 'Here's your proof.'

Kora's eyes widened. She took the armband. 'This pattern – it's *kengee*, sun ray. Every village has its own pattern. This one belongs to Jua Maji.'

In an instant, Kora was out of her chair. Fins flaring, she picked up a fighting stick, swung it over her head and brought it down on a table, smashing it to pieces. 'We have to get them out!' she cried. '*Now!* The kiongozi is gone, so we will do it – the Askari and I!'

Neela had forgotten what her friend was like when she was riled. It was hard to reason with her.

'*Whoa*, Kora,' she said. 'Hold on a second. You can't get them out. There are sea whips and guards. With weapons. As fearsome as you and the Askari are, you are no match for them. That prison is a fortress.'

Kora snorted. 'Every fortress can be taken,' she said. 'It's only a question of how.'

'You're going to get yourself killed,' Neela said, her voice breaking with exhaustion.

Concerned, Kora ordered her servants to take Neela to comfortable quarters. Neela followed them, barely able to swim another stroke, with Ooda close behind. At the edge of the arena, she turned and glanced back.

Kora and the Askari were casting songspells to transform themselves, changing their bold markings to muddy browns, greens and black, the colours of the seafloor and its flora. Neela couldn't believe what she'd set in motion. This was all happening so fast. But would it be fast enough? The guards had talked about moving the prison. Kora's people were suffering severely from the brutal conditions they were forced to endure. Many of them would likely die from the long swim to the new site.

When the transformation was complete, Kora threw her head back and uttered a bloodcurdling cry – a war cry. The Askari answered her. Their voices rose as one. They picked up their fighting sticks. And then they were gone, racing through the water. Heading for the prison.

THIRTY-ONE

NEELA BUCKLED a belt studded with black coral around her waist. Then she put on her turitella earrings and her shark-tooth necklace. Perfecting an ensemble always calmed her, and she needed calming.

Though she felt a bit better than she had when she'd first arrived in Kandina about eight hours before, she was still anxious and angry. The images of the people in that prison would not leave her. She'd slept much of the day, though, and had eaten a good meal. It was evening now, and she felt strong enough to talk about the prisoners without breaking down.

She'd heard whoops and shouts a few minutes ago, so she knew that Kora and the Askari were back. It had taken Neela and Ooda an entire night to swim from the prison to Nzuri Bonde, but the Askari were faster swimmers and they knew where they were going.

Neela asked a servant where she might find Kora, and the mermaid directed her back to the arena. Ooda, rattled by the Askari, had decided to stay in their room. As Neela approached the arena, she saw that the Askari were seated in a semicircle on the ground, sharing their evening meal.

Their camouflage was gone. They'd exchanged their breastplates for finely woven seaflax tunics. The light from their lava lamps played over their powerful bodies and shone in their dark, watchful eyes. Mermaids and mermen made up their ranks. Like their leader, they each wore a white coral armband notched for every Razormouth they'd killed. Some bore deep scars inflicted by the dragons. Neela knew that to these fighters, the scars were badges of honour to be proudly displayed.

Kora was not with her Askari. She was in the centre of the arena, silent and alone. Fighting dummies stood on poles near her. As Neela watched, she tail-slapped the stuffing out of one, knocked a second over with a fighting stick and gutted a third with a spear.

'Did you find the prison?' she asked an Askara, a mermaid named Basra.

Basra nodded. She was lithe and muscular and wore no jewellery except her armband. Like all the others, her black hair was cut close to her skull, to prevent enemies from grabbing hold of it.

There was a loud, guttural cry from the centre of the arena. Another dummy fell.

'What's Kora doing?' Neela asked.

'Thinking,' Basra replied.

'That's Kora thinking? I can't imagine what Kora fighting looks like.'

'No,' Basra said dismissively. 'You can't.'

Annoyed by Basra's curt tone, Neela glared at her. Just

then, Kora gave a piercing whistle. The Askari immediately stopped eating and swam to her. Neela followed.

Kora gathered everyone around her, then started drawing in the silty ground with the tip of her fighting stick. She sketched out the sea dragons' breeding grounds, and the prison.

'You saw them then,' Neela said to her.

'I saw them, yes. I saw my people . . . I saw . . .' Kora said. Her words fell away. She spun around and drove her tail into a dummy, decapitating it.

Remembering the effect the prison had had on her, Neela gave Kora time. She waited silently for her to speak again. 'I owe you an apology,' Kora finally said. 'I should never have doubted you. It's just that—'

'I looked insane. I know . . . the jersey, the hair, the nails. Anyone who dresses like that must be out of her mind,' she joked.

Kora put her in another headlock, then released her. Neela winced and rubbed her neck, listening as Kora spoke.

'We have two problems here,' she said to the group. 'We need to get our people out of a well-defended prison, and Neela needs to get a moonstone currently in the possession of Hagarla, the dragon queen.'

'I don't suppose we could just ask her nicely for it?' Neela said hopefully.

Kora smiled grimly. 'No. We could not.'

'I guess it means a lot to her. It's been handed down for generations, from queen to queen, right?'

Kora snorted.

'What's the snort for?' asked Neela.

'We live next to the dragons. We come of age in their domain. We suffer their attacks and sometimes lose our people to them,' Kora said.

Neela nodded, remembering that a dragon had killed Kora's father.

'The only way to defeat your enemy is to know her,' Kora continued, 'and we know the Razormouths. No rising queen would wait for an old queen to die and bequeath her such a treasure. That is not the dragon way. She would kill the old queen and take the treasure. *That* is the dragon way.'

'So sharing the moonstone's not an option,' Neela said.

'Hardly. Dragons are envious and greedy. They love things that sparkle or shine and comb shipwrecks for them, rob merchant caravans, even attack villages. They'll fight over a piece of beach glass, never mind a jewel. A huge mound of treasure is a Razormouth's greatest pride, and Hagarla lives in a cave filled with loot. She keeps her favourite pieces in a chest and sleeps by it. There is something else we know about dragons,' Kora said. 'They're gluttons. And the thing they like best to eat? Sea whips. They consider them a delicacy, stingers and all.'

'I think I see where you're going with this,' Neela said excitedly.

'I have a plan. It's very simple. We lead the dragons from their caves to the prison. After they've gobbled down every last sea whip, we draw them off again.'

Neela blinked at her. 'Wait a minute, Kora, I thought you said it was *simple*!'

'It is, in theory. The execution is a little trickier. If it works, though, I will free my people and you will get your moonstone.'

'And if it doesn't?' Neela asked.

'If it doesn't,' Kora said with a shrug, 'we're dead.'

THIRTY-TWO

'DUE SOUTH, the conch said. Not south-south-west, or south-south-east. *Due south*. It has to be here!' Serafina told herself.

She'd reached the waters off Saintes-Maries four hours before, after swimming for days, and had been searching for the *Demeter* ever since.

'Did I read this thing wrong?' she wondered aloud, looking yet again at the compass Fossegrim had loaned her.

According to the instrument, she was in the right place. Unfortunately, the *Demeter* was not.

A chilling thought gripped her: what if Traho had already found it? What if Mfeme had somehow lifted it aboard one of his massive trawlers? That would explain why it was nowhere to be seen.

As Sera was considering this possibility, she felt vibrations in the water. Only seconds later, something passed overhead. She looked up just in time to see two white bellies flash by.

Sharks. Big ones.

Serafina's heart lurched. They were tiger sharks, which were known to attack mer. They turned and started back towards her, picking up speed as they did. Hoping to drive them off, she reached for the Moses sole potion that Vrăja had given her, then remembered it was gone; she'd used it on the death riders. She looked down at the seabed, hoping to spot some cover – a cave, a reef, anything – but all that was there was a thicket of kelp. Could she get to it before the sharks got to her?

Her heart pounding now, Sera dived. The sharks followed her. She could feel them descending, knifing through the water, gaining on her with every second. Ten yards, five yards, three . . . and then she was in the seaweed, reaching for the seafloor so she could flatten herself against it. But there was no seafloor. There was nothing at all.

Sera found herself hurtling through the seaweed and into a deep black gully. The green fronds were so dense they'd obscured it. She stopped, turned and looked up. The sharks passed overhead, but didn't pursue her. A few weak sunrays penetrated the thicket. She wound them into a ball and held it in her hand. Then she looked down into the gully, and nearly dropped it.

The wrecked ship lay tilted on its side below. If the sharks hadn't chased her into the gully, she never would have found it. It was remarkably well preserved.

That should have been a warning to Sera, but she was so excited to have found the wreck, the fact that its masts, rigging and deck were still sound after four centuries didn't register.

She recognized the vessel as a three-masted caravel, a

ship used by the Spanish long ago. It was light, sleek and about sixty feet long – just the kind of fast, manoeuvrable ship a princess fearing a pirate attack would use. It had to be the *Demeter*.

As she swam closer, she saw that the hull was riddled with holes. She peered into one and saw crabs scuttling over wine casks, water barrels and baskets. Silver goblets and dishes lay on the bottom of the hold. Wooden chests, the sort that goggs from an earlier time used to contain clothing, were tumbled about like building blocks. Could these things have belonged to the infanta? Were her remains still on board the ship? Was Neria's blue diamond? Sera looked for human bones, but saw none. She would have to go inside and search the rest of the vessel.

The holes in the hull were too small for her to fit through, so she decided to swim topside and enter that way. She looked up, ready to head for the gunwale – and froze.

Someone was standing on the ship's deck. Watching her. It was a young woman with haunting black eyes. She was beautiful. Pale. And dead.

Serafina knew her instantly from the duca's painting. Her stomach clenched with fear. It was the infanta. The *Demeter* was a ghost ship.

Sera was in great danger.

CHAPTER 32

THIRTY-THREE

THE GHOST CONTINUED to stare at Serafina, saying nothing.

Sera knew she should swim away. Fast. This was no silly rusalka – this was something far worse. But she couldn't go; she needed Neria's diamond. She decided to speak to the ghost, but she would have to be very careful. Shipwreck ghosts were treacherous. They were hungry for life. They longed to feel the beat of a living heart, the rush of blood through the veins. Their touch, if prolonged, could be lethal.

Moving slowly, Sera swam up the ship's side. When she reached the top, she curtsied deeply. The infanta might be dead, but she was still royal, and Sera knew she must accord her due respect.

'Hail, Maria Theresa, most noble and esteemed infanta of Spain. I am the Principessa Serafina di Miromara, daughter of Regina Isabella,' Sera said, trying to keep her voice steady. 'I have come on a matter of state and humbly beg permission to board your vessel.'

'Hail, Serafina, principessa di Miromara,' the infanta said in a voice that sounded like a keening wind. 'You may board.'

Sera had addressed the infanta in Spanish, thanks to the bloodbind. She set her light ball down on the gunwale, then swam aboard the ship, careful to give the ghost a wide berth.

'Why have you come alone? Where is your court?' the infanta asked.

'My court is gone, Your Grace. My mother taken. My realm invaded,' she said.

The infanta's eyes darkened. 'Who has done this terrible thing?' she asked.

Serafina told her what had happened to Miromara and why. She told her of the monster in the Southern Sea and how the invaders were searching for the six talismans needed to free it.

'Your magnificent blue diamond is one of the talismans, Your Grace,' she said. 'I believe it was given by my ancestor, Regina Merrow, to one of your forebears. I've come to ask you for it. I need it to stop the invaders of my realm from unleashing a great evil upon the seas.'

'You ask a great deal. What are you willing to give in return?' the infanta said.

'Also a great deal,' Serafina replied.

'Sit with me a while, Principessa. It has been so long since I've had company.' The infanta settled herself on the gunwale and gestured for Serafina to join her.

Serafina obeyed, leaving several feet of rail between them. She sat lightly, ready to spring away if need be. She knew she was dancing with death. If the infanta lunged at her, if she grabbed her and held on, Sera would never leave the ship.

'*La Sirena Lácrima*,' the infanta said wistfully. 'The Mermaid's Tear. That is what my family called the famous diamond. My mother gave it to me on the occasion of my sixteenth birthday.' Her smile faded. 'You should be careful what you ask for, Principessa. That beautiful jewel cost me my life.'

She moved closer. 'I was betrothed to a French prince,' she said. 'The wedding was to be in Avignon. I sailed for France in the summer of my eighteenth year. We were heading for Saintes-Maries when the first mate raised the alarm. Amarrafe Mei Foo's ship had been sighted. I knew that name. Everyone did. Mei Foo was ruthless and cruel, a murderer. His ship was called the *Shāyú*. It was known that the diamond was part of my dowry. I knew he would take it. And me with it.'

The infanta smoothed her skirts, then continued. 'I vowed I would *not* be taken. I was a princess of Spain, meant to be wife to a French prince, not a wench to warm a pirate's bed. Our captain tried his best to outrun Mei Foo, but it was futile. I knew what I had to do. I waited until the *Shāyú* came alongside of us, until Mei Foo could see me. Then I called for my hawk, Miha, to be brought to me. I took my necklace off and gave it to her. "Fly!" I cried. Miha rose over the water with the diamond. Mei Foo had a bird too, a great black bird of prey. He sent it after my hawk. Miha was fast, but the pirate's demon bird was faster. As it closed in, Miha dropped the necklace. Mei Foo's bird tried to dive for it, but Miha fought it. She was killed, but she stopped the bird from getting the stone. It sank into the sea. The screams that evil bird made were nothing compared to the screams of Mei Foo. I mocked him, telling him an octopus would wear my diamond now, but at least it would not be in his filthy robber's hands.'

The infanta stretched out a graceful arm, and rested her bloodless hand on the gunwale, only inches from Serafina's. Spellbound by her story, Sera didn't notice.

'I angered the pirate so greatly that he did not take me with him,' the infanta said. 'He killed me instead. Which is what I wished. He boarded the *Demeter* and took the crew and my ladies to sell as slaves. Then he locked me in my cabin. He reboarded his ship and gave orders to bombard my vessel.'

The infanta's voice faltered. The pain of her memories was written on her face. 'I can still hear the cannonshot. I can smell the gunpowder. I faced death bravely, as a princess of Spain must. I had hoped Mei Foo would shoot me, that he would show me some small mercy, but he did not. Drowning is not an easy death.' She turned her dark, dead eyes on Serafina. 'After hearing my story, do you still wish to have the jewel? The invaders you spoke of, they will surely try to take it from you, as Mei Foo tried to take it from me. It may cost you your life too.'

'I still wish to have it. You told me where the diamond is – in the sea. Will you now tell me how far Miha flew? And in which direction? It will take me some time to find it, I think, and I don't have much.'

The ghost laughed. 'Oh, but, Principessa, I didn't tell you where the diamond is.'

'But you did, Your Grace,' Serafina said, confused. 'You said Miha dropped it into the sea.'

'I told you that Miha dropped the necklace I gave her. That necklace was a fake. I'd hidden the real diamond. To safeguard it. It's still aboard this ship.'

Sera's heart leapt with excitement. The diamond was *here*. Merrow's talisman was on board the *Demeter*!

'Will you allow me to take it?' she asked.

'For a price.'

'Whatever I can give you, I will.'

'Your life?' the infanta asked, reaching out to touch Serafina's cheek. Her fingers stopped only inches away from it. Serafina realized too late that she had allowed the infanta to come too close, but she did not flinch. She felt that the ghost was weighing her, testing her. She knew she must show no cowardice.

'Yes, Your Grace. If that's what I must give to save my realm,' she replied.

The infanta nodded approvingly. She withdrew her hand. 'You have a strong heart, Principessa. And a brave spirit,' she said. 'You will need both, for I wish to go home, and I require that you take me there.'

Serafina felt as if the breath had just been squeezed out of her. The infanta's request was a death sentence. She knew, as all mer did, that water bound human souls. If a human died on its surface, her soul went free, but if she drowned in its depths, her soul was trapped and became a ghost.

No soul wanted to be bound. It raged against its fate. The strength of that rage determined a ghost's power. Restless waters, like those of the shore with their ebb and flow of tides, or the rushing tumble of rivers, dissipated rage. Ghosts of those waters, like the rusalka, tended to be weak. They could slap and pinch, but not kill. They could take objects from the living, but couldn't hold on to them. They ranged freely through the waters where they'd died, more of a nuisance than a threat.

Shipwreck ghosts, however, were strong. A vessel made so well that it could keep an ocean out could also keep a soul in. The fierce life force that flowed out of a human at death was not dissipated on board a ship, but rather concentrated by being trapped within a cabin, galley or berth. It entwined itself with the ship, wrapping around its wooden beams or burrowing into its metal hull, which is why ghost ships did not rot or rust. Instead, they endured, drawing on the power of the souls onboard. And the souls endured too, bound forever to their vessels.

Unless a living creature agreed to free them.

'I have been trapped on this ship for four hundred years,' the infanta said. 'I pine for the sun, for the blue sky, for the warm winds of Spain. I long for the scent of jasmine and oranges. I want to be free, Principessa. I want to go home.'

If she agreed to the infanta's request, Serafina would have to take the ghost's hand and swim with her to Spain. She knew she had little chance of surviving the trip, because a ghost's touch pulled the life out of the living, little by little, until there was none left.

From stories told of shipwreck ghosts, Sera knew that the living could withstand minutes, even hours, of their touch, but days? No one had ever survived that long.

You have a strong heart, the infanta had said.

Is it strong enough? Serafina wondered.

'Your answer, Principessa?'

'My answer is yes,' Serafina replied.

The diamond was hidden beneath a floorboard in the infanta's cabin. Serafina swam below decks. Using a knife she found in the ship's galley, she started to prise the boards up, and suddenly there it was, glinting at her – Neria's Stone. It was a clear, deep blue, and as large as a turtle's egg. Serafina had seen many jewels – her mother's vaults were full of them – but she had never seen anything like the goddess's diamond. As she picked it up, she felt its power radiating into her hand. The sensation was both thrilling and frightening. She quickly dropped it into her bag. Even though she was no longer touching it, she could still feel its power.

'You've found it,' the ghost said, when Sera returned to her. 'I hope it brings help to you instead of harm.'

Serafina steeled herself. Now she had to uphold her end of the agreement. 'Your Grace,' she said, offering her hand.

The infanta took it and Serafina arched her back, gasping. It was as if the ghost had reached inside her and wrapped a cold hand around her heart. The ship groaned and shuddered in protest, as if it knew the infanta was leaving. A long crack split its deck. A piece of a mast broke off and crashed down to the seabed. Sera felt her heart falter; she felt her breath slow. For a few seconds, the world and everything in it went grey.

Fight it, Serafina! she told herself. *Fight it!*

She thought of her mother, fending off the invaders with her last breath so that, she, Sera, could escape. She thought of Mahdi, risking his life to defeat Traho. She saw her friends bravely taking the bloodbind with her, and Vrăja staying behind to face the death riders.

And then she summoned all the strength inside her and swam, pulling the infanta away from her ship and into the open, sun-dappled sea.

THIRTY-FOUR

'ARE YOU *SURE* ABOUT THIS?' Neela asked Kora.

'Not at all,' Kora replied.

'Wrong answer.'

Kora ignored that. It was the next morning, one day after Neela had arrived in Nzuri Bonde. They had all risen before dawn and had silently swum out of the village. Now Kora was going over the plan one last time with two of her Askari – Khaali and Leylo. Strong and powerfully built, they were not only formidable fighters, Neela had learned, they were also whale riders.

'Tell Ceto I'll give him my thanks in person when the deed is done,' Kora said when they'd finished talking. She touched her forehead to Khaali's, then Leylo's. She sent them on their way, then turned to the others. 'Ikraan, you need more green on the back of your neck. Jamal, I can see the tip of your tail fin. Neela . . .' She shook her head, sighing.

'What?' Neela said defensively. 'I camoed! I totally camoed!'

Basra snorted.

'I did! What's wrong with my camo? Don't you have anemones in Kandina?'

Kora sang a couplet. The bright purple and blue splotches on Neela's torso and tail disappeared. Kora sang again and Neela was instantly mottled in five different shades of mud.

Neela inspected her arms. 'Uck,' she said.

'You'd prefer to get them chewed off?' Basra asked archly, turning on her tail.

'You'd prefer to get them chewed off?' Neela mimicked.

Basra's superior attitude was getting to her.

Kora, Neela, Basra and several other Askari were at the edge of the Razormouths' breeding grounds. It was a barren, rocky place, littered with the rotting carcasses of sea creatures. Half the group, including Basra and Neela, were wearing camouflage. The other half were not.

'All right, the camoed group looks good. Are we all ready?' Kora asked.

Everyone nodded, though the Askari were more enthusiastic than Neela.

'You know the plan. We head to the caves together, then we split up. My team acts as bait and lures the dragons to the prison. Basra's team lies low in their camo. After the dragons give chase, they search Hagarla's cave for the moonstone and grab some swag. You have an hour, Basra, then you join us at the prison. If all goes well, we swim home together.' Kora paused, then shouted, 'Great Neria, favour us!'

'Great Neria, favour us!' the Askari shouted back.

'Great Neria, favour us!' Neela shouted, a little late. She

tried to sound as tough as the Askari, but didn't quite succeed. Basra rolled her eyes.

They started off, swimming straight into the heart of the breeding grounds. Basra and her group hugged the seafloor; Kora and her group swam high. Everyone swam fast. It was all Neela could do to keep up. About ten minutes later, Kora stopped and silently pointed to a cave. Its mouth was wide and high. Bones were scattered all around it. Neela's heart was in her throat. Once the dragons gave chase, Kora and her team would have to stay ahead of them for three leagues. And dragons were fast swimmers. Neela wondered if she'd ever see Kora again.

While Basra and her group remained on the seafloor, Kora's group hid behind an outcropping of rock. Kora did not join them. Instead, she positioned herself halfway between the rock and the cave. She took a deep breath and emitted a sharp distress cry – the sound a mermaid makes when she's hurt. She did it again, and then once more, but nothing happened.

'Come *on*, you smelly tub of guts,' Neela heard her say. 'You lowtide, stink-breath, sponge-brained—'

Then there was a sound – a slow, heavy pounding that shook the ground. Kora smiled grimly and cried out again. A few seconds later, Hagarla, the dragon queen, stuck her head out of her cave.

'Oh. My. *Gods*,' Neela whispered.

'Keep it together, *Princess*,' Basra warned.

'Bite me, sharkface,' Neela said, fed up with the snide remarks.

Basra gave her a look, but Neela didn't see it. Her eyes, as big as abalone shells, were on the dragon.

Hagarla was the size of a small whale. Her scaly skin was the blue-black of a bruise, her underbelly the colour of a drowned man. Six yellow eyes with black horizontal slits for pupils stared from a massive, serpent-like head. A forked black tongue flicked from her lips. She roared loudly, and Neela saw that she had rows of sharp teeth in her jaws. They spiralled all the way down her throat and were clotted with the bloody chunks of her last meal.

Kora cried out again. Hagarla's head whipped around, her eyes narrowing as she spotted Kora. She tensed then sprang, but Kora shot off. Other dragons came out of their caves. Hagarla turned and roared at them, possessive of her prey, but they wanted to eat Kora too, so they joined the chase.

When Kora gave the signal, the rest of her group swam out from behind the rock, all shouting and whooping. Their appearance sent the dragons into a frenzy. A dozen of them sprang at the mermaids. Kora and her warriors streaked off, and the dragons followed, propelling themselves with their great raylike wings.

Basra waved her group on. 'Let's go!'

Inside Hagarla's cave, the smell of decaying flesh was overwhelming, and Neela thought she was going to be sick. She shook off her queasiness and kept swimming, trying to stay focused on her mission. Twenty yards into the cave, the passageway widened into a large, high-ceilinged cavern.

'Holy sea cow,' Neela said, stunned by what was in it – a staggering amount of treasure. Gold plates, silver chalices, coins, glassware, porcelain vases, suits of armour, jewels, goblets, pieces of mirror glass, brass figures, statues of marble and alabaster, chunks of obsidian, malachite and lapis, several cars, a few bicycles, chrome coffeepots, cutlery, ropes of pearls, swords, scissors – anything with a sparkle or a gleam had been heaped into a small mountain.

'Naasir, grab some swag,' Basra ordered. 'Everyone else start searching.'

Naasir took a mesh bag from his pocket and started to fill it. The others dug into the treasure pile.

Neela started flipping bits and pieces of treasure off the pile with her tail. 'How am I ever going to find the moonstone in all this?' she said.

'Start with Hagarla's chest. It's by her nest. She keeps the best stuff there. Hurry. We don't have much time,' Basra ordered.

Neela found the chest and eased its lid back. She pulled out necklaces, golden crowns, gemstones, ropes of pearls as long as her tail – one after another. A few minutes later, she was at the bottom of the chest without having found the moonstone.

'Go help the others search the pile,' Basra said. She herself was looking around the edges of Hagarla's nest.

'Hey!' came a muffled voice. 'I think I found it!'

'Ikraan?' Basra called. 'Is that you? Where are you?'

'On the other side of treasure mountain.'

'What are you doing? Grab the moonstone!'

'Um, no can do, Chief,' Ikraan said.

Neela and the others dropped whatever they were holding and swam over the treasure pile. Ikraan was floating just above another nest – this one containing six tussling baby sea dragons, each as big as a great white.

One had a gold sceptre in its long black claws. Another had a soda can. A spiny sea urchin. A snorkeller's mask. A snorkeller's head. And a moonstone.

Neela caught her breath when she saw it. It was Navi's talisman; she was sure of it. It was the size of an albatross's egg, nearly six inches long. Silver-blue in colour, it glowed from within.

'Isn't that cute?' Basra said acidly. 'They're sleeping with their cuddly toys.'

The babies heard them. They hissed. One tried to scrabble out of the nest.

'How are we ever going to get that moonstone away from them?' Naasir asked.

Neela had an idea. She started to sing, soft and low.

'*What?*' Basra said. 'What's that going to do? We're going to have to take them out, one by one.'

'No, wait, Basra!' Naasir said. 'Look!'

The babies were swaying back and forth. They'd stopped hissing. Their scaly eyelids drooped over their yellow eyes. Neela was singing them an old Matali lullaby – one her mother had sung to her. After a few minutes they were almost out, when one suddenly slugged another one for no good reason. They all started tussling and hissing again, but Neela kept singing, and a few minutes later they were finally asleep.

'Nice work!' Ikraan whispered.

No longer singing, Neela swam towards the nest. It was for her to get the moonstone, no one else. She halted when a baby stirred, then hovered above the one who was holding the moonstone, clutching it to his chest. Working slowly and carefully, Neela prised his claws from around the talisman and took it. Then she turned to the others and smiled.

Which was a big mistake.

A swipe of pain across her back, sudden and blinding, made her scream. She dropped the moonstone. The baby dragon whose toy she'd taken had clawed her. He hissed angrily, then yawped for the jewel. Blood rose from the jagged tears in Neela's skin, curling through the water. Their sibling's noise, and the smell of blood, woke the others. Their eyes opened rapidly, their tongues flicked through their lips and they started to crawl out of the nest.

In agony, Neela swooped down and retrieved the moonstone. As soon as she had it, Ikraan and Basra grabbed her. Naasir and Jamal snatched pieces of treasure from Hagarla's pile and threw them at the babies, driving the creatures back into their nest. Furious at being deprived of a nice bloody snack and pelted with hard objects, they all started yawping loudly.

'Come on, we've got to go. *Now!*' Basra ordered.

Neela and the Askari fled. They swam away from the

nest, over the treasure pile and down the passageway to the cave's mouth.

'Thank gods they're too young to come after us,' Ikraan said, looking behind herself. She still had Neela's arm.

Basra, ahead of them all, stopped short. 'But he's not,' she said.

Ahead of them, standing in the cave's mouth, was a male dragon. He was smaller than Hagarla, but not by much. He growled at the mermaids, flattening his ears.

'Swim back to the treasure room. Very, very slowly,' Basra said quietly. 'It's our only chance.'

The mermaids did so, their eyes on the dragon. He followed them, snaking his head from side to side. Silvery strands of saliva spilled from his jaw. To Neela it felt like forever until they were back in the treasure room, but it had only taken a few seconds.

'Spread out and hit the ground,' Basra ordered.

They did and their camo blended them into the muddy, weedy cave floor. Confused, the dragon stopped short. He sniffed the water, then scuttled towards Neela, scenting her blood.

'Hey!' Basra yelled. 'Hey, silt-for-brains! Over here!'

The dragon's eyes narrowed. He lunged at her, jaws snapping. She darted backwards, just out of his reach.

'Get out of here, all of you!' she yelled, drawing the dragon further away from the passage.

Naasir, still holding his bag full of stolen treasure, made a dash for it, but the dragon sensed him. The creature whirled around and swung his massive head towards the merman. Naasir dived under the dragon's chest and around his foreleg, barely avoiding his snapping jaws. He tried to make the passage, but the dragon blocked him, roaring in anger.

Ikraan swore. 'We'll never get out of here,' she said. 'Basra, keep him engaged. I'm going to draw him over the treasure pile to the nest. Everyone else, get ready.'

While Basra clapped her hands at the dragon, luring him towards her, Ikraan darted backwards, grabbed a jewelled box from the treasure pile and then swam to the nest. Neela couldn't see what she was doing, but two seconds later, she heard a baby dragon's screech. *Ikraan must've thrown the box and hit one*, she thought.

At the sound of the screeching baby, the male roared. He turned his back on Basra and scrambled over the mountain of treasure.

'Go!' Ikraan yelled, her voice carrying up from the nest. 'Get out of here!'

Basra grabbed Neela's arm and yanked her towards the passageway.

'We can't leave her!' Neela cried.

'We don't have a choice!' Basra shouted. 'If we go back for her, we might all die!'

Neela didn't want to go with Basra. She wanted to go back for Ikraan. But Basra's grip was like a vice, and Neela was too weak from blood loss to break free. She knew that the Askari were trained to leave one of their own if saving him or her endangered them all. It was more important that the group, not the individual, survived. If Basra couldn't save Ikraan, how could Neela? Basra was so much tougher than she was and Basra had decided.

Someone is always deciding, Neela thought as Basra continued to pull her away. *My father and mother. Suma. My teachers. The grand vizier. Even the sub-assistant.*

They decided what she did. What she wore. What she studied. Where she went. All she could decide was what flavour of bingas to eat.

So she ate them. One after another. More and more. Stuffing down her frustration and her anger. Distracting herself from her pain with shiny wrappers. Eating sweets so she could stay sweet. So she could keep smiling, keep nodding, keep glowing – just a bit, not too much.

Someone was always deciding. And it was never her.

With a wild cry, she broke free of Basra and swam back into the cave.

'Neela, *stop!*' Basra shouted.

But Neela didn't listen. The talisman, heavy in her hands, was no longer pale. Neither was Neela. They were both cobalt blue and shining brightly. She raced towards the treasure pile. As she crested it, she saw Ikraan lying dazed on the ground near the nest. The dragon must have knocked her down. He was advancing on her now, lashing his tail, baring his horrible teeth.

Hardly knowing what she was doing, Neela held the moonstone out in front of her with one hand. Wisps of light emanated from it, curling like tendrils through the water. She wound the skeins of light together with her other hand until she had a large glowing ball. The dragon was standing over Ikraan now; he opened his mouth and hissed at her.

'Hey, tall, dark and ugly dragon! Over here!' Neela yelled.

The dragon looked up – and got a lightbomb straight to the face. He roared in pain and fell backwards, clawing at his eyes.

Neela shoved the moonstone into her pocket, then raced to Ikraan. 'Get up! Hurry!' she said, tugging her arm.

Ikraan rose woozily. Neela looped the Askara's arm over her neck and they swam over the treasure pile. The dragon was blinded, but he could still use his sense of smell. He crawled up the pile, swiping at them, but missed. He lost his balance and fell backwards, bringing a ton of treasure down on his head.

Neela and Ikraan hurried to the mouth of the cave. Basra and the others were waiting for them there. Basra was furious. She grabbed Ikraan with one hand and Neela with the other and swam, hard and fast, yelling at Neela the whole way.

Neela couldn't have cared less. Ikraan was with them. *Alive.*

After a tense, breathless half hour, they were out of the breeding grounds. Basra stopped at a reef, and ushered them all under an overhang of coral, where they would be out of sight. Naasir immediately set to work cleaning and dressing Neela's wounds. The Askari all carried small amounts of medicine and bandages on them, and they pooled their resources to tend to her back. Naasir tried to be gentle, but the slashes were deep and his ministrations hurt. Neela winced, but didn't whimper. When he was done cleaning the wounds, he hunted for some kelp fronds to tie across her back to keep the dressing secure.

'I got the scratches pretty clean, but you're going to have to see the healer as soon as we're back at Nzuri Bonde. Dragon claws are filthy. We need to make sure the cuts don't get infected,' he said.

'Merl, you're going to have some *serious* scars,' Ikraan said.

Neela turned to look at her, struck by the admiring note in her voice. 'You almost sound envious. I don't know why,' she said. 'I'll never be able to wear a backless dress again.'

'I'm *totally* envious! Nothing's hotter than dragon scars. Not to a Kandinian. Most mer who get that close to a dragon end up getting eaten. And you better wear backless dresses! I'm telling you, once those heal, every merboy in Nzuri Bonde will be after you. Right, Naas?'

Naasir smiled bashfully. He finished with the kelp fronds. 'That's going to have to do for now. We have to get to the prison,' he said.

While Naasir was tending to Neela, Basra sat off by herself, at the edge of the overhang. She didn't even come over to see if Neela was OK. Looking at her now, silent and stony-faced, Neela felt a flash of irritation. She'd risked her life, taken a hit from a dragon and saved Ikraan. What else did she have to do to prove herself to this merl?

Fed up, she swam over to her. 'I saved your friend, you

know. She was about to become baby food,' she said. 'The least you could do is say thanks.'

Basra, still looking straight ahead, shook her head. 'No, Neela,' she said, 'you saved my sister.'

She rose then, took her armlet off – the one made from coral, with all her dragon kills on it – and placed it on Neela's arm. 'It doesn't match your outfit, but I hope you'll take it anyway,' she said.

Neela looked at the armlet, then swallowed the lump in her throat. 'Matching is *soooo* yesterday,' she said. 'This season it's all about contrast.'

Basra touched her forehead to Neela's.

'Thank you,' Neela said. 'I'll always treasure this armband. It's totally invincible.'

Basra smiled. 'It is, yes,' she said. 'Just like you.'

THIRTY-FIVE

KORA, ARMS CROSSED over her chest, smiled broadly at the carnage before her.

If she was tired after her three-league race with Hagarla, she didn't show it. She and her group had led the dragons to the prison. As soon as Hagarla had spotted the sea whips, she'd stopped chasing the mermaids, who were hard to catch, and attacked the jellyfish instead.

She and the other Razormouths were in a feeding frenzy now. The sea whips were fighting back, lashing out with their powerful tentacles, but the dragons barely felt the stings through their thick scales. The prison guards tried to make the sea whips hold their formation, but it was no use; the sea whips broke rank and the guards abandoned their posts. As they fled, Nadifa and four other Askari shot through what remained of the fence and shepherded the terrified prisoners into the barracks.

'Now comes the hard part,' Kora said.

'Right,' Neela said. 'The hard part. Because it's all been a piece of spongecake so far.'

'Khaali, Leylo and Ceto are in position and waiting for us

just north of here,' said Kora. 'Basra, wait until I've drawn off the dragons, then you, Neela and Ikraan join Nadifa and help her get the prisoners out. The rest of you, divide up the treasure and get ready to swim.'

Naasir dumped out the bag of loot he'd taken from Hagarla's cave. As Kora and several Askari picked up the shiny objects, the dragons finished what had become an out-and-out slaughter of the sea whips. The water was clouded with blood, gore and wriggling tentacles.

'Let's move,' said Kora, pointing at the barracks.

A handful of dragons was moving towards the buildings. One had already landed on a rooftop and was pounding it with her long spiked tail.

Neela watched as Kora and her team readied themselves.

'On your marks . . .' Kora said.

The Askari waited, heads down, looking as if they were about to swim the race of their lives. '. . . get set . . .'

Heads snapped up, bodies tensed, tails coiled.

'. . . go!'

The warriors exploded off the seafloor, thrusting themselves up into the water. They whooped and called as they swam, making a commotion that no one could ignore. Hearing it, the dragons turned towards them.

'Hey, Halitosis!' Kora shouted at Hagarla in Draca. 'Look what we've got!' She held up a jewel-studded goblet. 'We took it from your cave!'

Neela understood what Kora was saying. It was the bloodbind again; it had to be. She'd never studied a word of

Draca in her life.

The other Askari, whooping and laughing, held up their plunder. 'We took the dragon treasure! We took the dragon treasure!' they sang.

'Your cave is *empty*! The treasure is *ours*, Hagbutt!' Kora shouted.

Hagarla's eyes widened. She roared loudly, insane with fury. Kora and her group tore off through the water, and the dragons followed – forgetting about the prisoners.

Basra signalled for her group to swim into the prison. They descended on the barracks, shouting that the sea dragons were gone, coaxing the prisoners to follow them to safety.

The prisoners were thin and weak. Parents were clutching their children to them as they swam, crying with joy at being reunited. The Askari moved them all along, kindly but firmly. If the dragons suddenly came back, they'd all be bait.

When they were a good distance north of the prison, Basra nervously said, 'Where are Khaali and Leylo and the Rorquals?'

Ikraan, listening hard, pointed. 'Over there! I hear Ceto!' she replied. 'This way! Come on!' she called to the column of prisoners.

Neela looked where Ikraan was pointing. She saw Khaali and Leylo and behind them, suspended in the water, what looked like several floating mountains. Two dozen humpbacked whales waited for them. When the whales saw

Basra and the freed mer, they divided themselves into two lines, with a wide space between them.

'Hail, Ceto, honoured leader of the Clan Rorqual!' Basra called out in Whalish, bowing to the largest humpback. '*Malkia* Kora sends her greetings and her deepest gratitude to you and your kin!'

Ceto dipped his magnificent head. 'Greetings must wait, Askara. Get your people within. Make haste!'

Basra and the others led the freed prisoners into the whalemade enclosure while Ceto and the other humpbacks began to sing. Their song was beautiful, but they were not singing to delight their listeners. Whalesong, mysterious and powerful, had strong magic. The humpbacks were casting a protective songspell over the prisoners, putting up a sonic forcefield around them.

As soon as all the freed merpeople were positioned between the whales, Ceto took his place at the front, and another whale took hers at the back. Two more swam above and below the mer. At Ceto's signal, they set off in formation. Khaali and Leylo, whaleriders, sat upon the two humpbacks flanking Ceto, scouting the waters for any sign of dragons.

They had smooth swimming, and encountered no dragons – until they were one league east of Nzuri Bonde.

'Trouble ahead!' Leylo shouted.

Seconds later, Hagarla and six other dragons appeared. Hagarla's ears were flat against her skull. Her tail lashed the water around her into a froth. She was looking for a fight.

'Leave, Hagarla. You are greatly outnumbered,' Ceto warned, in Draca.

'Our fight is not with you, Ceto Rorqual,' Hagarla hissed.

'We want the mer. Give them to us and we will leave your kin in peace.'

'Be on your way. You have no business here. Not with my kind or the mer.'

'The mer stole from me! They invaded my home! Upset my children!'

'And gave you a good feed,' Ceto said. 'You are very partial to sea whips. It is known throughout the seas. Go. I will not give you the mer. You must fight me for them and you will lose. Go, Hagarla.'

Hagarla's eyes narrowed. 'You will *pay* for this, Askari!' she growled. 'One day soon, when Ceto Rorqual isn't here to fight your battles!'

She let out an ear-splitting roar, then swam away. One of the other dragons made a rush at the whales, but was stopped by the forcefield. He joined the others in their retreat.

Shortly after their encounter with the dragons, Ceto and his charges arrived safely in Nzuri Bonde. Rescue workers had set up tents, canteens and hospitals to feed and shelter the stolen mer. Kora moved among the former prisoners, talking to them, listening to them, embracing them. When they were all settled, she turned to Ceto. Bowing to him, she thanked him and his kin for rescuing her people.

'Your thanks are not required, Malkia,' Ceto said. 'The Clan Rorqual remembers the harpoons your people have pulled out of us, the fishing nets cut from our children, the cruel hooks you have taken from our flesh. The Rorqual never forget.'

Kora swam up over the massive creature and touched her forehead to his. Ceto closed his eyes as she did, then took his leave. As he prepared to go, he glanced at Khaali and Leylo, who'd been hanging around him ever since they'd arrived back at Nzuri Bonde. They looked as if they wanted something, but couldn't bring themselves to ask.

Ceto looked at them knowingly with his wise whale eyes. 'All right,' he said. 'But only once. I'm getting too old for these exertions.'

'Yes!' Khaali and Leylo shouted, tail-slapping each other.

Kora shook her head. 'Those two never grow up,' she said. 'Come on, let's watch.'

'Watch what?' Neela asked. 'Where are we going?'

'Topside,' Kora replied.

Khaali and Leylo each grabbed one of Ceto's massive flippers. Ceto turned himself, and headed upward. He swam faster and faster. Kora, Neela and the others had to swim hard to keep up. A few yards from the surface, Ceto gave a thrust of his enormous tail and all three were suddenly airborne in a spectacular breach. Khaali and Leylo launched themselves off his flippers and flung themselves up even higher, doing backflips into the air. Ceto crashed down, and Khaali and Leylo cannonballed after him, hooting and yelling and laughing themselves silly.

Ceto laughed too, a sound that was as ancient and deep as

the sea itself, then he and his clan bade the mermaids farewell. Kora, Neela and the Askari returned to the arena. Kora, noticing Neela's bandaged back, took her directly to a hospital tent. A healer unwrapped the wounds. Kora let out a low whistle as the dressings fell away.

'Impressive,' she said. 'What happened?'

As Neela explained, Kora listened intently, eyeing the armband Basra had given her.

When the healer finished, Neela bade Kora good night. She was aching and exhausted.

'I'm going to my room,' she said. 'I'll see you all in the morning.'

'No,' Kora said.

'No? Why not? Do you have another death-defying rescue planned for the evening?'

'You will sleep in a room in the ngome ya jeshi. It's only fitting.'

Neela didn't understand. 'The ngome ya jeshi? But isn't that—'

'Yes.'

'But, Kora, I'm not . . .'

Kora smiled. She touched her forehead to Neela's. 'You are now. Welcome home, Askara.'

THIRTY-SIX

NEELA WAS HUNGRY. She was starving. But not for a binga.

She'd left Kandina four days before, after a huge send-off. Kora had swum with her to the outskirts of Nzuri Bonde.

'Dark days are ahead, I fear,' she had said on the way.

Neela had nodded. 'We liberated your people, but the death riders may strike again. And Abbadon will be freed if we can't find a way to stop it.'

'We will build up fortifications against any further raids,' Kora had said, 'and you and the others must call on us if you need help. We are always here for you.'

They said their goodbyes, and then, as Neela swam away, she had heard Kora call out, '*Kuweka mwanga, dada yangu.*' Keep the light, my sister.

'Come on, Ooda,' Neela said now. 'Let's see if we can find some jellies. A bit of algae. Anything.'

It was evening, and the sea's creatures were all rising to the warmer waters of the surface to feed. Neela joined them, scooping up handfuls of comb jellies and gulping them down.

She was hungry much of the time now. She had taxed her

body greatly and it had changed over the last few weeks. The long swim to the River Olt, her journey through Vadus to Matali and then the swim to Kandina had made her tail strong, her arms sinewy, her ample curves firm. She found herself craving leafy blues, slimy vegetables and crunchy proteins – preferably with their heads still on – instead of sweets.

Above her, floating on the surface, were clumps of tasty-looking red algae. Cautiously, she poked her head up, peering around for any danger. There was a large ship close by, and many more off in the distance, but they were no cause for alarm. Their presence was nothing unusual and a confuto would keep any gogg who saw her from telling another.

She ate her fill, then dived. Half an hour later, she and Ooda were at the outskirts of Matali City. She smiled as she spotted the shining domes and turrets of the palace. She'd never noticed how gracefully the sea grass swayed along the Royal Current. Or how the palace's centre dome turned from gold to silver in the late-day rays of sun. Her home looked more beautiful to her than it ever had before.

Maybe because I came so close to never seeing it again, she thought, remembering Hagarla's cave. She was so happy to see her city, and so relieved to be in a safe place after days in the open water, but as she gazed at the palace, her smile faded. She sensed something. The way Ava sensed things.

Ooda gave her a *What?* look.

'I don't know. Something's different. Something's *wrong*.'

Neela's gaze drifted over the myriad of buildings, the

turrets and spires, archways and porticos. She remembered the attack on Miromara. She'd seen the terrible destruction caused by the death riders. In only minutes, Blackclaw dragons had brought down huge sections of the city walls and flattened buildings. Nothing like that had happened here. Everything was intact. The flags were fluttering. And yet, she was uneasy.

Probably because my parents are going to kick my tail, she thought. Imagining the reception she was going to get when she swam into the Emperor's Chamber was almost enough to make her head straight back to Kandina.

Her father and mother would be angry. They would want explanations. And she would provide them, but she would not stand for being told she was crazy. Not any more. She'd taken the precaution of having Kora send her father a conch, telling him everything that had happened and asking him for troops to patrol her waters and prevent more raids.

Neela had done what she'd set out to do. She found the moonstone. And she'd found a new way of doing things – her way.

'It must be me, Ooda,' she finally said, shrugging off her uneasiness. 'I'm the thing that's different. Come on, let's go.'

As she swam under a soaring archway that led to the main current and the palace, Neela rehearsed what she would say to her parents. As soon as she'd spoken with them, and had placed the moonstone safely in the royal vaults, she would send word to Serafina and the others that Navi's talisman had been found.

It was weirdly quiet as she continued on, past shops and restaurants, embassies and government offices. Not many people were out. The current had picked up, and she could hear the flags snapping in it. There were so many of them flying tonight. Had she forgotten a holiday?

Neela was so preoccupied by her thoughts, she didn't realize at first that Ooda was nipping at her hand. It was only when the little blowfish swam right in her face and threatened to nip her nose that Neela stopped short.

'What *is* it?' she asked. She didn't see what could be upsetting Ooda. A school of butterfly fish? A few jellies? The flags?

'Cut it out, will you? We're here. I have to go inside now and deal with my parents.'

Visibily upset, Ooda streaked off.

'Come *back*!' Neela shouted.

But Ooda didn't listen. She swam high above Neela's head, to the top of one of the flagpoles. Then she swam around and around the flag itself at a dizzying speed.

'Come down right *now*!' Neela demanded. 'Ooda, I'm serious! Ooda, I *said* . . .' Her words trailed away as she saw what the fish had been trying to show her.

'*That's* what's different,' she said, staring at the flag.

It was red, like the old flag, which was why she hadn't noticed. But it didn't have the crest of the Matali royal family – the Razormouth holding the moonstone – in its centre. Instead, it had a huge black circle.

'What *is* that?' she said. 'Why has my father changed the flags? You don't change your realm's flags unless ...'

Someone forces you to.

Traho.

The scales on the back of Neela's tail rose. 'He's here, Ooda. He's taken over the city,' she whispered. 'Those must have been Mfeme's ships I saw. He must've transported Traho's troops.'

But that made no sense. Traho was working for Admiral Kolfinn. If he'd taken over Matali City, he'd be flying Ondalina's flag, not this one, wouldn't he?

Maybe Kolfinn doesn't want it known that Traho and Mfeme are working for him, she reasoned. *Or maybe the flag is intended to mislead people.*

Neela didn't know the answer, and she didn't have time to puzzle it out. If Traho was here, he'd know that she'd left the palace and he would have guessed why. The moonstone was in her messenger bag. Once he found her, it would take him all of two seconds to find it.

'Sudden change of plan, Ooda,' she said. 'We're out of here.'

Just as she turned to swim away, someone clapped a hand over her mouth.

She never had the chance to scream.

THIRTY-SEVEN

'CAN'T FAIL... can't die out here... Neria's Stone ... have to get it back ...'

Serafina was raving.

She'd been swimming for two days with little rest, ever since she'd pulled the infanta away from the *Demeter*. She was weak and disoriented now, barely able to follow the currents. The infanta was sapping her strength, taking her life force. Sera's eyes had dulled, her cheeks were sunken, but all the while, colour was seeping into the ghostly Spanish princess. A blush bloomed across her cheeks. Her lips reddened. Her dark eyes danced once again.

'Just a little further, Principessa,' she coaxed. 'Only a few more leagues.' Her grip on Serafina's hand tightened. Serafina moaned.

An octopus swam by. The creature made her think of Sylvestre. She had loved him very much. And the thought of him gave her strength. She would think of all the things she loved. That would keep her going.

'Sylvestre,' she said. 'And Clio ... Cerulea in the morning ... the Janiçari singing ... my parents dancing ... fencing

231

with Des . . . Neela's smile . . . keel worms and eel berries
. . . the Ostrokon . . . the ruins of Merrow's palace . . . Mahdi's
eyes, his smile . . .'

She struggled on, her fins shuddering with the effort.
'Gone off course . . . must have,' she mumbled.

She had aimed for Cap de Creus, a rocky outcropping of
land near Spain's border with France.

'Should have been there by now . . .'

'Oh, Principessa!' the infanta suddenly cried. 'Can you
smell it? Juniper! Bay leaves and roses! Oranges!'

'Why aren't we there? Gods, help me . . . *please* . . .'
Serafina begged.

'Palamós!' said the infanta. 'I remember it! I came here
as a child!'

Serafina's head was spinning. She was so weak, she didn't
realize they were in the shallow waters of a deserted beach.
She swam on and her head broke the surface. Gentle waves
lapped around her chest. But it wasn't over yet. The infanta
had to break her tie with the sea. She had to put a foot on dry
land. And Serafina had to get her far enough out of the water
to do it. With the last of her strength, she heaved her body
onto the beach, then handed Maria Theresa out of the waves.
The infanta stepped onto the shore and at last it was done.
She released Serafina's hand and walked out of the surf.

'I'm home,' she whispered. 'Thank you, Principessa. Oh,
thank you!' She kissed her palm and blew the kiss to Serafina.
Then she turned and walked on, her head back, her arms
outstretched to the bright-blue sky, laughing like the girl she

once was. Her body glittered now, became a million points of silver light, and then crumbled into a fine, shimmering dust. As Serafina watched, the warm Spanish winds swept her away, until all that remained was the echo of her laughter.

Serafina could barely breathe now. Her exhausted body was failing. She tried to push herself back into the sea, but she didn't have the strength. The ghost had taken too much from her. Her chest was hitching. Her face was turning blue. She collapsed on the sand and rolled onto her back.

The sun blinded her. She closed her eyes, knowing she was going to die there.

Knowing she had failed.

And then she felt hands on her.

They were pulling at her. Her body was being dragged over the rough sand, inch by inch. It was the terragoggs. They were dragging her out of the water to put her in a tank. That's what they did to sea creatures.

Sera struggled, but didn't have the strength to fight them. The infanta had taken too much from her. *Please, gods, don't let the humans take me. Let me die*, she prayed.

But no, she was being dragged into the sea. She suddenly felt the life-giving water all around her body. Her head went under.

'Serafina!' A small, worried face smiled at her. 'We're not too late! You're alive!'

'Coco?' she rasped. 'How ... how did you ...' She couldn't finish. She was back in the water, but breathing was still so hard.

'The conch! The one you were listening to in the Ostrokon before you left. After you swam away, I picked it up and listened to it. I figured out that you were going to the *Demeter*, so I followed you!'

'By yourself . . . How?' Sera asked, coughing.

'No. I went for help.'

'Serafina . . . Oh, gods, Sera, what have you done?'

Serafina knew that voice. It was Mahdi. He'd pulled her back into the water. He had her in his arms now.

She smiled at him. 'It's OK . . . I found it.' She was gasping now.

'It's *not* OK. Look at her, Mahdi! I'm scared!' Coco said.

'Take a breath, Sera . . . Just take a deep breath.'

'She's turning *blue*!' Coco cried. 'Do something, Mahdi!'

'Come on, Sera . . . stay with me . . . Don't *do* this, Serafina! Breathe! Please, please breathe!'

THIRTY-EIGHT

NEELA FOUGHT like a tiger shark.

Her attacker had dragged her off the current and down behind a coral reef. He was still behind her, his hand pressed to her mouth, his arm around her waist, squeezing her tightly.

This filthy death rider is not getting the moonstone, she thought wildly. *He's* not.

She whipped her tail back and forth, battering it hard against his. She grabbed his arm and dug her fingernails into it. She sank her teeth into his hand.

'*Ouch!* Quit it!'

Quit it? Neela thought. *Since when do death riders say 'Quit it'?*

'Neela, it's *me*, Yazeed!'

Neela stopped moving. Her attacker released her and she turned around. Her hands came up to her mouth. The boy in front of her was thin and weary-looking, but he was Yaz.

'Oh, my *gods!*' she said, throwing her arms around his neck.

She'd nearly beaten her brother to a pulp. Now she hugged him so hard, he could barely breathe.

'I'm sorry, Yaz! I'm so sorry! I didn't know it was you. You're alive!'

'I *was*,' he grumbled.

She let go of him and swam back a few strokes, her hands on her hips. 'Where the hell have you been all this time? Why didn't you let anyone know you're OK?'

'It's a long story. I'll tell you later.'

'Why did you grab me just now? You scared the silt out of me!'

'To save you from a whole squad of death riders. They were just about to swim out of the main gate. They would have seen you. There was no time to explain. Sorry.'

'What's going on? Why are they here? Why are these flags flying?'

'Because Matali belongs to them now.'

Neela shook her head, distraught. *I was right*, she thought. 'And Mata-ji . . . Pita-ji?' she asked tearfully.

'They're OK. They're alive. Traho's got them under house arrest, but he hasn't hurt them.'

'Traho's in the palace?'

Yazeed nodded. 'His boss too.'

Neela's blood ran cold. 'Kolfinn? *He's* here?'

Yaz shook his head. 'No, Neels . . . *she* is.'

THIRTY-NINE

'**S**HE?' NEELA SAID. 'Kolfinn's a *he*.'

'It's not Kolfinn. Here,' Yazeed said, handing her a transparensea pearl. 'Cast it. I'll show you.'

Yazeed cast a pearl too. When they were both invisible, he led Neela through the Emperor's Courtyard and into the palace. They swam just below the ceiling, and over the heads of dozens of death riders.

Seeing the invaders in the palace, in her home, made Neela's blood boil. *Murdering sea scum*, she thought. *You have no right to be here.*

'Stick close,' Yazeed whispered.

They made their way into the Emperor's Chamber and hovered under one of the chandeliers. Burly death riders holding swords lined the chamber's walls.

'There she is,' Yazeed whispered, pointing to the mermaid seated on the emperor's throne. 'Meet the mastermind.'

Neela looked down. The mermaid had long auburn hair, emerald eyes and a stunningly beautiful face.

'Portia Volnero!' Neela hissed.

'The one and only,' Yazeed said.

Portia was a duchessa, one of Miromara's highest-ranking nobles. She was also Lucia Volnero's mother.

'It's *not* Ondalina. Astrid was telling the truth,' Neela said. She had to get word to the others.

'What are you talking about?'

Neela was about to explain, when Khelefu, the grand vizier of Matali, swam into the room. Seeing him, Portia spoke. Her commanding voice carried up to Neela and Yazeed.

'You've opened the vaults as I requested, Khelefu?'

'I have, Your Grace.'

Khelefu all but spat the words. And though his face was composed, Neela – who had known this proud and loyal merman all her life – could see the hatred in his eyes.

'Very good,' Portia said. She rose from the throne and swam to him. 'I wish to have Ahadi's diamond tiara for Lucia's coronation in Miromara. The one with the Pearl of the Maldives in its centre. And she'll need something for her betrothal too. Sapphires, I think, to go with her eyes. And for her future husband, Crown Prince Mahdi, the Bramaphur Emerald. It will look wonderful on his turban.'

'Say *what?*' It was all Neela could do not to shout the words.

'Shh!' Yaz said.

'I was not aware the crown prince was to be betrothed to your daughter, Your Grace,' Khelefu said. 'I thought he had been promised to Serafina, principessa di Miromara.'

Portia's eyes darkened at the mention of Serafina's name.

'He *was*, but unfortunately the poor principessa is dead. We believe she was killed in the attacks on Cerulea. Our diligent Captain Traho put signs up throughout the realm, seeking her return, but we've heard nothing of her. Although it pains us greatly, we must accept this difficult truth.'

'How very sad, Your Grace.'

'Tragic,' Portia said. 'I'll need those things packed immediately, Khelefu. I plan to leave for Miromara in the morning.'

'We've got to warn Sera!' Neela whispered to Yazeed.

'I shall have the proper forms prepared and brought to you, Your Grace,' Khelefu said. 'You will need to fill them out before you remove the jewels from the vaults.'

'Actually, I *won't*,' Portia said.

'But that is the way things are done. That is the way things have always been done,' Khelefu protested.

Portia nodded at two of her guards and they seized the grand vizier. She drew a crimson-tipped finger across her throat and they dragged him away.

Portia smiled as she watched them go, then said, 'Not any more.'

FORTY

SERAFINA OPENED HER EYES. She didn't know where she was. The waters around her were dusky. She was lying on something soft. A lava globe glowed on a table nearby.

Noiselessly, she snaked a hand towards her hip, and the dagger hidden there.

'It's all right, Sera. You're safe.'

'Mahdi?'

'We're in a farmhouse in a village off the Costa Brava. It belongs to a couple named Carlo and Elena Aleta Roja. They're loyalists.'

Serafina propped herself up. She was woozy. Her body ached. She saw that she was lying in a narrow bed in a small, rustic room. Curtains framing the room's single window fluttered in the night current. A pot of tea and two cups had been placed on a table under the window.

Mahdi was sitting on a chair next to the bed. He took her hand. 'How are you feeling?'

'Better now that I'm holding your hand instead of a ghost's,' she said weakly.

'It was a shipwreck ghost, wasn't it? That's what Coco said. Sera, tell me you didn't do what I think you did.'

'I had to. She had something I needed. It was the only way to get it.'

'How long were you in contact with her?'

'I don't know. Two days, maybe? Three? It's all kind of foggy.'

'That can't be right. No one could survive contact with a shipwreck ghost for that long.'

Sera shook her head, trying to clear it. Had she somehow got the number of days wrong? She was so exhausted it was hard to think straight.

'What happened after you and Coco pulled me back into the water?' she asked.

'You blacked out. You weren't getting enough oxygen. You turned blue and stopped breathing. I gave you mouth-to-mouth. You coughed up a lot of air, then started breathing again.'

'I would have been dead without you, Mahdi. You saved my life,' Sera said, squeezing his hand. 'How did you get out here? Aren't you supposed to be on patrol in Cerulea?'

'I caught a very lucky break. A few nights ago, Coco came to me in a panic. She told me you'd set off to find the *Demeter* and that she was worried about you and begged me to go after you. Two nights before that, I was at the palace, having dinner with Traho. Turns out he has a new acquisition – a painting that Rafe Mfeme took from the duca. He's cast some sort of spell on it, to protect it from water. It's hanging over a lavaplace and—'

'—it's a portrait of Maria Theresa, an infanta of Spain,' Serafina said.

Mahdi gave her a quizzical look. 'How did you know that?'

'I admired the portrait when I first arrived at the duca's, and he told me that she was an ancestor of his.'

'Traho didn't tell me that. He told me the story of the *Demeter* though, and of the infanta's blue diamond. He said it's very valuable and that he wants it.'

'Yes, he does,' Serafina said darkly. She remembered how it felt to hold the diamond in her hand. The sensation of power was like nothing she'd ever felt before, both frightening and intoxicating.

'After I spoke with Coco I was worried about you too, so I came up with a way to leave my command,' Mahdi said. 'I went to Traho and told him it would be a great honour if he would allow me to find the infanta's diamond for him. He was so pleased, he immediately gave me permission to search for it. I have a dozen death riders with me.'

'Nearby?' Serafina asked, alarmed.

'About a league east of here. At my suggestion, we fanned out to look for the shipwreck. Except for me. I went to look for you.'

'They'll never find the wreck, and even if they did, they'll never find the diamond,' Serafina said. 'The infanta was the only one who knew where it was and I just set her free. She's gone. The wreck is empty.'

'And the diamond?'

Sera didn't answer.

'Back at the safe house, you asked me to tell you what was going on. You asked me to trust you. Now I'm asking you to trust me.'

'I've got the diamond.'

'Wow. OK,' Mahdi said, clearly surprised. 'You found it on the wreck?'

Sera nodded.

'That's weird,' said Mahdi.

'Why?'

'Traho told us to find the wreck, then search the seabed half a league due north of it. He said that the infanta had a hawk, and that the bird took off with the necklace and dropped it there.'

Serafina released Mahdi's hand. She sat bolt upright. '*What?* That's impossible! How does he *know* that? Only a handful of people could have known that, and they're all *dead*!'

'Wait, I don't understand . . . know what?'

'Don't you see? Only the infanta, the pirate who attacked her and the rest of the people on their ships could know that the hawk carried the necklace away. The infanta certainly didn't tell Traho and, up until yesterday, she's the only one who could have. Mei Foo and his crew didn't tell him. According to the conch I listened to, they were all hanged ashore centuries ago. The *Demeter*'s crew and passengers didn't either, since they all likely died ashore as slaves. So how does Traho know where the necklace is?' She frowned. 'Or rather, how does he *think* he knows?'

'What do you mean?'

'The infanta fooled Mei Foo,' she said. 'The necklace her hawk flew away with was a fake. She kept the real diamond necklace hidden.'

'What are you not telling me about this diamond, Sera? Why is it so important? Why is it worth your life? Are you going to sell it to fund the resistance?' Mahdi asked.

'It's worth much more than my life, and I would never sell it. It's powerful, Mahdi. Really powerful. I think it's the reason I survived the infanta. Its power protected me from her.'

Mahdi gave her a long look. 'There are other things – things besides the diamond – that you're not telling me about, aren't there?'

'I wanted to tell you. At the safe house. I would have, if the death riders hadn't raided it.'

'Tell me now.'

Serafina glanced at the teapot. 'Could I have a cup of tea first? I'm going to need one.'

Mahdi poured. As he handed Sera a cup of the hot, soothing drink, she started to talk. She told him everything that had happened to her since she and Neela fled the duca's palazzo. An hour later, she finished.

Mahdi sat back in his chair, dazed. 'You could've been killed, Sera,' he said. 'By death riders. By Rorrim. By Rafe Mfeme. By the Opafago. Why didn't you come back? Why didn't you let me help you?'

'Hmm, let's see . . . because I had no idea you were Blu? Because you never told me?'

'And you think Ondalina's behind all this? You think Kolfinn's the one who wants to unlock the monster's cage?'

'I was sure it was Ondalina until I met Astrid. She was summoned by the Iele too. She fought the monster so courageously and she swore that her father had nothing to do with the attack on Cerulea. But then she left us. She won't fight with us. And now I don't know what to think.'

Mahdi digested this. 'I don't know either, Sera, but I do know this: that story you told me about the infanta's hawk and the fake necklace? That's some very good news.'

'Why?'

'Because Traho believes the hawk dropped the *real* necklace. If I can find the fake necklace for him, he'll have a fake talisman, but he won't know that. And he – or Kolfinn – will fail if they try to use it to free Abbadon.'

'You're right. You have to find the fake, Mahdi,' Sera said. She told him exactly where the wreck was, so that he could search north of it. As she finished talking, there was a knock on the door.

'Come in,' Mahdi said.

'You're awake!' said Coco, swimming into the room with Abelard right on her tail. She hugged Serafina tightly. 'Elena wants to know if you're feeling up to dinner.'

'Is it that late?' Mahdi said, looking out of the window. The waters were dark now.

'Can I tell her you'll come down?' Coco asked.

Serafina smiled. 'Yes, you can.'

As Coco left, Mahdi turned back to Serafina. 'I'll need to leave right after dinner. I have to get back to camp.' He hesitated, then added, 'Sera, there's news of your uncle. Good news, I think.'

'What news? What's happened?' Sera asked excitedly.

'I don't want to get your hopes up, but he's been seen in the waters off Portugal with an army of Kobold at his back.'

'Mahdi, are you *serious*?'

He nodded and Serafina whooped for joy.

'I also hear that Portia Volnero has left Cerulea for parts unknown.'

'Does anyone know why?' asked Serafina. 'Was she a collaborator? Did she side with Traho?'

'It's possible. And if she was, she might've left because she was worried about what would happen when your uncle retakes the city.'

'What about Lucia?' Sera asked.

'I don't know. I haven't seen her for days. Kind of makes me nervous. She's like a rockfish – the most dangerous when you can't see her.'

'Oh, Mahdi, this is such good news. I want to have hope, I can't help it, but I'm almost afraid to,' Serafina said.

Mahdi's face grew solemn. 'You should be, Sera,' he said quietly.

'Why? What's wrong?' she asked him.

'When the death riders came to Cerulea, it was an invasion. When Vallerio returns to the city, it will be out-and-out war.' He took her hand again, then said, 'No matter what happens, I want you to know that I love you, Sera.'

'Oh, Mahdi,' Sera whispered.

'I've loved you since the day I met you. Really met you. In the garden.' He smiled. 'When you were listening to a conch and knocked the sea fan down to get my attention.'

'*What?* I didn't *knock* it down! It fell!'

'Uh-huh. Sure it did.'

'Mahdi!' she protested. And then she leaned over and kissed him. Slowly and sweetly. 'I love you too. Always have. Ever since you made Ambassador Akmal knock the sea fan down. To get *my* attention.'

'Sera,' he said, serious again, 'I don't know what will happen when your uncle tries to re-enter the city. I'm moving people between safe houses. I'm helping Fossegrim and the Black Fins. Traho could find out at any time, and if he does . . .' He paused for a moment, as if to work up his courage, then all in a rush he continued. 'I want us to say our vows to each other.'

Sera blinked at him. 'Mahdi, I . . . I just . . . I mean, *wow*. This is sudden.'

'Once I told you that you were my choice. Am I yours?'

'Yes,' Serafina said. 'Always.'

'Then let's do this. Carlo and Elena's neighbour is a justice of the seas. His name is Rafael. I've already talked to him. It won't be a big-deal state ceremony with you promising the realm a daughter and all of that. In fact, it won't be much of a ceremony at all. No glittery ring, no fancy dress. It's hardly what a merl dreams of, I know, but it's still a Promising. We'll vow to be together one day. Even though Traho wants to rip us, and everything else, apart. No matter what happens, I want to know that you're mine, and I want you to know that I'm yours. Always.' He took her hand in his again. 'Will you?'

I know why he's doing this, Serafina thought dully. *A war is coming and he doesn't think he'll survive it.* A pain, familiar now but still terrible, tore through her. Traho had taken everything from her – her family, her people, her realm. And still he wanted more.

Well, this time, he wouldn't get it.

She would take her vows.

She would take this night and these few precious hours.

She would take this merman for her own.

'Yes, Mahdi,' she said. 'I will.'

FORTY-ONE

CARLO ALETA ROJA SMILED. 'Time to go,' he said.

He offered Sera his arm, and together they swam out of the farmhouse's kitchen to its garden. Short and wiry, with greying hair, Carlo had the gnarled hands and stiff movements of one who had wrested his living from a rocky seabed. He and Elena farmed oysters.

'You couldn't ask for a better night,' he said. 'The tide's high, the waters are calm and the moon is full.'

Sera tried for a smile.

'Are you all right, Principessa? Are you nervous?'

'Very,' she admitted.

'Just remember,' Carlo said, covering her hand with his own, 'no matter how nervous you feel, Rafael feels a thousand times worse!'

Sera laughed. Carlo was right. Sera had overheard Rafael fretting. She'd been on the landing outside her bedroom door, adjusting her dress, and he had been on the lower level of the farmhouse, talking to Elena. Their voices had carried up to her.

'I can't *do* this!' Rafael had said. 'I'm just a little backwater justice of the seas and they're royalty! My voice, my powers . . . they're not strong enough. Mahdi and Sera need a better songcaster. They need a canta magus. They need—'

Elena cut him off. 'What they need is *hope*. So give them some. They're two young people in love. Don't you remember what that feels like? *I* remember when you met Ana, gods rest her. You couldn't take your eyes off her.'

'I never did take my eyes off her. Not once in fifty years. She was everything to me,' Rafael said wistfully.

'And Mahdi can't take *his* eyes off Sera. They don't need a canta magus. They have love. It's enough,' Elena said. 'Love's the greatest magic of all.'

Sera took heart at the memory of those words. She had already learned that love was hard and demanded sacrifices. Now she knew that it also demanded courage. It was hard to speak betrothal vows to Mahdi when he might be taken away from her at any moment, but she wasn't going to let fear stop her.

'Are you ready?' Carlo asked. They had reached the garden's entrance. Like most mer gardens, it was not only fenced, but also roofed. Slender kelp stalks, woven together, discouraged pests from swooping in.

'Yes, I am,' Sera said, squaring her shoulders. 'Thank you, Carlo. For swimming me up the aisle. For sheltering me. For everything that you and Elena have done.'

Carlo smiled sadly. 'It should be your father at your side tonight, Principessa. He was a good merman.'

Sera nodded, missing both her parents so badly that it

hurt. 'He's in my heart,' she said. 'And you're at my side. I'm a lucky merl to have two good mermen with me.'

Carlo kissed Sera's cheek, then opened the door to the garden. As they swam inside, Sera's eyes lit up with surprise and delight.

'Oh, how beautiful!' she exclaimed.

Hundreds of moon jellies formed a glowing canopy over the garden. Darting among them were dozens of minnows, their silver scales winking with reflected light. In the garden itself, anemones of all hues bloomed. Mauve stingers – purple jellyfish with long ruffled tentacles – floated like lanterns. Sea roses – flat, fluttery worms – twined themselves into red blossoms, and exotic sea lilies waved their feathery arms. Urchin shells filled with tiny lava globes shone softly atop rocks and corals.

Elena had done all this. Sera was so touched by the gesture that tears came to her eyes.

The setting was enchanting, and Sera loved its every detail, but it was the sight of Mahdi waiting for her at the end of the garden that made her heart swell.

He was wearing a dark-blue seaflax jacket, fashionable three decades ago, that he'd borrowed from Carlo. He had not wanted to wear the uniform of the death riders for his betrothal. Elena had smartened the jacket by attaching a bright-yellow anemone to one lapel. His dark hair was loose and hanging down his back. His face was solemn, but his warm, brown eyes were smiling. For her.

As Sera smiled back at him, she felt her nervousness

disappear. Her worries and fears too. Death riders were nearby, hunting for a talisman. Traho held Cerulea and would not give it up without a battle. She didn't know what the future held, or if she and Mahdi would live to find out. And yet, when she looked into his eyes, she felt strong enough to face whatever was coming.

Elena was right: love was enough.

'Sera, you look . . .' he started to say.

'. . . *soooooo* pretty!' Coco chimed in.

Sera laughed. Coco was on Mahdi's left, wearing a pink dress that had belonged to one of Elena's grown daughters. Abelard swam in circles around her. Elena was next to them in a pretty blue seaflax dress, her silver hair in a braided coil at the nape of her neck.

Sera herself was dressed in Elena's own betrothal gown. It was made of palest green sea silk and had fitted three-quarter sleeves, a square neckline, a cinched waist; and a skirt that gracefully skimmed Serafina's curves. She wore a brilliant-blue starfish in her short hair and was holding a bouquet of white and red coral that Elena had gathered for her.

Carlo escorted Sera to Mahdi's side, then joined his wife. Then the whole tiny betrothal party turned to Rafael, who was floating just behind Mahdi.

Rafael nodded at them all, then started to sing. His voice was not the most robust, but it had warmth to it, and a rustic sincerity that conveyed the emotion of the betrothal vows perfectly.

The sea is still and bathed in light
As we begin these hallowed rites.

With Neria's help, I now will sing
The sacred vows of Promising.

Sera turned to face Mahdi, as tradition dictated. She raised her right hand and he put the little shell ring he'd once made for her on her ring finger. Then he raised his left hand and she put a gold band, studded with emeralds, on his ring finger. Carlo had given it to Mahdi. He'd found it many years ago in a shipwreck. As Mahdi and Sera pressed their palms together, Rafael wound a rope made of kelp around their wrists and knotted it.

Around your limbs these ropes do wind,
Just as your hearts these vows will bind.
What the goddess joins forever
Is not for mortal mer to sever.

Be sure before you sing your oath,
You truly wish to plight your troth.
These vows of love and faith once spoken
Must forever be unbroken.

Rafael paused here to allow his words to sink in, and to give Mahdi and Sera a chance to change their minds. When he was certain they did not wish to, he continued, looking at Mahdi.

> *Let no rough waters rend apart*
> *Two who have become one heart.*
> *For love's not love that can't withstand*
> *A rogue wave breaking on the sand.*

Mahdi responded to Rafael, singing his vows perfectly.

> *As strong as the pull of the tides,*
> *As strong as the wind and the weather,*
> *My love has the force of ten oceans.*
> *I vow it will keep us together.*

Rafael addressed the next verse to Sera.

> *Love must be constant, not ebb and flow,*
> *Like storms and frets, tides high and low.*
> *For love's not love if one must force*
> *The beloved one to stay the course.*

It was Sera's turn now. She looked at Mahdi as she sang.

> *As sure as the seabirds in flight,*
> *As sure as the endless deep blue,*
> *My love is as certain as sunrise.*
> *I vow it will keep us both true.*

Rafael sang once again.

Stay heart to heart and hand to hand,
As close as water touching land.
For love's not love if feelings fade
And hearts grow cold, despite vows made.

Mahdi and Sera sang the next response together.

As long as the pale moon rises,
As long as waves break on the shore,
Our love will go on never-ending.
As the whales in the deep, evermore.

Rafael smiled. He was almost done.

You've taken vows, you've given rings.
Now comes the end of Promising.
Go forth, be true, be kind and strong.
Live a life both good and long.

But most of all, never forget
It's what you give, not what you get.
In seas below, or far above,
Be guided, evermore, by love.

The last note of Rafael's song rose and faded. The rope binding Sera and Mahdi unwound and sank slowly to the seafloor. As it did, Mahdi, overcome by emotion, cupped Sera's face in his hands and kissed her, and Sera kissed him back, forgetting there were others nearby.

The sound of clapping, however, quickly reminded her. Carlo and Rafael were applauding with gusto. Sera blushed furiously. Elena dabbed at her eyes. Coco made a face.

With the ceremony over, Rafael led Serafina and Mahdi back inside the house. They both had to sign a parchment attesting to the fact that they had indeed spoken their betrothal vows. Carlo and Elena signed afterwards, as legal witnesses.

'Now for dinner!' Elena said, when they'd finished. 'I've kept it warm all this time. Come, everyone, let's eat!'

She led the way to her kitchen, with Coco close on her tail. Mahdi didn't follow them. Instead, he bent over the parchment-work.

'Aren't you coming?' Serafina asked him.

'I am,' he said, smiling at her. 'I'm just checking that everything's filled out properly. You go ahead. I'll be right there.'

Serafina swam to the doorway, then looked back. Mahdi's smile had disappeared. He was holding up the parchment, scrutinizing it.

'If one of us was to actually marry anyone else now, that marriage would be . . .' he said to Rafael.

'Null and void,' Rafael said. 'Why?'

Serafina thought it was the strangest question. Why would Mahdi ask about marrying anyone else? But then, as quickly as it had gone, his smile was back again.

'Just want to make sure you won't try to steal her from me, sir,' he said.

Sera realized he was only joking. She swam to the kitchen. The sound of Rafael's laughter followed her. 'Ah, son,' he said, 'once upon a time, maybe. Back in the day . . .'

A pretty table awaited Sera in the kitchen, set with Elena's best shipwreck china and old, burnished silver. There was a vase arranged with colourful sea fans. Bright ribbon worms were wound around them.

'Everything's so beautiful,' Serafina said, hugging Elena. 'Thank you so much.'

Elena flapped a hand at her. 'I'm sure it's much grander at the palace, Principessa,' she said.

'It is, but I like this so much better. No table could ever be as lovely as this one. And no meal could be as special.'

Everyone sat down to eat. Elena's cooking was delicious and Sera found that she was starving. There were sea lettuces with spicy pink shoal peppers, saltmarsh melons stuffed with beach plums, and the farm's own oysters glazed with snail slime. Dessert was silt-cherry seafoam.

Serafina's heart was so full as she looked around the table. The marriage ceremony, which would happen when she came of age at twenty – *if* she came of age – would be a huge ceremony of state, and would legalize her union with Mahdi. But this night wasn't about realms and alliances; it was about true love. If only her mother and father could be here, and Mahdi's parents too. As if sensing her sadness, Mahdi took her hand. She smiled at him. He was hers now, and she was his.

'I have to go,' he said quietly.

Serafina nodded. She knew he had to get back to his mer men, and to the camp they'd made. He was supposed to be searching for Neria's Stone. He said his goodbyes, thanking Carlo, Elena and Rafael profusely, and then Sera swam outside with him.

The moonlight shone down through the depths, glinting off the scales of bluefish and bonito, silhouetting sharks and rays.

'If I swim all night, I can make camp by morning. I'll find the *Demeter* tomorrow and, with any amount of luck, the necklace too. I'll be a hero in Traho's eyes,' Mahdi said bitterly.

'You *are* a hero,' Serafina said. 'To me. To our people. One day, everyone will know it.'

He looked down at her. '*Mērē dila, mērī ātmā,*' he whispered. It was Matalin mer for *My heart, my soul*. He took her in his arms and held her close. 'I love you, Serafina. No matter what happens, remember that,' he said fiercely. 'You are mine. Always. Believe that. Tell me that you do.'

'Stop, Mahdi. You're scaring me,' she said. 'It sounds like you're going to die.'

'There are things in this world worse than death,' he said. 'Tell me, Serafina. Right now. Say you believe me.'

'I believe you.'

'We'll meet again one day. In a better place,' Mahdi said, his voice husky. He turned away from her then, and swam into the dark waters.

'I love you, Mahdi,' Sera said.

But he was gone.

FORTY-TWO

'NOT MUCH FURTHER NOW,' said Serafina encouragingly.

Coco was exhausted. They'd been on the currents for four days. Sera had tried to get her to stay at the farm. It was safe there. Carlo and Elena doted on her. But Coco refused. She would not be separated from Serafina.

They were about five leagues from Cerulea now and entering the small village of Bassofondo. Serafina headed towards an inn she'd seen signs for, but it was full. She tried two more, but they, too, had sold out every room. She wondered what was going on. Finally, they found a small hotel on the eastern edge of the village.

'We have one room left. It's small. You'll have to share a bed. Are you headed to Cerulea too?' the mermaid at the desk asked her.

Serafina hesitated, wary of revealing her plans. 'Well, we—' she started to say.

'Oh, of course you are! Everyone's going. Isn't it *wonderful*? He's coming back! Principe Vallerio, the high commander! He's heading straight into the city and there's going to be a big betrothal ceremony when he gets there. To make up for the one that never happened.'

'There is?' Serafina said, astonished.

'Yes! In the Kolisseo. Vallerio's riders have been going village to village, ordering every merperson within two leagues of Cerulea to attend.'

'The high commander sounds very confident. His army must be a powerful one,' Serafina said, trying to get as much information from the mermaid as she could.

'They say it's fearsome. Much bigger than Traho's. The death riders must be terrified. I'm sure they're packing their bags as we speak and I say good riddance.' The mermaid handed her a room key. 'Here you go. Room Four. Sleep well.'

'Mahdi must know all about this!' Coco said excitedly, as soon as she and Sera were in their room.

'I think you're right,' said Sera. 'He must've deserted Traho and told Vallerio that he was only pretending to be on the invaders' side.'

'He must've told Vallerio about you too,' Coco said. 'Your uncle knows you're alive and that's why he's having the betrothal ceremony! As soon as they take back the city, you and Mahdi can do a *proper* betrothal. Just like you were supposed to do before Cerulea was attacked. We have to get back to the city, Sera! You *have* to be there! Mahdi and Vallerio are going to be waiting for you!' The little merl was nearly bouncing off the walls.

'And you have to get some sleep. We have five leagues to

cover tomorrow.'

She gave Coco some of the food Elena had packed for them. Coco gobbled it, then fell into bed. Abelard snuggled next to her. Seconds later, both Coco and her little shark were fast asleep. Serafina locked the door, turned off the lights and crept into bed herself. Not that she was able to sleep.

At Elena and Carlo's, Mahdi had said that Vallerio was seen in the waters of Portugal. That was four days ago – he might be nearly as close to the city as she was now. If that was so, then as soon as tomorrow, she and her uncle might be reunited. She could barely believe this happy turn of events.

Sera closed her eyes, and for the first time in a long time, she fell asleep with hope, not fear, in her heart.

Finally the tide was turning back towards peace.

FORTY-THREE

'I'M SO GLAD you're not dumb, Yaz,' Neela said.

Yazeed shot her a sidelong glace. 'I thought you were going to say *dead*.'

'That too.'

'Hey, thanks.'

'You really had us fooled, you and Mahdi. We had no idea you were Blu and Grigio. We thought you were just a couple of idiots.'

'That was the idea.'

Neela looked at her brother. 'I'm actually going to miss him.'

'Who?'

'The old Yazeed.'

'He's still around,' Yaz said. He affected a vapid expression. 'Merl, you look fresh to *death* in that dress! Wanna go to the Sand Bar tonight? The Nepp Tunes are playing. They have the *best* kombu smoothies. They're like, *totally* seagan,' he said.

A second later, the vapid expression was gone and the

Yazeed Neela now knew was back. A Yazeed with a hardness to him.

'Wow. You know, that's actually kind of scary, Yaz. I had no idea you were such a good actor.'

'And I had no idea you were such a good songcaster. Can you try a convoca again? I really need to talk to Mahdi.'

'Sure, but I need to stop and sit down somewhere. The last two times I tried, it was a total fail. I'm hoping it was because I was tired.'

'I see a place down there,' Yaz said, pointing to a hollow under a coral reef.

He and Neela swam to it. Neela sat down for a moment, caught her breath and tried her hardest to cast a convoca, but once again, she failed.

'You're beat, that's all,' Yaz said.

'No, it's more than that,' Neela said dispiritedly. 'Vrăja told us our powers are strongest when we're all together. The convoca's one of the hardest songspells there is. I can't seem to cast it without the others near me. Come on, Yaz, let's get going. We've got to find Mahdi and Sera.'

'Rest for two more minutes, then we'll swim again,' Yaz said. He sat down on the silty seafloor and leaned his back against the coral, but didn't close his eyes. He just stared ahead, a grim expression on his face.

Neela and Yazeed were on their way to Cerulea. They'd been swimming for days, stopping to sleep for only a few hours each night. They'd left the palace as fast as they could after Khelefu had been murdered. They'd wanted to be well out of Matali City when their transparensea pearls wore off.

The first night of their journey, they'd sheltered in a sea cave. There, Yazeed had told Neela why he and Mahdi had joined the Praedatori, and she had told him about her nightmare, where it had led her and what she'd learned.

'Yaz? I think we should get going now,' Neela said, rising. 'Yaz? Yaz!' She snapped her fingers in his face.

'Sorry. You ready to go?' he asked, getting up. He still wore a dark expression.

'What is it?' Neela asked, not used to this serious, sombre new brother. 'Where were you?'

'Back at the palace. Watching Portia Volnero send our grand vizier to his death.'

'We can't think about that now. Or Mata-ji and Pita-ji. We have to keep going. Find Mahdi. Warn Sera. Get help.'

'She's going to pay for what she did, Neela. Khelefu was an innocent merman. He didn't deserve to die.'

'Portia's completely insane,' Neela said. 'Her plan can't work. How can she have Lucia crowned regina? Only a mermaid with Merrovingian blood in her veins can sit on the throne of Miromara. There's only one of those, and it's *not* Lucia. Alítheia is going to rip her head off.'

'I guess that's some consolation,' Yazeed said.

'But how can Portia *do* it? That's what I don't get. She knows what will happen. How can she sit by and watch her only daughter be killed by a bloodthirsty monster?' Neela shook her head. 'All this time, Sera and I were sure that Traho had been sent by Admiral Kolfinn, but it turns out

Portia's the one behind all of it.'

'She must've been collaborating with Traho from the beginning,' Yaz said.

'She helped him take Cerulea so he could have access to Miromaran waters to search for a talisman – the same one Sera's searching for right now,' said Neela.

'And in return, Traho's allowing her to make her daughter the ruler of Miromara, and to betroth her to Mahdi, the future ruler of Matali – a ruler Traho already controls. Or thinks he does.'

'In a realm he already controls. And whose waters – and people – he's using to try to find Navi's moonstone. My gods, Yaz, where is it all going to end?' Neela asked.

'Hopefully in Cerulea,' Yaz said.

'What do you mean?'

He told her that the Praedatori had credible information that Miromara's high commander, Vallerio, had been successful in his bid to align with the Kobold goblins.

'If the info I have is good, Vallerio's approaching the city as we speak,' Yaz said.

'Is he strong enough to stop Traho?' Neela asked.

'We don't know. It depends on how many troops the Kobold gave him. And it depends on the dragons. Do the Kobold have any? Because we know the death riders do,' Yazeed replied.

'Where *are* we, anyway? Are we any closer to Cerulea?' asked Neela, worry in her voice.

'We're in Miromara. Specifically, we're in what the goggs

call the Mediterranean. Just like the last time you asked.'

'*Still?* When are we going to hit the Adriatic?'

'By tomorrow morning, if we can keep up a fast pace.'

'We've got to get there in time to warn Sera about the Volneros. Portia's way ahead of us.'

'Yeah, that happens when your ride is a chariot drawn by twelve hammerheads. Best we've been able to do is hitch on the back of a whale shark. When did you learn to speak Whalish, anyway?'

'I didn't. It's the bloodbind,' Neela said. 'At least I still have those powers.'

Yaz looked up. 'I see a giant manta above us,' he said. 'Lay some RaySay on him, will you, Neels? See if we can catch a ride. And catch up to Portia.'

FORTY-FOUR

SERAFINA HEARD the Kobold army before she saw it. Unlike the mer, goblins had feet, and the seafloor shook violently beneath them as they marched.

'Do you hear that, Sera? There must be a million of them!' Coco whispered. 'Just look at that silt cloud rising! I'm heading down to the Corrente with the others. I want to see them up close.'

Serafina grabbed her arm. 'Oh no you don't, Coco. You wait right here. Traho's death riders might be waiting to ambush them.'

Serafina and Coco had hidden themselves behind an outcropping of rock above the Grande Corrente, the main route into Cerulea. From their high vantage point, they would be able to see Vallerio and his troops as they neared the city.

Thousands of mer had gathered at the edges of the Corrente, to watch and wait.

Sera was worried for them. If Traho attacked, they'd be caught right in the middle of the fighting.

'Sera, look!' Coco said, pointing.

The first of the fighters crested a ridge. Broad-backed and

muscular, with thick, powerful limbs, they carried a lethal assortment of weapons – double-bladed axes, long swords, halberds and flails – all cast from Kobold steel. They had the facial features of the Feuerkumpel tribe: two nostrils but no nose, transparent eyes, lipless mouths full of sharp teeth, and ears that were mangled or torn off from fighting.

Sera's uneasiness grew as she remembered the vision she'd had back in the Iele's caves of a goblin attacking her.

'Where's my uncle?' she asked, straining to pick him out. 'I can't see him. Wait ... there he is!' Coco said. 'In the distance!'

Vallerio, magnificent in a shining suit of armour, rode in a silver chariot in the middle of the Kobold. In one hand, he held the reins of four magnificent black hippokamps. With the other, he saluted the Miromarans.

As the people saw him, a tremendous cheer went up. They rushed into the current, happily greeting their liberators.

Serafina kept a fearful eye on the city gates, on nearby rocks and reefs, and on the waters above, expecting Traho's troops to come charging at any second. But they didn't. The waters were eerily quiet.

Vallerio's chariot passed by, and the cheers of the people became deafening.

'Come on! We're missing it all! Let's go!' Coco said. And then she shot off, Abelard zipping after her.

'Coco!' Serafina shouted. 'Come back here!'

But the little merl was too far away to hear her. Serafina had no choice but to follow. She was still disguised as a swashbuckler, but she doubted anyone would have noticed her even if she was dressed in full court regalia. They only wanted to see Vallerio.

'Coco!' she called. 'Coco, where are you?'

As she searched, she saw a small boy push through the crowd and swim up to a goblin. Instead of smiling at the child, the creature kicked him away. A few yards up the Grande Corrente, a mermaid offered another goblin a laurel made of seaweed. He backhanded her.

My uncle doesn't know, Sera told herself. *He doesn't know that his troops are behaving badly. As soon as I can get to him, I'll tell him what they're doing. They can't treat our people this way.*

As she watched the Kobold, row after row of them, continue to march along, she saw a bright bronze tail flash by. 'Coco!' she shouted. She zipped after her and grabbed her arm. 'Don't you do that again!'

'Come on, Sera! Let's follow them!' Coco said, carried away by the excitement.

'No, stick close to me. I'm still wondering about the death riders. Where are they?'

'There! By the gates. It's OK, Sera. See?' Coco said.

Sera looked at the gates. Coco was right. Death riders hadn't been there before, but they were there now, and they weren't poised to attack. They were lining both sides of the current, spears held upright before them in tribute to her uncle.

'They've surrendered!' she said excitedly. 'Traho must know he's outnumbered. He's handing over the city peaceably,

Coco. There won't be any fighting.'

'I told you!' Coco said.

Joy flooded Serafina's heart. She let go of Coco's arm and took her hand. 'Let's go! We've got to get to my uncle!' she said.

The goblins' behaviour still unsettled her, and the presence of any death riders – even peaceable ones – made her uneasy, but what mattered most was that her uncle was home and that the city was his. She pushed her misgivings aside and swam ahead, eager to take part in his triumphant return. Eager to see Mahdi too, and take her place at his side for a public betrothal. When the ceremony was over, she would ask Vallerio if he had any news of her brother. Then she'd show him Neria's Stone and tell him what needed to be done.

She and Coco followed the other Miromarans to the Kolisseo. That was where it had all begun, and that was where it would end.

The fighting was done.

The invaders were routed.

At last, Serafina thought, *it's over*.

FORTY-FIVE

VALLERIO'S BLACK HIPPOKAMPS drew his chariot to the centre of the Kolisseo. He alighted to cheering.

With Coco right behind her, Serafina tried to make her way through the dense crowd to get to him. He needed her for the Promising.

She was rudely stopped by a Kobold with a pike. '*Gå tilbake!*' he growled in a deep voice. *Go back.*

'But I have to see the high commander. He's—'

'*Tilbake!*' the Kobold shouted, thrusting the weapon's steel tip in her face.

Serafina understood him and did as she was told. She and Coco swam into the amphitheatre and sat down. Abelard swam under Coco's seat and peered out from her tail fins. Sera decided that she would wait until the crowd settled and her uncle announced the betrothal. Then she would make her presence known. All around them, people were still cheering for Vallerio, but Serafina noticed that the loudest cheers were coming from the Kobold troops and the death riders. Something had changed. The festive atmosphere of the Grande Corrente was gone. The mer of Cerulea looked wary and mistrustful. Some looked downright scared.

A few rows in front of her, a merman was cheering half-heartedly.

A goblin noticed, and punched him. '*Heie høyere!*' the creature shouted. *Cheer louder!*

Serafina looked around and saw that death riders ringed the top of the Kolisseo, in a dense, tight formation, spears in their hands.

If we wanted to leave, we couldn't, she thought uneasily.

And then she saw something that made her fins prickle. Above the heads of the death riders, flags rippled. They were red with a black circle in their centres – the same flags she'd seen in the Lagoon.

'Something's wrong, Coco,' she whispered. 'Whatever you do, keep smiling and keep cheering.'

'Something's *way* wrong,' Coco said, nodding towards the royal enclosure.

Serafina followed her gaze. In front of the enclosure, resting on a dais, was Merrow's golden crown. Behind it were two ornate thrones. The last time Serafina had been here, they'd been occupied by her mother and Emperor Bilaal. This time, her mother's was empty and Mahdi was sitting in the other one.

His expression was sombre. His hands, resting on the arms of his chair, were clenched. He was dressed in the black uniform of the death riders, and wearing a matching sea-silk turban. In the centre of it was the magnificent Bramaphur Emerald. Serafina recognized it. Bilaal had worn it. Why wasn't Mahdi smiling? Why wasn't he searching the crowd for her?

Sera continued to scan the royal enclosure, hoping for answers. Directly behind Mahdi sat Portia Volnero, resplendently dressed in a gown of gold sea silk. She should have been sitting with the other duchessas of the realm, but was sitting apart in a chair only slightly less ornate than the two thrones. She was smiling serenely. The other duchessas were not.

Sera's feeling that something was wrong grew stronger.

She needed to talk to Mahdi and find out what was going on. Hoping that no goblin was watching her, and that her voice would be drowned out amidst all the cheering, she closed her eyes, bent her head and quietly sang a convoca, calling to him. It failed. She took a deep breath and, summoning all her powers, tried again.

Mahdi . . . Mahdi, it's me! Please answer!

She opened her eyes and looked at him, willing him to hear her. This time, the songspell worked. Mahdi's eyes widened. He looked around, scanning row after row of faces.

And then Serafina heard his voice. Inside her head.

Sera! Is that you?

Yes! I'm here in the Kolisseo. On your left. Midway up.

She risked a small wave. Mahdi saw her. Even from where she was sitting, she could see his face go white.

Sera, get out of here!

Why? What's wrong?

Leave the Kolisseo. Hurry!

I can't! The death riders are blocking the exits.

You're in serious danger. If they find out . . . if they see you . . .

If who finds out? What do you mean?

Before Mahdi could answer, trumpeters blasted a deafening fanfare. The noise broke the convoca.

Vallerio swam to the royal enclosure amidst more cheering. 'Miromarans, thank you!' he shouted, holding up his hands for silence. 'Thank you for this heartfelt welcome! I am glad to be back among you. You have suffered. You have lost your regina. You have lost your royal city. I am here today to restore them to you.'

Cheers went up again, but they were not enthusiastic enough to please the Kobold. A few seats away, a goblin soldier threatened a family. '*Heie, dårer! Før du blir goblin kjøtt!*' he said. *Cheer, fools! Before you become goblin meat!*

'I have made peace with our enemies,' Vallerio continued. 'I have brought friends from the north to help keep this peace and rebuild our city. But that is not enough. Our realm needs a leader if we are to move past the darkness we have endured into a bright new dawn. We all mourn our beloved Isabella, taken from us too soon. We mourn her daughter, Serafina, killed in the attack on the palace.'

'*What?*' Serafina whispered. 'He thinks I'm *dead*?'

She started to rise. Goblins or no goblins, she was going to swim to her uncle now and show him that she most certainly was not dead.

Sera, no! He'll . . . you, don't . . . a voice said inside her head.

It was Mahdi. His words were faint and broken up. She looked at him. He was looking in her direction. Slowly, almost imperceptibly, he shook his head. It was a warning. Sera sat down again.

'I have your new regina here with me today,' Vallerio continued, his voice jubilant. 'I have the one who will lead Miromara out of the pain and sorrow of the past and into a brilliant future!'

Vallerio swept his arm towards the opposite side of the Kolisseo. As Serafina watched, a mermaid appeared in the arched doorway there.

Serafina knew her all too well. She knew the ebony hair, the cobalt eyes, the mocking smile.

It was her old enemy.

Lucia Volnero.

FORTY-SIX

GASPS WENT UP from the crowd. Even fear of the brutal goblins couldn't make the people cheer.

Lucia, stunningly beautiful in a gown the colour of midnight, swam into the Kolisseo. As she did, twenty burly mermen, each wearing armour and carrying a shield and a lava torch, followed her. Serafina knew who the mermen were, and what they did.

'My gods, no. She'll *die*!' she whispered.

Vallerio spoke. 'In accordance with Merrow's decree, and the laws of this realm, we will ask Alítheia to judge this mermaid fit to occupy the throne of Miromara . . .' He paused, then added, '. . . or *not*.'

What is he doing? Serafina wondered, panic-stricken. *She's not a Merrovingian. Alítheia will kill her.*

Serafina remembered Mahdi saying the Volneros might have collaborated with Traho. Was this Vallerio's way of punishing them for it? He'd always been hard and uncompromising towards the realm's enemies, but never vicious. Had he changed?

Surely Portia would stop him. Lucia's mother wouldn't

allow her child to be led to the slaughter. She would beg Vallerio for Lucia's life. They'd been in love once, Serafina remembered. Her words would soften him. But Portia didn't move. She wasn't distraught. She wasn't weeping. She was perfectly fine.

Lucia took her place in the centre of the Kolisseo, and the burly mermen swam to the iron grille covering Alítheia's den.

'Release the anarachna!' Vallerio ordered.

The next few minutes felt like a dream to Serafina – a nightmare in which something horrific was happening, but she couldn't speak or move or do anything at all to stop it. She watched as the terrible bronze spider hissed at Lucia, calling for her blood, for her bones – just as the creature had done to Sera herself only weeks before.

Sera knew that the spider's task was to make certain only blood descendants of Merrow ruled Miromara. Legend had it that when Merrow was close to death, she asked Neria, the sea goddess, and Bellogrim, the god of fire, to forge a creature of bronze to protect the throne from pretenders. As the Kobold were smelting the ore for the monster, Neria slashed Merrow's palm and dripped her blood into molten metal so that the spider would have the blood of Merrow in her veins and know it from imposters' blood.

'Stop this, uncle, *please*,' Sera whispered. 'If she's guilty of something, she deserves a trial, not cold-blooded murder.'

But Vallerio did nothing and Sera, along with everyone else in the Kolisseo, had to watch as Lucia faced Alítheia.

They watched as the Mehterbasi, leader of the Janiçari

guards, handed her his scimitar.

As Lucia drew the blade across her palm.

And as Alítheia bent to drink from the wound.

And then, Sera couldn't watch any more. She bent her head, not wanting to see the spider do her dark work.

'Alítheia!' Vallerio bellowed. 'What say you?'

Serafina clenched her hands, waiting for Alítheia to attack.

But the spider didn't.

Instead, she spoke.

Hail, Lucia, daughter of the blood, rightful heiresssssss to the throne of Miromara . . .

Serafina's head snapped up. '*What?*' she said.

She watched in disbelief as the creature scuttled to the royal enclosure, took Merrow's crown from its dais, and placed it on Lucia's head – the very same crown that she, Serafina, had worn.

This isn't happening, she thought. *It can't be happening. Alítheia was made by the gods themselves. She's infallible.*

Vallerio swam to Lucia. He took her by the arms and kissed her forehead.

Then he turned to the crowd and, smiling triumphantly, said, 'Good people of Miromara! I give you your new regina . . . Lucia Volnero . . . *my daughter.*'

FORTY-SEVEN

SERAFINA WAS REELING. It all made sickening sense now. How could she not have seen it? Lucia, with her jet-black hair, deep-blue eyes and silver scales, looked exactly like Vallerio. Like Isabella too, for that matter. She looked more like a true Merrovingian than Serafina did.

No wonder Vallerio had never married, and no wonder Portia had. She'd married a man who looked like Vallerio only weeks after Regina Artemesia, Sera's grandmother, had forbade their marriage. Because she was carrying Vallerio's child. That man – Sejanus Adaro – had died soon after Lucia's birth. Had Portia and Vallerio continued their affair in secret all these years?

The Kobold had once again bullied the crowd into cheering, and Vallerio once again held up his hands to quiet them.

'Yes, it's true, good people. Lucia Volnero is my daughter, conceived with her mother, the duchessa, nineteen years ago. She is a Merrovingian, as Alítheia has confirmed. Lucia wished to keep the truth of her parentage a secret and to spend her life in quiet service to the realm. But since we have lost our regina and our principessa, and since only a mermaid of Merrovingian blood may sit upon the Miromaran throne, she has bravely and selflessly decided to offer herself as your ruler.'

Exultant beside her father, Lucia smiled her barracuda smile.

Vallerio held up his hands for quiet again. 'In accordance with Merrow's decrees, Lucia will now continue to the casting, the second part of her Dokimí, by performing the required songspell.'

Lucia swam forward and began to songcast. Serafina expected her to stumble, to make mistakes. The casting was torturously difficult. She herself had spent the better part of a year practising it. But Lucia didn't stumble. Not once. Her mastery of magic was excellent. Her singing was flawless. Her beautiful voice was beguiling.

How can that be? Serafina wondered. How can she sing Merrow's songspell so perfectly when she's never even practised it? With a chill, she realised the answer: Lucia *had* practised. She'd prepared for this moment for a very long time.

When Lucia finished the songspell, the amphitheatre erupted. The cheers were deafening; the applause was long. As before, the most enthusiastic responses came from the Kobold and the death riders.

'Thank you! Thank you, good people!' Vallerio shouted, as the noise subsided. 'To ensure the stability of the realm and the continuity of Merrow's line, Lucia will now undertake her betrothal, during which she will recite vows with her intended and promise to give this realm a daughter.'

Vallerio turned to the royal enclosure and looked at Mahdi. 'Your Grace, if you would join us . . .'

FORTY-EIGHT

MAHDI ROSE FROM HIS THRONE.

'You can't do this,' Serafina whispered. She rose from her seat too.

'Sera, don't!' Coco said, pulling her back down.

'Coco, I have to. I—'

. . . don't move . . . please . . . in danger . . .

That was Mahdi. He was inside her head again.

Mahdi, you can't do this . . . she said to him.

SERA, YOU SIT DOWN RIGHT NOW!

The voice was so loud, Serafina thought it would shatter her eardrums.

Neela? she said weakly, when the pain subsided.

You heard me? Oh, thank gods! I didn't know if my convoca would work.

Heard you? You nearly blew my head apart! Where are you?

Here in the Kolisseo. Stay where you are, Sera. Do. Not. Move.

But I have to tell my uncle—

Nothing. You tell him nothing. You do nothing.

But it's all a huge mistake! My uncle's doing this for the sake of the realm. *He brokered a truce with the death riders. He only put Lucia on the throne because he thinks I'm dead. Now he's going to betroth her to Mahdi. If I just go to him, if I tell him . . .*

If you move out of your seat, you die.

That was a new voice, but Serafina recognized it.

Yazeed? she said. *What are you talking about? Why do I have to . . .*

Stay put until this is over. Then meet us outside the Kolisseo.

I can't watch this, Yaz. I can't.

You don't have a choice. Portia . . . back from . . . death riders . . . and then . . .

Yazeed was breaking up.

Please, Sera . . . do not move.

That was Neela. Then the convoca faded and she heard no more.

Serafina did as they asked, though it nearly killed her. She sat in her seat, stared straight ahead and watched the merman she loved declare his love for another.

Mahdi took Lucia's hand. He looked into her eyes. He smiled at her. Said his vows. And tore out Serafina's heart.

But even as she was blinking back tears, Serafina noticed something odd – Mahdi was wearing a yellow anemone on his black jacket. As she stared at it, straining to see it clearly over the distance between them, she realized it was the one he'd worn at their betrothal. It was vivid; its tiny tentacles were moving. He'd obviously tended it and kept it alive. She saw something else too. He kept tugging at his ear. At a gold hoop that dangled from his lobe.

That's strange, she thought. *He wasn't wearing an earring at Carlo and Elena's. He gave his earring to that mother in the Lagoon so she could sell it to buy food for her children. Back when he was Blu.*

As the ceremony finished, and Mahdi kissed Lucia's cheek, another cheer went up, started – yet again – by the soldiers.

Do you recognize it? Mahdi suddenly said. Inside Sera's head. *It's the ring you gave me at our Promising. It was Carlo's. I've had to take it off my hand, but I found a way to keep wearing it.*

Oh, Mahdi . . .

Don't be upset, Sera. Please. Not over this. It means nothing to me.

Then why are you doing it?

To stay close to them. To stop them. Traho, the Volneros . . .

My uncle too?

I don't know. I don't know if he really thinks you're dead or not. Be careful of him, Sera.

You belong to her now, to Lucia.

No, I don't. You know that.

A memory came to her of their betrothal. They had signed the parchment. She'd started towards Elena's kitchen and Mahdi had lagged behind to talk to the justice of the seas.

That's why you questioned Rafael about the ceremony, isn't it? Why you asked him if the betrothal was binding even if one of us was to marry another.

Yes. I was worried Portia and Lucia were plotting something like this. That's why you're in such danger, Sera. Portia knows the laws too. If she finds out about us – about you and me – she'll do anything she can to break our vow. Anything. Do you understand?

Sera did.

You mean she'll kill me.

Yes. That's why you have to get out of here. Leave Cerulea. Get as far away from the Volneros as you can and don't come back.

I can't do that, Mahdi. This is my home. These are my people.

The convoca began to fade.

. . . have to go . . . please be care— . . . love you . . .

Will I ever see you again?

She listened for his answer.

But it never came.

FORTY-NINE

'WE GOTTA MAKE WAKE,' Yazeed said quietly, as he swam up behind Serafina. 'If Portia Volnero hears you're in the city, you're chum.'

Serafina turned around. She threw her arms around Neela, and then Yazeed, and then introduced them to Coco. They were all outside the Kolisseo in the middle of a surging crowd of soldiers and civilians. The royal party had already left for the palace.

'Yazeed, I'm so glad you're all right. Neels, what are you doing here? You're supposed to be safe and sound at home,' Sera said.

'Home's not safe any more. Or sound. It's not even home.'

'What do you mean?'

Neela told her that Portia had taken Matali City. Yaz explained that she'd also plundered the Matalin vaults and murdered the grand vizier, and that they'd hightailed it to Miromara to warn Sera about her.

'Plus, that thing we need? I got it,' Neela said, glancing around at the soldiers.

Sera understood. There were too many enemies around to

speak freely. 'That's awesome, Neela. Likewise.'

'Excellent,' Neela whispered. 'Have you seen any prison camps, Sera? Has Traho set any up here?'

'Camps?' Sera echoed.

'Save it for later,' Yazeed said. 'We got here in the nick of time to find you,' he said. 'And now we've got to get out again. Let's go.'

'I can't, Yaz. Not yet. I have to get Coco to safety first,' Serafina said.

'Principessa,' a voice whispered.

Serafina turned around.

'Niccolo!' she said, recognizing her friend and fellow resistance fighter.

'Smile at me as if I'm an old friend,' Niccolo said, smiling like an idiot himself. 'And keep swimming, as if we're going back to our old neighbourhood. Don't stop. Two Kobold soldiers are watching us.'

They all did as he instructed.

'Busted,' Yaz said grimly.

'I don't think so,' Niccolo said. 'The principessa looks so different now. I only recognized her because I've seen her in her swashbuckler clothes. And because she has Coco with her. Are you heading to headquarters?'

'Yes,' Serafina said.

'I thought so. That's why I came over. Forget about it. It was just raided by the Kobold. We set off a bomb under the death riders' barracks last week.'

'That was you guys?' Yaz said admiringly. 'Nice work!'

Niccolo continued. 'Yeah, it was, but now Traho wants revenge. The goblins are going house to house, looking for members of the . . . er, our friends. Most of us made it out, but Fossegrim, Alessandra and Domenico didn't.'

Coco bit her lip. She squeezed Serafina's hand painfully. Abelard, sensing her upset, swam around her in quick, worried circles.

'Me . . . our friends . . . we're all swimming separately to the pit – the refuse dump north of the city. We're going to meet in the kelp forest on its western edge. We'll wait until it's dark, then head for a new safe house in the azzuros, the blue hills. You must join us. All of you. It's too dangerous for you here.'

Serafina looked at Neela and Yazeed. They nodded.

'Thank you, Niccolo,' she said. 'We'll see you there.'

As soon as he left, Serafina told Yaz how to get to the kelp forest.

'Wait a minute, why are you telling me?' he asked. 'You're coming with us.'

'I'm going to meet you there. There's something I have to do first. Do you have any transparensea pearls?'

'Why do you need—' Yazeed started to say. Then he shook his head. 'No way, Sera. Are you out of your mind?'

'Give me a pearl, Yaz. I have to know if he's part of this.'

'Sorry, fresh out.'

'I'm going anyway.'

Yaz swore, but he gave her a pearl.

'I'll meet you in the forest,' Serafina said. 'In one hour.'

'One hour,' Yazeed said. 'Or I'm coming after you.'

'Please, Sera . . .' Coco said, her eyes large and fearful.

'I'll be there,' Sera said confidently, smiling at her. 'I'll make it. I promise.'

As Neela led the child away, Serafina's smile faded. She grabbed Yazeed's hand and put something into it. He looked down and saw that he was holding a necklace with a big blue diamond in its centre.

'Give it to Neela if I don't,' she said.

FIFTY

SERAFINA, STILL VISIBLE, cautiously swam into the ruined stateroom of Cerulea's palace.

She'd taken a secret passageway from the stables to get here. It was a risky move, but she didn't have a choice. Transparensea pearls often wore off without notice, and she didn't want to activate the one Yaz had given her until she was well inside the palace. It was an enormous place and she knew it could take time to find her uncle.

Sneaking by two grooms and three death riders to get inside the stables had taken some doing. Luckily, they'd been so busy drinking posidonia wine in celebration of Lucia's Dokimí that they hadn't noticed Sera as she'd crossed the exercise yard, swimming low behind bales of sea hay.

Now, as she crossed the stateroom, she looked at the gaping hole where its east wall had once stood. A mournful current swept through it. Anemones and seaweeds grew along its broken edges. She swam to the throne, then bent down to touch the floor near it. Head bowed, she stayed there for quite some time, remembering her mother. Then she rose and backed away from it.

As she did, a movement behind the throne startled her. She spun towards it, dagger out, then realized she was seeing herself in the floor-to-ceiling mirrors on the wall.

For a moment, she worried that Rorrim might be lurking behind the network of cracks in the silver glass, or, worse yet, the eyeless man. But the mirrors were empty.

She took the transparensea pearl out of her pocket and cast it. Now all she had to do was figure out where her uncle was. His living quarters were in the palace's north wing, so she decided to start there. To get to them, she had to swim past her mother's presence chamber into the north corridor. As she approached the chamber, she saw that its door was closed. But voices were carrying through it.

Careful not to make any noise, she pressed an ear to the door. The voices belonged to Vallerio and Portia. But she couldn't make out what they were saying.

Sera quickly swam through a hole in the stateroom wall and around the side of the palace to see if the presence chamber's tall windows were open. Luckily, one was. She squeezed through the opening, and swam silently into a corner to listen and watch.

'If the people knew . . . if they ever find out . . .' her uncle was saying.

'The people are fools. No one has any idea you were behind the invasion. You covered your wake well. You warned Isabella that Ondalina would wage war. Kolfinn inadvertently helped us by breaking the permutavi.'

'I still don't know why he did it,' Vallerio said.

'Nor do I. And I don't care. It was a real piece of luck for us. So was your begging Isabella to declare war on the very day of the attack. The councillors who survived will remember your words and tell the people how wise you were.'

'But how were the payments made? If they find that gold is missing from the vaults . . .'

'*He* paid Traho. As promised. And the councillors will have no problem paying the Kobold, because they saw how you used them to *liberate* the city,' Portia said, laughing.

Sera wondered who this *he* was.

'*That* was a stroke of genius, my darling,' Portia continued. 'Making it look as though you and the Kobold frightened Traho into surrendering. Now that the beasts are here, they can root out the resistance for us. Miromara is ours. Matali is ours. Soon Qin will be too. Mfeme is on his way there as we speak. Atlantica will fall next, then Ondalina, and finally the Freshwaters. Soon our daughter will rule all the waters of the world!'

'Nineteen years,' Vallerio said. 'That's how long I've waited for this. How long I've waited to make you mine. To be the family we always should have been. To put our daughter on the throne.'

Serafina put a hand against a wall to steady herself. She felt as though she'd been gutted.

It wasn't Admiral Kolfinn who'd ordered Traho to attack Miromara. And it wasn't Kolfinn who'd collaborated with the gogg Mfeme. All this time, it was Vallerio, *her own uncle*. He hadn't escaped to the north to bring liberating troops back

CHAPTER 50

293

to Cerulea. He went there for reinforcements – for goblin thugs who would make sure that no one challenged Lucia's coronation. And he and Portia weren't going to stop with Miromara; they planned to invade *every* mer realm. As soon as she was in the azzuros, and the safe house, she would warn the others. Astrid too. Astrid *had* been telling the truth; Ondalina had nothing to do with the invasion.

Portia picked up a bottle of posidonia wine on a table and filled two glasses. She handed one to Vallerio. 'Things are going so well. Even better than I'd hoped,' she said, touching her glass to his. 'He's pleased, and why wouldn't he be? He has the black pearl, and now Mahdi's found the blue diamond for him.'

Serafina's heart nearly stopped. Who in the gods' names was *he*? She had to find out. Whoever this person was had Orfeo's talisman. She and her friends would have to get it from him.

'He'll want the other talismans too,' Vallerio said. 'They were his price for helping us. We mustn't keep him waiting.'

'We won't,' Portia said. 'The camps are full. The prisoners are working day and night to find the talismans.'

Camps? Prisoners? What is she talking about? Serafina wondered. Then she remembered that Neela had mentioned something similar. Was Traho taking people prisoner and forcing them to work?

'All obstacles are being overcome, Vallerio,' Portia continued, 'and all threats to our power eliminated. That fool Mahdi is on our side and will continue to be as long as we keep giving him money. Bilaal and Ahadi are dead. Aran and Sananda are our hostages. Bastiaan is dead. Happily, Isabella is too.'

'Happily?' Vallerio echoed. 'It's not a happy thing, Portia. She was my sister. I wish it could have ended differently.'

Portia had no such sentiments. 'Come, Vallerio, this is no time for regrets. What we've done, we've done for the good of the realm.'

'She was only following Merrow's decree, that only a daughter of a daughter can rule Miromara, not a daughter of a son,' Vallerio said, gazing into his glass.

Portia snorted. 'Of course she was! That was one of Isabella's so-called strong points – slavishly following Merrow's absurd decrees. It's time for some new decrees – *our* decrees. Handed down to the people by *our* daughter.'

Vallerio nodded. 'You're right, my love. Of course you are.'

Portia smiled. 'You mustn't lose your nerve. Not now. We're almost there. Soon, nothing will be able to stop us.'

'Is there any news of Desiderio?' Vallerio asked. 'Of Serafina?'

'We have death riders tracking Desiderio. They haven't found him yet, but they will. As for Serafina, she's proving to be tougher to capture than I anticipated. But sooner or later, her luck will run out. I tell anyone who asks that she's dead, and soon she will be. The death riders have their orders and they'll carry them out. Our daughter's rule is not assured as long as Isabella's daughter lives.'

There was a knock on the door.

'Enter!' Vallerio said.

A servant swam into the room. 'Your Graces,' he said, 'the betrothal dinner is about to begin.'

Vallerio offered Portia his arm and they left the presence chamber together. As the door closed behind them, Serafina felt an overwhelming urge to destroy the room, to smash everything Vallerio and Portia had touched. She fought it down. Only fools alerted enemies to their presence.

She swam back out of the window, and headed for the kelp forest and her friends. Yazeed was right. They had to get out of Cerulea. The sooner, the better.

As Sera swam, she quietly sang a lamentatio, a mer funeral dirge.

She had just lost another member of her family.

FIFTY-ONE

SERAFINA LEANED HER head back and stared up through the fronds of the kelp forest. Night was falling. She could see the rising moon's pale rays on the water.

'"Happily." That's what she said. "Happily", Isabella is dead . . . As she smiled and sipped her wine.'

Her voice caught. Coco twined her arms around her waist. Neela kissed her cheek. Yaz took her hand.

'Oh, Sera,' Neela said. 'I'm so, so sorry.'

Finally, when she was able to speak again, Sera said, 'Somebody has a talisman. Orfeo's black pearl. I don't know who he is, only that Vallerio and Portia are helping him. Yaz, Neela, do you know? And do you know anything about labour camps and prisoners?'

Neela told her everything that had happened to her after they'd parted company in the Incantarium.

Sera was sickened by her description of the labour camps. 'How could they do such a thing? How could my uncle?' she asked. 'Nothing can explain it. Not even his nineteen years of pain.'

'We've got to find out who this *he* is,' Yazeed said,

releasing her hand.

'We've got to get the black pearl from him,' said Serafina.

'We've got to get out of here first,' Neela said.

The kelp they were hiding in grew so densely that they had to float upright in it. They could not sit down and stretch their tails out.

'Who are we still missing?' Yazeed asked.

'Bartolomeo and Luca,' came the reply from further in the kelp. It was Niccolo.

'We wait for another half hour, then we head for the safe house,' Yaz said.

Serafina felt a thump. Coco had nodded off, floating upright. The child's heavy head had fallen on her shoulder.

'I'm going to swim a little further into the forest,' she whispered, picking Coco up. 'See if I can find a place where she can stretch out. I won't go too far. Give a whistle when the others get here.'

Yazeed nodded and Serafina pushed her way through the tall, leafy stalks. Abelard followed her. A few minutes later she came across a small clearing – only it wasn't empty, as she'd hoped. It contained two long earthen mounds. Each had broken bits of bronze statuary lying on top of it. She saw a torso on one. A hand. A plaque. Fins. Part of a tail.

She bent over and carefully lowered Coco to the ground. The little merl woke instantly. 'What's going on?' she asked fearfully. 'Death riders?'

'Shh, Coco, it's OK. I was just trying to find a place for you to sleep,' Serafina said.

Coco blinked at the mounds. 'What are those? Graves?' she asked.

'I think so,' said Serafina.

She swam closer and saw that the broken pieces had been arranged in an orderly fashion, with the tail fins at the bottom of the mounds, and faces at the top. She leaned over to have a look at the bronze faces, and realized, with a gasp, that she knew them. They were the faces of her parents.

Fresh sorrow welled up inside Sera. She dropped to the seafloor, wondering how it was possible that her heart could break over and over again and still keep on beating.

The pieces scattered across the graves, she thought. *They're from statues that used to stand in Cerulea.* She recognized one of her mother. It had stood in a square in the fabra and had been very good likeness of her.

Hand-lettered markers at the heads of the graves proclaimed the occupants to be the Regina Isabella and her consort, Principe Bastiaan. MAY YOU REST IN STILL WATERS was written under each of their names.

As Sera traced the letters of her father's name, she heard an agitated rustling in the kelp stalks. A few seconds later, an angry old merman with a rusty spear stormed into the clearing. He looked like a stickleback – grey on top and orange underneath, with short, spiky fins.

'What are you doing here?' he asked crossly, pointing his spear at her.

'We're paying our respects,' Serafina said.

'Oh,' he said, lowering the spear. 'Well, that's all right,

then. I was worried you was some of them filthy marauders who killed the regina and her husband.'

'No,' Serafina said. 'We didn't even know their graves were here. Who buried them?'

'I did. Name's Frammento. I live just over there.' He hooked a thumb behind him. 'I make my living picking the dump and selling what I find. Found a bit more than I bargained for one night – two bodies wrapped up in a blood-soaked carpet.'

Sera flinched at his words, but quickly masked her grief. She didn't want the old merman to guess who she was.

'They was Isabella and Bastiaan,' Frammento continued. 'Traho's thugs must've wanted to get rid of 'em all quiet-like so none of their subjects would have a place to gather. I was heartbroken when I found 'em. Mad as hell too. I carried 'em away and gave 'em a proper burial.'

'That was very good of you,' Sera said, more grateful to the merman than she'd ever be able to say.

'It's not much. Wish I could've done more. I had nothing to fancy the graves up with at first, but then Traho started pulling down statues and I was able to collect some pieces and bring 'em here. No one knew about the graves at first, but then one or two people happened on 'em and word spread. More and more come to pay their respects now. I'll leave you in peace to pay yours.' He tipped his cap and then he was gone.

Coco, who was peering closely at the graves, said, 'Oh, no. Sera, look at that.' She pointed to a small pile of rubble near the top of Isabella's grave.

It was the crown that had rested on the statue's head. It had been made not from gold or silver, but from red coral branches – a gift from the sea.

'It must've cracked and fallen off when Frammento put the head here,' Coco said as Abelard nosed the pieces. 'I'll fix it. I'm really good at canta prax. I was always breaking Ellie's stuff and I always fixed it before she found out.' She sat down on the ground and started to fit the pieces back together.

Serafina barely heard her. She was looking at her mother's beautiful face. Strong and serene, it gazed out at her now. She touched its cold cheek.

'The resistance is so brave, but it's weak and scattered, Mum,' she whispered. 'Safe houses are being raided. There isn't enough to eat. Some of our people are very sick. So much needs to be done. Here in Cerulea against Vallerio and Portia. Out in the seas against Abbadon. I don't know where to start.'

Her mother always had the answer. And Sera desperately needed it now. But the bronze face was silent.

'Got it!' Coco suddenly said. The coral crown was whole again. She lifted it off the seafloor, carried it to Serafina and placed it on her head.

'This was Isabella's crown but she's gone, so it's yours. You're the regina now. Not Lucia,' she said. She threw her arms around Serafina's neck and hugged her tightly.

Sera hugged Coco back, grateful for the little merl's faith in her, and for her constant love. As Sera released Coco, her eyes fell on the plaque that had adorned the base of Isabella's statue. She could see the words incised upon it. She knew them well. They had been the motto of Merrow, and of every Merrovingian ruler since.

The love of the sea folk is my strength.

That was it. The answer she needed. It had been there all along.

She heard Thalassa's voice now: *a ruler's greatest power comes from her heart – from the love she bears her subjects, and the love they bear her.*

Vrăja's: *nothing is more powerful than love.*

And Elena's: *love's the greatest magic of all.*

Love was Merrow's greatest power. And her mother's. It would be hers too. She would fight to the death for her people. She would take her city, and her realm, back. She would stop the evil in the Southern Sea. Not with terror, cruelty and hatred, like Traho. But with love.

'Thank you, Mum,' she whispered.

'Come on,' she said to Coco, as she rose. 'Let's go. It's time we got to the safe house and got ourselves organized again. I have a resistance to lead.'

As the two swam off to join the others, Serafina's back was straight, her head was high.

There was a dangerous new light in her eyes.

FIFTY-TWO

IN THE EAST CHINA SEA, a large trawler moved slowly through the water. Rafe Iaoro Mfeme was sitting in a chair on the ship's aft deck, watching the last rays of the sun paint the sky. His hair was covered by a baseball cap. His eyes were hidden behind sunglasses. A flawless black pearl dangled from a chain around his neck. His right hand was bloodied.

Across from him was a mermaid bound to a chair with rope. Blood dripped off her chin. Her head lolled on her chest. One of her black plaits had come loose.

Her sword rested on top of a table. Her bag had been torn apart. Its contents lay strewn across the deck – a few cowries, some transparensea pebbles, a water apple, and letter tiles from a terragogg word game.

'This is getting tedious,' Mfeme said, turning to her.

The mermaid lifted her head and spat out a mouthful of blood. Her lip was split. One of her eyes was swollen shut.

'Sorry to hear you say that,' Ling said. 'I'm having a fabulous time.'

Mfeme cracked his knuckles. 'I'll ask you again: where is the talisman?'

'And I'll tell you again: I have no idea,' Ling said.

'Do you think I'm joking? I'll cut your ears off and throw them to the sharks.'

'Good. I won't have to listen to you any more.'

Mfeme grabbed Ling's hair and yanked her head back.

'There are all kinds of pain, Ling. There's the kind you're feeling right now, but there's a worse kind too. The kind you're going to feel when I find your father, haul him up on this boat and cut off *his* ears, all because you won't tell me what I want to know.'

'Good luck with that. My father's dead. I don't *know* where the talisman is. Even if I did, I wouldn't tell you.'

Mfeme let go of her. 'I'd like to kill you. I'd like that very much.'

'Then do it and stop wasting my time.'

'Unfortunately, I can't. You're valuable to me and you know it. You're smart, Ling, but you're not smart enough. All this time, and you still have no idea who you're dealing with, do you?'

'Actually, I do. You're Traho's boat boy. His gogg lackey.'

'I'm afraid you have that the wrong way around,' Mfeme said.

He removed his sunglasses.

Ling gasped. His eyes had no irises, no white. They were entirely black.

Mfeme swept his hand through the air and her letter tiles slid across the deck. As Ling watched, they spelled out his name.

RAFE IAORO MFEME

Then slowly the tiles rearranged themselves.

'*No!*' Ling said in horror, as she saw what they spelled. 'It *can't* be. You're dead. You've *been* dead for four thousand years!'

I AM ORFEO FEAR ME

ACKNOWLEDGEMENTS

THIS PAGE IS where you thank the people who helped you make a book, and once again, I'd like to thank my wonderful family, and the awesome team at Disney, for their support and enthusiam for *Rogue Wave* and the whole Waterfire Saga. But there's one person in particular I'd like to thank here – the person who first introduced me to my mermaid friends: my longtime agent, Steve Malk.

An agent's role in a writer's life is huge – he's a business partner, confidante, cheerleader, adviser, and if you're as lucky as I've been, a friend. I can't adequately thank Steve for all he's done for me in these few lines, but I'm going to try anyway. Here goes.

Thank you, Steve, for your insight, wise counsel, and constant good humour – all of which I prize so highly. Thanks for loving music and chocolate as much as I do. I'd split my last ginger-sesame-wasabi truffle with you, and I know you'd do the same for me. Thanks for talking me off the ledge more times than I can count. Thanks for caring enough to always tell me what's wrong with a manuscript as well as what's right. Thanks for your genuine and enduring love of children's books. Most of all, thanks for helping me make my living doing what I love. My whole life, I've wanted to be a writer. Because of the hard work you do on my behalf, I get to be.

GLOSSARY

Abbadon an immense monster, created by Orfeo, then defeated and caged in the Antarctic waters

Abelard Coco's sand shark

Acqua Guerrieri Miromaran soldiers

Agora public square

Ahadi, Empress the previous female ruler of Matali; Madhi's mother

Alítheia a twelve-foot, venomous sea spider made out of bronze combined with drops of Merrow's blood. Bellogrim, the blacksmith god, forged her, and the sea goddess Neria breathed life into her to protect the throne of Miromara from any pretenders.

Alma the woman Orfeo loved; when she died, he went mad with grief

Amah nursemaid

Amarrefe Mei Foo a pirate who attacked the *Demeter*, looking to steal the infanta's blue diamond

Apă piatră an old Romanian protection songspell that raises water and hardens it into a shield

Aran, Emperor the current male ruler of Matali; Neela's father

Armando Contorini duca di Venezia, leader of the Praedatori (a.k.a. Karkharias, the Shark)

Askari members of Kora's personal guard in Kandina (*Askara*, sing.)

Astrid teenage daughter of Kolfinn, ruler of Ondalina

Atlantica the mer domain in the Atlantic Ocean

Atlantis an ancient island paradise in the Mediterranean peopled with the ancestors of the mer. Six mages ruled the island wisely and well: Orfeo, Merrow, Sycorax, Navi, Pyrra, and Nyx. When the island was destroyed, Merrow saved the Atlanteans by calling on Neria to give them fins and tails.

Ava teenage mermaid from the Amazon River; she is blind but able to sense things

Baba Vrăja the elder leader – or obârşie – of the Iele, river witches

Baby Ava's guide piranha

Baltazaar first minister of finance from the start of Merrow's reign

Barrens of Thira the waters around Atlantis, where the Opafago live

Bastiaan, Principe Consorte Regina Isabella's husband and Serafina's father; a son of the noble House of Kaden from the Sea of Marmara

Becca a teenage mermaid from Atlantica

Bedrieër one of three trawlers that Rafe Mfeme owns

Bella Italian for *beautiful*

Bengalese Bluefin Dragon gentle, calm, good for pulling

wagons and carriages

Bilaal, Emperor   the previous male ruler of Matali; Mahdi's father

Bing-bang   a Matalin candy

Bioluminescent   a sea creature that emits its own glow

Black Fins   members of a Cerulean resistance group headquartered in the Ostrokon

Bloodbind   a spell in which blood from different mages is combined to form an unbreakable bond and allow them to share abilities

Bloodsong   blood drawn from one's heart that contains memories and allows them to become visible to others

Blu, Grigrio, and Verde   three Praedatori who help Neela and Serafina escape Traho

Brack   a frothy ale brewed from sour sea apples

Buono   Italian for *good*

Caballabong   a game involving hippokamps, similar to the human game polo

Canta magus   one of the Miromaran magi, the keeper of magic (*magi*, pl.)

Canta malus   darksong, a poisonous gift to the mer from Morsa, in mockery of Neria's gifts

Canta mirus   special song

Canta prax   a plainsong spell

Cara   Italian for *dear one*

Carceron   the prison on Atlantis. The lock could only be opened by all six talismans. It is now located somewhere in the Southern Sea.

Cerulea   the royal city in Miromara, where Serafina lives

Ceto   leader of the Clan Rorqual, humpback whales

Chillawonda   a Matalin candy

Clio   Serafina's hippokamp

Commoveo   a songspell that can be used to push objects

Conch   a shell in which recorded information is stored

Confuto   a canta prax spell that makes humans sound insane when they talk about seeing merpeople

Convoca   a songspell that can be used for summoning and communicating with people

Corrente Largo   the Lagoon's main thoroughfare

Cosima   a young girl from Serafina's court; nickname: Coco

Council of the Six Waters   a meeting of representatives from all of the water realms

Currensea   mer money; gold trocii (*trocus*, sing.), silver drupe, copper cowries; gold doubloons are black market currensea

Daímonas tis Morsa   demon of Morsa

Dankling   a person's deepest fears; Rorrim Drol feeds on them

Darksong   a powerful canta malus spell taht causes harm; legal to use against enemies during wartime

Death riders   Traho's soldiers, who ride on black hippokamps

Demeter   the ship that Maria Theresa, an infanta of Spain, was sailing on when it was lost in 1582 en route to France

Desiderio   Serafina's older brother

Dokimí   Greek word for *trial*; a ceremony in which the heir to the Miromaran throne has to prove that she is a true descendant of Merrow by spilling blood for Alítheia, the sea spider. She must then songcast, make her betrothal vows, and swear to one day give the realm a daughter.

Draca the language spoken by dragons

Duchi of Venezia created by Merrow to protect the seas and its creatures from terragoggs

Eelish the language spoken by eels

Ekelshmutz one of the four goblin tribes

Elysia capital of Atlantis

Eveksion the god of healing

Fabra marketplace

Feuerkumpel goblin miners, one of the Kobold tribes, who channel magma from deep seams under the North Sea in order to obtain lava for lighting and heating

Filomena Duca Armando's cook

Fossegrim one of the Miromaran magi, the liber magus, the keeper of knowledge

Fragor lux a songspell to cast a light bomb (*frag*, abbr.)

Freshwaters the mer domain that encompasses rivers, lakes, and ponds

Ghost ship a shipwreck entwined with the life force of a human who died onboard; it does not rot or rust

Great Abyss a deep chasm in Qin where Sycorax's talisman is believed to be located, and where Ling's father disappeared while exploring

Hagarla queen of the Razormouth dragons

Hall of Sighs a long corridor in Vadus, the mirror realm, whose walls are covered in mirrors; every mirror has a corresponding one in the terragogg world

Haraka   a form of marital arts practiced by the Askari

Hippokamps   creatures that are half horse, half serpent, with snake-like eyes

Höllebläser   goblin glassblowers, one of the Kobold tribes

Horok   the Keeper of Souls in Atlantis, who took the dead to the underworld, holding each soul in a white pearl

Iele   river witches

Illuminata   a songspell to create light

Illusio   a spell to create a disguise

Incantarium   the room where the incanta – river witches – keep Abbadon at bay through chanting and waterfire

Iron   repels magic

Isabella, La Serenissima Regina   Miromara's ruler; Serafina's mother

Janiçari   Regina Isabella's personal guard

Janteeshapta   a Matalin candy

Jua Maji   a village in Kandina

Kandina   a region in the western part of Matali, near the Madagascar Basin, ruled by Kora

Kandinian   from Kandina; the language spoken in Kandina

Kanjaywhoohoo   a Matalin candy

Karkharias   'the Shark', or leader of the Praedatori

Kengee   sun ray in Kandinian; the symbol of Jua Maji

Khelefu   the grand vizier of Matali

Kiongozi   Kora's general

Kiraat   Matali's medica magus

Kobold   North Sea goblin tribes

Kolfinn   Admiral of the artic region, Ondalina

Kolisseo   a huge open-water stone theatre in Miromara that dates back to Merrow's time

Kootagulla   a Matalin pastry with many layers

Kora   the mermaid ruler of the Matalin region of Kandina, as a vassal of the emperor; leader of the Askari

Kuweka mwanga, dada yangu   Kandinian for *Keep the light, my sister*

Kyr   Neria's youngest son, whom Merrow saved from a shark attack

La Sirena Lácrima   *The Mermaid Tear*, the blue diamond given to Maria Theresa, an infanta of Spain, on her sixteenth birthday

Lagoon   the waters off the human city of Venice, forbidden to merfolk

Lagoona   a resident of the Lagoon

Lakshadwa Blackclaw dragon   one of the many types of dragons that breed in Matali and are the main source of the realm's wealth; huge and powerful and used by the military

Lava globe   a light source, lit by magma mined and refined into white lava by the Feuerkumpel

Liber magus   one of the Miromaran magi, the keeper of knowledge

Ling   a teenage mermaid from the realm of Qin; she is an omnivoxa

Lucia Volnero   one of Serafina's ladies-in-waiting; a

member of the Volnero, a noble family as old – and nearly as powerful – as the Merrovingia

Madagascar Basin   where the Razormouth dragons breed; in western Matali, near Kandina

Maggiore   Italian for *bigger*

Mahdi   crown prince of Matali; Serafina's betrothed; cousin of Yazeed and Neela

Maria Theresa   an infanta of Spain who was sailing to France on the *Demeter* in 1582 when it was attacked by a pirate, Amarreffe Mei Foo

Markus Traho, Captain   leader of the death riders

Mata-ji   Matalin term for *mother*

Matali   the mer realm in the Indian Ocean. It started as a small outpost off the Seychelle Islands and grew into an empire that stretches west to the African waters, north to the Arabian Sea and the Bay of Bengal, and east to the shores of Malaysia and Australia.

Matalin   from Matali

Medica magus   mer equivalent of doctor

Meerteufel   one of four goblin tribes

Mehterbaşi   leader of the Janiçari

Mēērē dila, mērī ātmā   Matalin for *My heart, my soul*

Merl   Mermish equivalent of *girl*

Mermaid Tear   another name for Neria's Stone, the blue diamond that Neria gave to Merrow

Mermish   the common language of the sea people

Merrovingia   descendants of Merrow

Merrovingia regere hic   *The Merrovingia rule here*

Merrow   a great mage, one of the six rulers of Atlantis, and Serafina's ancestor. First ruler of the merpeople; songspell originated with her, and she decreed the Dokimí.

Merrow's Progress   Ten years after the destruction of Atlantis, Merrow made a journey to all of the waters of the world, scouting out safe places for the merfolk to colonize

Mgeni anakuja   Kandinian for *A stranger is approaching*

Miromara   the realm where Serafina comes from; an empire that spans the Mediterranean Sea, the Adriatic, Aegean, Baltic, Black, Ionian, Ligurian, and Tyrrhenean Seas, the Seas of Azov and Marmara, the Straits of Gibraltar, the Dardanelles, and the Bosphorus

Molluska   the language spoken by octopi

Moonstone   Navi's talisman; silvery blue and the size of an albatross's egg, with an inner glow

Morsa   an ancient scavenger goddess, whose job it was to take away the bodies of the dead. She angered Neria by practicing necromancy. Neria punished her by giving her the face of death and the body of a serpent and banishing her.

Moses potion   a liquid from the Moses sole in the Red Sea that puts people to sleep

Näkki   murderous shapeshifters in the northern Atlantic

Navi   one of the six mages who ruled Atlantis; Neela's ancestor

Neela   a Matalin princess; Serafina's best friend; Yazeed's sister; Mahdi's cousin. She is a bioluminescent.

Neria   the sea goddess

Neria's Stone   a blue, tear-shaped diamond that Neria gave to Merrow for saving Kyr, her youngest son, from a shark attack

Nex   a darksong spell used to kill

Ngome ya jeshi   the compound of the Askari, Kora's personal guard

Nocérus   a darksong spell used to cause harm

Nyx   one of the six mages who ruled Atlantis; Ava's ancestor

Nzuri Bonde   the village in Kandina where Kora lives

Omnivoxa (omni)   mer who have the natural ability to speak every dialect of Mermish and communicate with sea creatures

Ondalina   the mer realm in the Arctic waters

Ooka   Neela's pet blowfish

Opafago   cannibalistic sea creatures that lived in Miromara and hunted mer until Merrow forced them into the Barrens of Thira, which surround the ruins of Atlantis

Orfeo   one of the six mages who ruled Atlantis; Astrid's ancestor

Ostroki   the mer version of librarians

Ostrokon   the mer version of a library

Palazzo   Italian for *palace*

Pani Yod'dha'om   Matali's water warriors

Permutavi   a pact between Miromara and Ondalina, enacted after the War of Reykjanes Ridge, that decreed the exchange of the rulers' children

Pesca   the language spoken by fish

Petra tou Neria Neria's Stone, a blue, teardrop-shaped diamond that Neria gave Merrow for saving Kyr, Neria's youngest son, from a shark attack

Pita-ji a Matalin term for *father*

Pompasooma a Matalin pastry

Portia Volnero mother of Lucia, one of Serafina's ladies-in-waiting; wanted to marry Vallerio, Serafina's uncle

Posidonia a sweet wine made from fermented seaweed

Praedatori soldiers who defend the sea and its creatures against terragoggs; known as Wave Warriors on land

Praesidio Duca Contorini's home in Venice

Prax practical magic that helps the mer survive, such as camouflage spells, echolocation spells, spells to improve speed or darken an ink cloud. Even those with little magical ability can cast them.

Principessa Italian for *princess*

Priya a Matalin term of affection

Pyrrha one of the six rulers of Atlantis; Becca's ancestor

Qin the mer realm in the Pacific Ocean; Ling's home

Rafael the justice of the seas who officiates at Mahdi's and Sera's exchange of vows

Rafe Iaoro Mfeme worst of the terragoggs; he runs a fleet of dredgers and super trawlers that threaten to pull every last fish out of the sea

Razormouth dragon one of the many types of dragons that breed in Matali and are the main source of the realm's wealth; they are feral and murderous and prevent invaders from getting past the Madagascar Basin

Reggia   Merrow's ancient palace

Regina   Italian for *queen*

River Olt   the Freshwater region where the Iele's cave is located

Robus   a songspell used to push

Rorqual   humpback whale

Rorrim Droll   lord of Vadus, the mirror realm

Royal Arabian dragon   one of the many types of dragons that breed in Matali and are the main source of the realm's wealth; they are so dazzling and so costly that only the wealthiest mer can afford them

Rursus   the language of Vadus, the mirror realm

Rusalka   a ghosts of a human girl who drowned herself because of a broken heart

Sagi-shi   one of three trawlers that Rafe Mfeme owns

Saintes-Maries   the wreck of the *Demeter* lies twenty-five leagues due south of this point in France

Salamu kubwa, Malkia   Kandinian for *Greetings, Great Queen*

Sanada, Empress   the current female ruler of Matali; Neela's mother

Sea whip   the most deadly jellyfish in the world

Sejanus Adaro   Portia Volerno's husband, who died a year after Lucia's birth

Serafina   principessa di Miromara

Shipwreck ghosts   hungry for life, their touch – if prolonged – can be lethal

Sí   Italian for *yes*

Siren a mermaid who sings for currensea

Soldati Italian for *soldiers*

Suma Neela's amah, or nurse

Svikari one of three trawlers that Rafe Mfeme owns

Swash Mermish slang; a shortened version of *swashbuckler*, suggesting a flamboyant adventurer

Sycorax one of the six rulers of Atlantis; Ling's ancestor

Sylvestre Serafina's pet octopus

Talisman object with magical properties

Tavia Serafina's nursemaid

Terragoggs (goggs) humans. Before now they haven't been able to get past the merpeople's spells.

Thalia, Lady a vitrina who knows what the six talismans are

TideSides small freestanding snack bars

Tortoisha the language spoken by sea turtles

Transparensea pearl a pearl that contains a songspell of invisibility; transparensea pebbles are not as strong as transparensea pearls

Trouncer large jellyfish who float above entrances to nightclubs and prevent anyone from sneaking in without paying

Vadus the mirror realm

Vallerio, Principe del Sangue Regina Isabella's brother; Miromara's high commander; Serafina's uncle

Vitrina souls of beautiful, vain humans who spent so much time admiring themselves in mirrors that they are now trapped inside

Vortex a songspell used to create a whirl

Waterfire magical fire used to enclose or contain

Wave Warriors humans who fight for the sea and its creatures

Yazeed Neela's brother; Madhi's cousin

Zee-zee a Matalin candy

Zeno Piscor traitor to Serafina and Neela, in league with Traho

MEET THE AUTHOR

1. Which character in the series do you most relate to?

That would be Astrid – the difficult one!

2. Which Mer realm is your favourite?

I love them all, but I think Ondalina, which is made entirely of ice, is my very favourite.

3. Who would be at your dream dinner party?

Pippi Longstocking, Annika and Tommy, Mr Nilsson and Pippi's horse.

4. Is there a book you wish you had written?

When deadlines are pressing in, then whatever book I happen to be writing at the moment is the book I very much wish I'd written!

5. What advice would you give to aspiring young writers?

Listen to your own thoughts and feelings very carefully, be aware of your observations, and learn to value them. When you're a kid – and even when you're older – lots of people will try to tell you what to think and feel. Try to stand still inside all of that and hear your own voice. It's yours and only yours, it's unique and worthy of your attention, and if you cultivate it properly, it might just make you a writer.

6. Where is your favourite place to write?

My office, at home. It's the only place I can write.

7. Who is your favourite author and why?

James Joyce. His books gave me the keys to the kingdom.